BRING ME TO LIFE

Elaine Robertson North

For Steve

1

She hadn't meant to kill her. Not initially, anyway. She'd entered the room knowing only that this woman was ruining her life and that, as a consequence, something had to be done about it. She'd thought they would talk, that she would definitely be forceful, perhaps a little threatening even, but she hadn't considered actually ending her life. Not until her hands were wrapped tightly around her neck, willing the very last breath from her body, had she realised that death wasn't just an option, it was the only option.

The eyes that stared back at her had been full of terror but that hadn't been enough to make her blink, never mind look away. She'd needed to see it, to look right into the depths of her blackened soul and be reminded of how she'd sucked every inch of joy from her life, leaving her with a cavernous hole of frustration and loneliness that she had never been able to fill.

"Do you see what you've done to me? What you've turned me into?" She had forced the words out through gritted teeth, not sure in the moment if the droplets of liquid that fell on to the face beneath her were saliva or tears. It mattered not. The response to her desperate questions was a look that turned from terror to sadness and it was this complete woefulness that proved to be the most powerful, causing her to look away for the first time. But it was only momentary and did nothing but make her squeeze tighter still, her knuckles slowly turning white with the strain.

"Why won't you just die?" she had pleaded, terrified that she would run out of strength. She'd grabbed for a nearby cushion and pushed it hard over pleading eyes, then lay on top of it using her entire body weight in a desperate attempt to get the job done. She'd held her own breath as arms and legs had flailed and then twitched, the movements clearly muted by a body already wasting away and ravaged by drugs, a circumstance they were both now grateful for.

And then finally it had stopped.

Now, as she walked briskly away from the large red-bricked building, she felt her gait slowly change from a hurried flustered scurry to a slower, more confident stride, her pounding heart calming as the distance between them widened, her neck lengthening, her head rising. She gave herself a little shake and felt the last knots of tension fall away, and then she smiled.

So this was what freedom felt like.

2

Grace

"Is there an update on the idea we discussed Grace?"

Grace smiled at the deputy editor with as much enthusiasm as she could muster. She felt her bottom lip lower tentatively in preparation for what she hoped would be some carefully selected words of wisdom although she had absolutely no idea what those words might be. This would be interesting. And then suddenly she was looking at the broad back of the sales director who had stepped between them with his usual air of self-importance, oblivious to the fact that he might be interrupting something. Not that Grace was about to object. She was off the hook for the time being at least and, seeing her opportunity to escape, she quickly left the meeting room.

For some unfathomable reason, the deputy editor saw a free frozen chicken for every reader as the ultimate in newspaper giveaways and Grace had given up trying to persuade her otherwise. A bloody chicken! If Grace didn't know how serious she was, it would almost be funny. But she was serious. Like a dog with a bone. Or a wishbone, Grace thought and she smiled at her own joke, but the smile quickly faded.

Grace wound her way along the corridor until she was back in the main lobby of the building, one cell of lunacy now safely behind her, a whole different kind of madness waiting for her back on the twelfth floor. With a loud ping, the lift cheerfully announced its arrival and Grace stepped inside. As the heavy doors then slowly encased her, she was immediately aware of a familiar sense of being trapped, feeling like someone who had been wrongly admitted to the most grim mental health facility imaginable.

Another loud ping and the lift doors swung open again and, reluctantly, Grace stepped out. She could hear Peter shouting long before she reached the marketing department. As she arrived at the door she stopped for a moment, her hand reluctantly reaching out to push it open. She was about to walk in at just the wrong moment and there was nothing she could do about it.

"Grace! Where the hell have you been? I've got Sebastian screaming at me that this weekend's promotion is a piece of worthless crap. For fuck's sake do something useful for a change and go and sort it out!"

Grace immediately turned around and walked straight back out again, her heavy heart feeling like a dead weight in her chest as she headed for the editorial department. She spotted Sebastian straight away, holding court at the front bench where the news editor and her team were busily pulling the next day's paper together. He caught her eye and waved with a smile that Grace happily returned. She had worked really hard at their relationship and, despite Peter's determination to convince everyone otherwise, they worked well together with genuine mutual respect. As the newspaper's editor, she had of course taken Sebastian through the weekend's promotion in great detail and he wasn't just happy with it, he was delighted, convinced that the chance to win a posh(ish) holiday home was more than perfect for their middle-England audience. She also knew Peter was a bully and out of his depth which made him a double pain in the backside, or thorn in her side or any other equally poetic, pain-inducing idiom you cared to use.

Grace walked past the rows of desks that were slowly starting to fill as the momentum of the day picked up. The atmosphere was always intense and yet it was surprisingly quiet. That said, Grace could sense the growing swell of energy as the first deadlines loomed.

She was suddenly aware of an approaching presence in the shape of the tall, slightly twitchy deputy news editor who had fallen into step beside her. "Grace, about these sales figures." She braced herself as he waved a crumpled sheet of paper at her. "Cutting the price last week brought in loads of new readers but now the price has gone back up again, they all seem to have gone?"

And then he was looking at her, genuinely puzzled by the situation he had just outlined. She sighed. A well-educated quick-thinking man who couldn't work out that, at half the price, some new folk were prepared to give the paper a try. They think it's rubbish but it's cheap so they keep buying it. Then the price goes back up and now it's just expensive rubbish so they go back to their usual paper. It surely wasn't that hard to grasp? Grace snatched the report from his hand. "Don't worry. We're going to fix it with a frozen chicken." Before he could come up with a response, Grace had already moved on. She quickened her pace until she reached a small row of offices and then disappeared into the second one.

Sam was on the phone as she entered. He smiled at her, gesturing towards the empty desk opposite him for her to sit down. He knew why she was there and knew too that she wouldn't be moving until she was confident Peter had left for the evening. In any other situation she would find his pity completely unbearable. She would be thoroughly embarrassed by the knowing looks, the gentle squeeze of her shoulder that Sam all too often now administered. Particularly as he was so strong, both mentally and professionally, and already incredibly successful for his late thirty-something years. In a relatively new role created to straddle the print and digital sides of the business, he was definitely one of the company's high-fliers. He was basically everything she felt she was not.

Grace slipped into the empty chair and opened her notebook as Sam chatted away. By the time he was finished, Grace was on a call of her own and so it continued until Sam stopped for a moment and waited patiently for Grace to finish her latest conversation. She laid her phone down and looked at him. "Afternoon!" she said with a smile.

"Good afternoon to you too," he replied. "How's it going?"

Before Grace could answer her phone started to ring again and she visibly pulled back at the sight of Peter's name staring back at her.

"What is it?" Without hesitation, Sam leapt up and grabbed her phone, Grace's temporary paralysis preventing her from reacting quickly enough to stop him answering on her behalf. "Peter, hi it's Sam. Yes, good thanks. Grace is on the editorial floor somewhere. Can I pass a message on?" Grace held her breath. "Of course, I'll tell her. Cheers mate."

As Sam handed back her phone, Grace's fear was immediately replaced by shame. So much so that she couldn't look Sam in the eyes.

"Something and nothing. Just checking up on you before he heads out." Sam waited. "It's okay Grace, really."

"Yeah, I know," she said, as nonchalantly as she could manage, busying herself collecting up her things. "It's just…" And then she stopped as she felt her eyes fill with tears. She took a deep breath. She absolutely must not, would not cry. "I'm just being stupid. As always."

"He's an arse. And you're amazing." Sam shrugged with a blush-fuelled smile as Grace finally looked at him. "Well you are. And it makes me really angry that he's allowed to treat you the way he does. Shall I talk to him for you? Would that help?"

Grace smiled. "Thank you but no, I don't think it would help. It's okay, I'll work it out."

"Sam! Conference!" The voice of the editor's secretary could be heard loud and clear as she started to round everyone up for the daily afternoon meeting where the content and layout of tomorrow's paper would be finalised. Sam hesitated for a second but they both knew he couldn't be late.

"It's okay, you go."

Sam picked up his laptop and headed for the door. And then he stopped. "You know where I am."

Grace smiled and then she slowly exhaled as she watched him go. What a complete mess. She had gone from a job she loved with a magazine publisher where the pressure was manageable, her colleagues reasonable and her goals achievable, to one where the pressure was literally crushing her soul, where many of her colleagues were borderline certifiable and her targets were so far out of her reach that the reward and praise she had become used to had been substituted with constant disappointment and the fear of imminent failure.

"You're the only one for the job, Grace," the wily headhunter had said, his tone deep and seductive. "You're the only one who's capable of taking it on. And what a job! Head of marketing for the biggest publishing company in the country!" And then he had sat back, eyes wide, almost breathless with the sheer excitement of it all. It had all been so convincing, so rousing, that Grace had said yes. Or had she just found it too difficult to say no? She had spent many wistful moments since, wondering which was the more accurate reflection.

The jewel in the company's crown was a national newspaper along with all the accompanying digital formats and, with the help of a small team, this was where Grace's ever-depleting energy was focused. And if the job itself wasn't stressful enough, there was Peter, her aggressive, ignorant and complete shit of a boss. Grace had long since given up trying to work out why she allowed him to intimidate her the way he so clearly did, a knot of fear now permanently in situ in the pit of her stomach. Or why she tolerated the continuous mental abuse. Suffice to say she hadn't been raised to admit defeat and walk away.

The marketing department was almost empty when Grace eventually walked back in and a glance in the direction of

Peter's office thankfully confirmed he had indeed gone. The lights were out and the door was closed, causing her shoulders to spontaneously and painfully start to lower. She was physically exhausted and emotionally drained and, as she slumped into her chair, she was horribly aware that on top of everything else, she now had some serious catching up to do. As she prepared to dive in, her phone rang. She sighed. She was never going to get out of here at this rate.

"Hello?"

"Grace, it's John. I have to see you. I'll be round at eight." And then he hung up. Grace's heart was now so heavy she wondered for a moment if she might literally fall off her chair.

3

Grace

At five past eight, Grace and John sat opposite each other, their awkwardness at complete odds with the intimacy they had, until recently, shared. Grace could feel John staring at her but she was determined not to even look at him, furious with herself that she had even let him in. Why had she done that? Why hadn't she stood up to him and said no? She felt the corners of her mouth twitch into the smallest of wry smiles. If she had been able to stand up to John, this whole sorry mess would have been over long before now.

At least here in her own home she felt more secure, in a room that had been dressed with real love and care. There were a couple of striking pictures, a small fortune spent on one elaborate mirror that sat elegantly above the fireplace and a selection of unusual bits and bobs collected over a number of years, each a memory of a special day out, a trip with friends or just a casual solo mooch around a market. She was still wearing a smart fitted shirt, tailored trousers and heeled boots with her hair swept back in a tight ponytail. She knew she looked severe and business-like but felt mildly comforted as a result. Anything to hide how she was really feeling.

She distracted herself by staring out of the large, sash windows. It had started to rain, falling in perfect straight lines but she could hear nothing. The water just seemed to be melting silently into the ground. She pulled her focus back to the pane of glass in front of her and watched the tiny drops of water race down the window, stopping and turning as if unsure of their way, before collecting finally in little rivers on the ledge. And then she jumped.

"For God's sake Grace, this is so childish!"

As she looked at him, it was hard to miss how tired and disheveled he looked. His face was unnaturally pale, his dark eyes tired and weary with equally dark circles surrounding them, giving his skin an almost grey hue. His clothes were creased, his palms sweaty. He was a mess but hey, what did she care?

"Please talk to me!"

"I can talk as much as you like," she said, as confidently as she could manage. "The question is, will you listen?"

"Yes of course I'll listen! Just talk to me. You did agree to see me."

"Actually I didn't. You just told me you would be here and, as always, you just expected me to comply. But I did let you in. It seems rolling over is a surprisingly hard habit to break. Or maybe I was just hoping I could make this the last time. The moment when you finally accept it's over."

"I'll never accept that," he said with real force as he shot to the edge of his seat, his eyes suddenly wide and fierce. Grace immediately sat as far back as possible, hoping she didn't look as terrified as she now felt.

"Let me go, John, please."

"No, I can't. I won't."

His determination was matched only by her own desperation and, as he put out a hand to grab her, Grace jumped up and hurried towards the bathroom. "You can let yourself out," she shouted over her shoulder as she disappeared inside, locking the door quickly behind her. She moved to the edge of the bath and sat down, her foot tapping nervously on the floor and then she waited, her ears on high alert, listening for any sound of movement.

"Grace!" She started at the sound of his voice just the other side of the door. "Come out of there!"

Grace held her breath. There was a loud knock.

"Grace!" Louder this time. Then the thud of a fist.

"Fine!" Louder still. "Have it your way."

Grace felt a tightening in her lungs but still she waited. And then there it was; the satisfying sound of the front door opening and then closing behind him. Finally she exhaled.

She wasn't sure how long she stayed there, sitting in an uncomfortable hunched position, head down, foot tapping again but eventually she forced herself to move. She unlocked the bathroom door and then waited a beat before opening it. When she was sure she could hear nothing, she walked slowly back into the lounge and then on into the kitchen, her eyes searching every corner until she was convinced he had gone. As she came back into the lounge, she turned the radio on her way to her bedroom. The room behind her immediately filled with the sound of Phil's voice and, as the dulcet tones of her best friend swept over her, she felt her shoulders lower and the tightness in her neck slowly start to loosen.

As Grace wandered back into the lounge a few moments later, comfortable now in an over-sized sweatshirt and leggings, with her hair loose and falling gently around her shoulders, she could hear Phil chatting with a female caller. She was annoyingly giggly and, if Grace wasn't mistaken, she had just announced to the nation that she had recently had sex with one of his fellow presenters, throwing in enough colourful adjectives to make it clear she was mocking him and his clearly lacklustre performance. It was beyond cringeworthy and sure to get Phil into all sorts of trouble. Grace should call him but knew she wouldn't. Shameful as it sounded, she was way too deep in her own mess tonight to help Phil out of his.

Getting dressed for work the next morning, Grace was on reluctant auto-pilot. As she slowly stumbled from being barely awake to fully alert, her troubles were busy rebuilding themselves into an impenetrable wall of frustration and then she jumped as the silence of the room was shattered by the sound of her phone ringing. It was Phil.

"Bit early for you isn't it?" Grace immediately found herself smiling.

"I've been summoned by the master. Bit of trouble on air last night. So tell me what John had to say?"

"There was very little conversation last night. I'm sure he thinks I'm just fighting the urge to go running back into his arms, saying everything's okay and can't we try again."

"The man is truly deranged. Are you okay?"

"Never felt better."

"That good eh? I'll be round later after my show. Try to have a good day in the meantime."

"Thanks, but unlikely"

"Yeah, that makes two of us."

Within a few hours, Grace was in a meeting finding it increasingly difficult to concentrate. The combination of a warm room and a rubbish night's sleep was making her feel horribly nauseous as her body coaxed her towards sleep, her eyes heavy and desperate to close, while her mind struggled to drag her back from the edge of slumber and keep her alert. The battle was exhausting which clearly wasn't helping the situation at all. She gave herself what she hoped was a subtle little shake and straightened herself up.

"Anything to add Grace?" The lofty sales director looked at her, eyebrows raised but with little expectation of anything interesting to come.

"Just to say the latest reader research has been completed and will be sent round this afternoon. And following last month's comments, we've reshaped the way we report on our social media which should make it more useful for everyone."

"Excellent. Right, unless there's anything else, I think we're done."

Chairs were pushed back and the room slowly emptied amidst a gentle buzz of conversation. Grace followed on behind, wondering how bad things would have to get before she actually needed to be woken up to make her valuable contribution to this particularly tedious monthly meeting. Taking a detour to pick up a very large strong coffee, Grace checked her phone for messages. In amongst the usual stuff were five from John, each one slightly more frantic and hyper than the one before. She genuinely didn't know what to do for the best so immediately elected to do nothing.

By the time she had listened to the last message she was back at her desk but had barely got her bottom on her chair before Peter came flying out of his office.

"Grace! In here now!" The hairs on the back of her neck leapt to attention as she gathered up her notes and reluctantly disappeared into Peter's office, closing the door quietly behind her.

The end of the working day couldn't come soon enough and after a particularly tough week, Grace was desperate to escape for the weekend and hurried to her car. With the office sitting just on the edge of town, she had quickly got into the habit of driving to work, happy not to have to sweat along with the rest of London on the underground every day. She knew she probably worked longer hours as a result, coming in early and often staying late to avoid the worst of the rush hour traffic, but it was a fact she chose to ignore in favour of a comfortable, well-ventilated and peaceful commute.

It was past ten when she finally turned into the small car park beside the beautiful old mansion block that housed her flat only to find John lurking there. As she got out of her car he was beside her in a shot, rambling in an absolute frenzy. "I had to see you Grace. I need to talk to you. I know how difficult these past few months have been. We have to talk about it!"

"We have nothing to talk about as you well know." Grace tried to walk past him, her eyes fixed on the front door.

"It was a tough few months Grace, I get that."

Grace stopped and turned to face him. "You know shit about the last few months and our relationship was over long before I finished it so just leave me alone!" With a renewed determination, she quickened her pace.

"Can't we at least be friends?"

And then she stopped again and turned back to look at him. "Why on earth would I want you as a friend? Just let it go, John. It's time to move on."

Grace started walking away from him again until her hand was finally pushing a key into the door. But John wasn't finished. "I know you were just trying to make a point. Well you have my attention now. Come on Grace, we have to make this work! You belong to me."

Grace immediately stopped what she was doing. Her hand froze and her keys fell to the ground. Had she really heard that correctly? She felt a sudden tightening deep in her gut and tears stung her eyes. As her heart started to race, she realised what she was feeling was fear. She'd felt it when he'd been in her flat earlier that week and it was back, even sharper now and easier to define. In fact it was so real she could taste it, clawing at the back of her throat and threatening to choke her. But she couldn't back down now or she would never be free of him.

Slowly she walked back towards him until she stood inches from his face. "Finally your true colours are shown in all their technicolor glory. Belong to you? You're insane. You screw around behind my back, humiliate me, make a complete mockery of my love and now that you've been exposed and I've taken a stand, your best shot is that I belong to you?" Grace paused, struggling for a moment to maintain composure. "It's time for you to leave me alone."

"We both know what this is really about. It was only ten minutes in a clinic Grace, not the end of the world."

Grace raised her hand and slapped him hard across the face in one swift fluid movement that left her fingers tingling and John clutching at his cheek. Before he had a chance to recover, she turned and ran back to the door but as she fumbled to pick up her keys, John's hand was on her arm. She gasped as he swung her around to face him and then suddenly, he was being dragged away from her.

Grace hadn't noticed Phil pulling up but here he was, landing an almighty punch in John's face that sent him flying. John was taken completely by surprise and, before he had time to react, Phil was standing over him, pinning him to the floor.

"What do you think you're doing?" Phil yelled furiously. John stared up at him with terrified eyes, his nose and lip bleeding. "Haven't you done enough?" Clearly frightened by his own strength of feeling, Phil then roughly let him go. "Get out of here before I really lose it."

John staggered to his feet. "This is nothing to do with you. I just want to talk to Grace."

"Well she doesn't seem to want to talk to you. What does it take to make you understand that?"

Grace watched on as Phil squared up to him, daring John to say another word or make the slightest move towards her. It was clear he wasn't finished but what words could he possibly find that could be deemed even remotely appropriate? Would he tell her again that he loved her? That she was all he wanted and that the extra-curricular sex had all meant nothing? That the unplanned pregnancy was just collateral damage, the ensuing termination something she would get over in time? The minute Grace had taken a stand and finished things, his only focus in the aftermath had been to convince her to take him back, promising to change, although somewhat unconvincingly she had felt. Either way, it really didn't matter. There would be no second chance.

Grace glanced up again to see John touching his bloody nose. She imagined he was thinking that he should be the one seeing Phil off, the anger in his eyes making the left one twitch intermittently. For a moment, his back straightened and Grace watched as Phil immediately moved closer, his eyes willing John to make a move so he could justify hitting him again. And then John visibly shrunk before him, his head falling.

As John turned and walked away, Phil finally took Grace into his arms. "Come on, it's okay now. He's gone." She clung to him for a moment and then taking the keys, Phil took her inside the building and into her flat.

"What did I do to deserve all this?" she said, dropping herself down on to the sofa. "I must have been truly wicked in a past life and I'm being suitably punished for it in this one."

"You could never have known what a complete maniac he would turn out to be," Phil said as he sat down next to her. "After everything he's done, how could he think for one minute he deserves another chance? We can all forgive one mistake, one moment of madness but fucking hell! The extent of his cheating, the lies, the way he made you feel paranoid for ever doubting him, chipping away at your self-confidence, keeping you away from your friends. Not to mention his behaviour over the pregnancy. What was next? Locking you in the bloody basement?" Phil shook his head. "Just talking about him makes me so angry." He put his arms protectively around Grace again and for a moment they sat in silence and then she turned to look at him with a smile.

"Quite the hero of the hour aren't you?"

Phil was immediately smiling back. "I can do butch when butch is required!"

Grace then felt the sudden lightness in her demeanour slowly seep away again, horribly aware that this was the second time in one day that someone had offered to fight her battles for her or, in Phil's case, actually do the deed without feeling the need to ask permission first. Alongside Sam's offer to talk to Peter, it made her feel like a child, a thought that immediately sent its own icy shiver down her back. She gave herself a shake. A change of subject was needed.

"So, tell me about your day. Exactly how much trouble were you in?"

Phil grimaced. "I'd say about thigh deep in crap. The papers had a bit of fun with it all. The boss man was not amused. 'Confessions of a DJ – Listener Tells All!' 'Listener reveals sex with married DJ live on air.'" Phil put on his most sensational voice as he mimicked the headlines and then he sighed. "I did point out that there wouldn't have been anything to write about if Chris hadn't actually had sex with the bloody women in the first place but I'm not sure that really helped."

"It's his poor wife I feel sorry for. What is it with men? Bunch of shits the lot of them." Phil raised his eyebrows. "Just the straight ones, obviously," Grace quickly added with an apologetic smile.

They slipped into a peaceful silence until Grace decided it was time to call it a night. "I think it's time I went to bed."

"You sure you'll be okay?"

She nodded, knowing he was really looking for a sign that it was okay to ask about the termination. Seeking her permission to talk about the one element of this whole sorry episode that had left the ugliest of scars, still so deep and raw that she found it impossible to talk about. "Honestly I'm fine," she said, forcing a smile. "I'll call you tomorrow."

Phil waited for just a moment and then, admitting silent defeat, he gave her one last hug before heading out the door. As the sound of it closing faded, Grace was suddenly aware of the silence but she felt surprisingly calm. There was simply no energy left to feel anything else and, thoroughly exhausted, she headed straight for bed.

Moments later, it was the smell that set her nerve ends jangling. She sat up, immediately on high alert. There was a fire. Her eyes were suddenly wide open but she could see nothing. The room was already filled with a thick, choking smoke that grabbed her throat in a stranglehold and stung her eyes until any sight she had was lost behind a film of grit. Arms outstretched, she stumbled to the door, immediately snatching back her hand with a yelp as she touched the door handle, already red hot. She put her ear close up to the door and was greeted by an eerie silence, interrupted by the occasional snap and pop or a cracking sound as something crumbled. With every whooshing sound she imagined the flames licking up the walls, engulfing the building and swallowing it one terrifying gulp at a time.

And then she heard it. The distant haunting sound of a baby crying. She was suddenly overwhelmed by a mind-blowing sense of panic. She rattled the door handle, oblivious to her flesh burning as she did so. She twisted and turned it, shook it violently, her strength fuelled by the most extreme sense of terror. "My baby!" she screamed, her fists now banging on the door. "Somebody save my baby!"

Grace sat bolt upright, awake this time, her breathing frantic, her body covered in a thin film of sweat, her eyes blurred with tears and flitting around the room as she looked for confirmation that it had indeed been just a dream. As she slowly started to accept that all was okay, she sat for a moment, concentrating on nothing but her breathing until she felt her sense of balance restored. Then she reached for her phone and called Emily.

4

Anna

Stepping into the revolving door of No.1 Brockley Court, Anna was aware of the familiar shift in her posture that happened every time she entered this magnificent building. Her head went up, her shoulders uncurled, her back straightened and then she smiled in preparation for the young, glamorous receptionist whose eyes would be waiting for her as the revolving doors took her from pavement to the interior in one fluid movement.

"Morning Anna. How are you today?"

"Good Imogen, thank you. You?"

Immaculate Imogen waved with a smile by way of a response as she answered a ringing phone, her free hand quickly pushing her headset into position, oozing polished efficiency as she did so. Anna had often tried to imagine Imogen away from work, the envy of her suburban friends that she worked 'up west' in a role that required her to dress in a way she probably thought was smart and business-like. Anna, however, considered it borderline sluttish, the dresses a little too short and figure hugging, the heels an inch too high. Not to mention the make-up. Goodness only knew how long that took to apply. Anna imagined her needing a blow-torch to remove it every night and then she silently scolded herself. She really shouldn't knock her.

Anna headed for the lift and the third floor, stepping out into a foyer that was markedly different to the glass-dominated main reception with its smart but almost clinical meeting rooms, the sea of grey suits, the air heavy with determined deal-making and the pressure of winning in whatever form that took. Up on the third floor there were warm colours on the walls, relaxed sofas and armchairs, a coffee machine and all the accompanying paraphernalia and a careful selection of stylish pictures on the walls. She swept past the array of comforts on to the familiar room that had become a space she loved. A desk, a small sofa and chair, both incredibly comfortable, and just enough extra stuff to make it look like somewhere you could relax and be yourself while still maintaining the belief that this was a place of business. There was a large window behind the desk (an office with a view came at quite a premium but it was definitely worth it) and Anna sat for a moment, just watching the madness of the world outside before firing up her laptop to remind herself what lay ahead today.

First up was Amanda Clark. Anna liked talking to her. She was smart and ambitious but, like most of her clients, lacked that level of self-belief required to really fulfil her potential. She would get there and Anna would play her part which would be hugely satisfying. Not least because Amanda's employer was paying so Anna got to enjoy inflated corporate rates for empowering this young professional who would in turn excel in the workplace and increase her corporate value. So, a win for all concerned. Then there was a new client, Malcolm, who, judging from their initial phone conversation, had fallen victim to a classic mid-life crisis.

Lost his way at work and having an affair. Text book stuff. And then it was lovely Lucy and their final 'haven't you done well' session before Anna unleashed her back into the big bad world, her confidence restored, her future goals realigned, her expectations from personal relationships explored and firmly established. A job well done, even if she said so herself.

Anna wandered back to the coffee machine for a quick caffeine injection before Amanda arrived, nodding and smiling to her fellow office dwellers as she went. No suits allowed here. The men were mainly in jeans with logoed t-shirts or sweatshirts and just the occasional shirt amongst them. Anna constantly monitored what the women were wearing, her hands unwittingly touching her own clothes on occasion, as if looking for reassurance that she had it right, that she appeared to belong. It was a genius idea to create an environment more aligned to the creative, the free-thinkers and artists in the midst of the more traditional business going on beneath them. They knew little about each other but enjoyed a shared sense that they had escaped to a higher plane.

Nothing of note happened in her session with Amanda who was soon replaced by Malcolm. Anna listened to his unenthusiastic description of life – a boring job where he'd been passed over for promotion on countless occasions and a monotonous home life with children long since departed and a wife who, according to Malcolm at least, had simply given up. After twenty minutes in his company, Anna's over-riding thought was no bloody wonder. What she was desperate to do was give this man a massive and literal kick up the backside but sadly this was neither a recognised nor accepted method in any training course she had attended. Or, better still, she would like to swap him for his wife, investing her time in boosting her self-confidence, encouraging her to establish some self-worth and recognise that she still deserved to live an exciting and fulfilling life so she could put her own boot in his backside and propel him straight out the front door. Malcolm told her his family meant everything to him causing Anna to suggest that having an affair was possibly not the best way to demonstrate this. Malcolm immediately made to respond but Anna put her hand up to stop him.

"Okay Malcolm, here's what we're going to do. We'll focus on work and by fixing this problem, we can then enjoy the positive knock-on effect to your personal life. We're going to turn problems into goals and devise a strategy to achieve those goals. We're going to replace negative self-beliefs with positive ones and embed some vital new patterns of thinking". She paused for a moment. Malcolm looked slightly bemused but no matter. He would pick it up as they went along. "You have to accept some responsibility for life as it is Malcolm," Anna told him, "but, more importantly, you have to believe it is possible to change." She smiled. "The good news is you're here which means you do want things to be different, so the rest will be easy." Anna stood up and Malcolm immediately did the same. "I'll see you next week." Taking his cue, Malcolm muttered that indeed she would and then quietly left.

Anna headed to the building's café for some lunch. It was part of what made this place so perfect; a chance to be around fellow workers when your own working life was actually quite solitary. It was a way for Anna to feel connected to the wider workforce, to feel like she hadn't quite left the buzz of corporate life which, in a past life, had made her feel so alive. Working where she did made her feel like she still counted and, as so many of her clients worked in large companies, she felt she needed to offer an environment that would sit comfortably with what they were used to. That somehow they would immediately feel she understood them if she too operated from an enormous glass-fronted, smart and shiny building. Even if it was from the cosy and rather cool third floor.

Anna picked up her usual salad and a bottle of water and headed for a quiet table where she could enjoy watching the comings and goings around her. The place was a blur of suits and, as always, most of them were grey. There was the odd splash of colour from a tie or scarf and she was immediately aware of her own bright blue cardigan – azure if you're so inclined – as she celebrated her smart yet casual attire, her vibrancy in the midst of this spectacular dullness. No wonder people often started to feel suffocated in business when they simply didn't allow themselves any room at all for self-expression or individualism. She smiled at her smugness. There's nothing like feeling you've escaped from something to give you an air of superiority.

"Do you mind if I sit here?"

Anna looked up with what she hoped was only a small start to see a tall attractive man whom she guessed was in his mid to late fifties in a grey suit, obviously. But her eyes were immediately drawn to the shocking pink tie. His shirt was threaded with pale blue and pink and the overall look yelled effortless style, and expensive style at that.

"Of course," she said, busily moving her bag and papers to make room. Not that she'd been looking at anything in particular. She just liked to appear as though she was on her own for a reason. He put down his sandwich and coffee, took off his jacket and sat down.

"That's better," he said as he loosened his tie and then removed it completely. "I've felt like I was being strangled all morning." Anna smiled as he put out his hand. "Matthew."

"Anna," she said, taking his hand as he gripped hers firmly.

"Busy today, isn't it?" he said as he tucked into his sandwich. "It's nice to find a corner to get away from it all." Anna wasn't sure if she was expected to answer, a dilemma immediately eliminated as he continued. "Fascinates me, the people in this place. See that group over there?" She followed his eyes to a table of three men and a woman, a laptop open with all eyes on it as they chatted and ate. "Consultants," he said. "See that chap there, loading his coffee with sugar? Consultant. And that pair? Consultants. They're everywhere. Charging thousands for their perceived wisdom." He shook his head as he took another large bite of his sandwich, quickly chewing and swallowing so he could carry on. "Genius if you can get away with it," he said before taking a few mouthfuls of coffee, lost in his own little world for a moment, and then he turned towards her. "Sorry. You were probably hoping for some peace and quiet."

"Not at all," Anna said with a smile. "I've often wondered what all these people were up to and now I know. Although, if I'm honest, I had hoped for a little more diversity." He smiled, nodding as he polished off the last of his lunch. "What do you do?" Anna waited while he drank more of his coffee and then he looked at her, really looked at her this time, and it may only have been by millimetres but she drew back, an involuntarily reaction to the dark but bright eyes staring at her, so intense, so challenging, so alive.

"I'm a consultant," he said with a straight face. There was the briefest of pauses and then they both laughed.

"How very disappointing," she replied.

"I know, I'm sorry. The truth is, I do all sorts of things. Sometimes it's just easier to use the same label as everyone else. What about you?"

"I'm a life coach."

There was a flicker of something, so fast that Anna couldn't quite grasp its meaning, but his expression definitely changed.

"How very interesting," he said as he turned his chair towards her, suddenly giving her the full focus of his attention.

5

Grace

When Emily arrived at their favourite café bar, Grace was already on her third coffee, her nerve ends tingling as a result. It was an environment they felt wonderfully comfortable in, loving the feel of the place from the very first time they had wandered in. There were the most beautiful paintings on the walls and solid wooden tables and chairs. Then there were the little touches. Muffins baked in flower pots, cappuccinos served in small bowls, tea in vintage floral cups and saucers and fresh flowers on every table. In the evenings, it underwent a seamless transition into an equally stylish bar. They had subsequently spent many an hour putting the world to rights over a cappuccino and a pain au chocolat during the day and more of the same with a beer or a glass of wine and a bowl of assorted nuts in the evening.

"Finally!"

Emily looked at her watch. "I'm not late am I?"

Emily was always late. Oblivious, she sat down and immediately looked around for Warren. Catching his eye, she shouted over to him. "Hey Warren! Two more coffees please, when you've got a mo." He smiled in response as Emily turned back to look at Grace, her eyes narrowing slightly. "So, how are things?"

How to answer? Grace thought for a moment, searching for a new and fresh way to say things were absolutely desperate when Emily jumped in and saved her the trouble. "That good, eh? So Peter's been an arse. Despite pulling off the impossible, none of it's been good enough. Your ears are ringing from the shouting and swearing and, don't tell me, John's been round again, all pathetic looking and begging for forgiveness?"

Grace couldn't help but smile, despite knowing how horribly tragic it was that her life had become so predictable. "One interesting twist though. Phil turned up when John was there and punched him in the face. Knocked him to the ground in one Rocky-style blow."

"You're kidding?" Emily's look of surprise quickly turned into a huge grin. "I bloody love Phil. The man deserves a medal."

"Yes, it was quite a moment." Grace paused as her focus was drawn back to the weariness she carried with her constantly feeling it, as she so often did, resting heavily on her shoulders. Her smile subsequently disappeared. "What am I going to do Em? Something needs to change. Everything needs to change. I just don't know where to start." Grace sat back in her chair with a sigh as Warren appeared with two fresh coffees. He hesitated for just a moment and then chose to retreat, surmising correctly that this was not the right time to pull up a chair and join in the chat. "I mean, we can't keep having the same conversation week in, week out," Grace continued as she watched him go. "I'm boring myself to death with all the whining and complaining so goodness knows how you must feel."

Emily looked at her with genuine concern. "Pretty helpless, that's how I feel."

There was silence for a moment and then, sitting forward again, Grace reached into her bag for a newspaper supplement she'd been carrying around for some time now. It was already open at a particular feature that she'd read numerous times already, a fact made evident by the curled up corners and its overall crumpled look. She pushed it across the table and, picking it up, Emily started to read. Grace watched Emily's facial expressions change – the occasional raised eyebrow, the odd grimace, small movements of the head from left to right as she weighed it all up – and then finally Emily put the magazine down and looked at her. "Life coaching? Really?"

Grace immediately felt embarrassed. "Why not?" She watched Emily struggle to find an answer.

"I don't know," Emily said carefully. "I just wouldn't have thought it was something you'd go for. The whole handing over control thing."

"But that's just the point. It's about being empowered to fulfil your goals, finding ways to push past difficult situations and emotional barriers." Grace had read the article so many times, she could now quote it verbatim. "No one will be telling me what to do, just helping me work stuff out. I'm sorry, I just need some help."

"Why on earth are you apologising? Of course you should try it! It's a very compelling feature. It's got to be worth a try."

Emily smiled at Grace, her face full of reassurance and encouragement and Grace slowly smiled back, trying to dismiss the paranoia that Emily was holding something back. She wasn't sure why she needed affirmation but she clearly did. No doubt a symptom of Peter's bullying, rendering her incapable of trusting her instinct. And her instinct was screaming loud and clear that she needed help. She wanted to make big changes to her life but her self-confidence had been beaten to a pulp which meant she simply couldn't do this on her own. And so she wouldn't. She would forge ahead with the help of Anna, an accredited life coach who featured prominently in the article and, with Emily's approval, however forced it may have seemed, she now felt it was okay to make contact. Her heart enjoyed a little celebratory flutter that the journey towards salvation may finally be about to start.

"Earth to Grace?"

Nothing.

"Grace!"

And then Grace jumped, jolted back into the here and now, having been momentarily lost in thought. "I'm so sorry. So what's new with you?"

Emily immediately perked up. "A better question might be to ask what I'm doing tonight."

"You're kidding?" Emily clearly wasn't and Grace beamed with joy, spontaneously straining out of her chair to give her friend the best hug she could manage from a partial sitting position and with a solid table separating them. "You actually did it? I'm so proud of you!"

"Well you've all been nagging me for what feels like an eternity so I decided maybe it was time. If for no other reason than to just shut you all up." Grace watched as

Emily's gaze suddenly dropped. When she looked up again, her eyes were full of sadness. "I told you James and his new girlfriend are pregnant?"

Grace laid her hand on top of Emily's. "It'll happen for you too Em, I know it."

"Four failed IVF attempts might suggest otherwise."

Grace hesitated. "But your infertility is unexplained. That means there's still hope. Wrong husband maybe?"

"Yes, let's blame James!"

Grace was relieved to see Emily smile. "Totally and utterly his fault. I always thought so. So, who did you choose?"

"Brian," Emily said. "Classic good looks and he's an accountant so good with figures! He's perfect. Or at least according to his profile he is so you know, best not to get too carried away just yet. What are you doing tonight?"

"A long soak in the bath, some trashy TV and then a late drink with Phil when he gets off air." Grace then started to gather up her things. "Come on Em, therapy time. Let's go spend some money."

First on the shopping list was a killer outfit for Emily's big date. She was tall, her hair short and very dark, her eyes a surprisingly bright blue for her colouring and she had fantastic curves so finding her a perfect dress should have been an easy and enjoyable task. The reality was that an hour later, she'd tried on a host of dresses that perfectly showed off her considerable attributes and yet, despite this, she still wasn't satisfied. Grace waited patiently outside yet another changing room for Emily to appear once again.

"What on earth is that?"

Emily looked instantly disappointed. "Don't you like it?" She had emerged in a dark brown, shapeless dress that was beyond unattractive.

"No I don't. What was wrong with the little black one? It was much more you."

"Yes, but was it Brian?"

"You're not expecting him to wear it are you?"

"Very funny. I just felt this was more what he would like."

"Please don't do this!" Grace immediately regretted her tone as she watched Emily flinch. "I'm sorry Em, really. I just wish I could find that magic switch that would reboot your self-confidence. I just want you to be yourself. Choose something that says something about you, something you'll be comfortable in."

Emily looked at her with watery eyes. "I'm just not sure what that is," she said with an apologetic shrug.

Grace grabbed for her hand and squeezed it tight. "I get it Em, I do. You've forgotten who you are on your own but you'll work it out. And the truth is, you'd look amazing in any one of these dresses."

Emily smiled. "The black one it is then."

With the dress bought, they headed next to Grace's favourite deli so she could prepare for her own Saturday night. She was basically planning to eat and drink her way through it and quickly armed herself with enough tasty treats to feed a small family and sufficient wine to more than adequately wash it all down. She would be fit to burst with all edges suitably blurred by the time she met up with Phil. Perfect.

6

Grace

It was Monday morning. Grace had spent the perfect Saturday night with Phil. At least she thought she had. She didn't actually remember very much of it. She did very little on Sunday as a result and was now regretting her general lethargy. The weekend always seemed longer when she made the effort to do stuff whereas her routine weekend had flashed by in a non-eventful blur but there was obviously nothing she could do about that now. She had to get up but her body was refusing to co-operate. She waited till the last possible moment then threw back the duvet, struggled to a sitting position and then finally to her feet.

An hour or so later, she was taking an all too familiar deep breath and walking into the office. Peter was already pacing up and down, waiting for his first victim. "What did Gary say about the production problem with next week's promotion?"

Good morning to you too Peter, she thought. Yes, I had a very pleasant weekend thank you so much for asking. "I was just going to see him now."

"Why didn't you see him on Friday? How could you let the weekend go by without sorting it out?" The level of his voice began to rise as he built momentum. "You have no concept of the word 'urgent' do you? I don't know what goes on in that head of yours sometimes!" He was really shouting now and pointing so aggressively that Grace's head involuntarily rocked backwards and forwards as if he was actually jabbing her head with his finger. "I'm not going to do your job for you. Get a fucking grip and sort it out – NOW!"

Grace's heart sank to a new low. She put down her bag, took off her coat and, with the air of the walking dead, she went in search of Gary. When she returned half an hour later, Peter burst out of his office. "Where's Robert?" he yelled as his assistant leapt to attention.

"He's in an editorial meeting."

"Well get him back then!" He narrowed his eyes and stared at Grace with a look of pure menace. She did a quick double take, convinced for a moment that he had actually sprouted horns. "You first."

A brutal fifteen minutes later, Grace slowly closed the door behind her as she left Peter's office. No need to dwell on what happened in there. Suffice to say, Peter had spent almost all of that time shouting at her. She wasn't sure what about. She had stopped listening a long time ago when she realised the rants served no purpose. Not for Grace any way so she sincerely hoped Peter got something out of it. She would hate to think it was all for nothing.

Although, if she was honest, she had known he would be gunning for her even more so than normal after an unfortunate incident that had taken place during a meeting the previous Friday. It was a regular gathering of editors and directors from across the company and she had only been there to deputise for Peter who had thought he couldn't make it (at the request of the meeting's organiser, not Peter, who would obviously never see Grace as a suitable filler of his clearly unfillable shoes). When he had burst in half way through, she had been unsure whether to stay or go but the disruption caused by Peter taking a seat – interrupting someone's flow as he apologised for being late, asking for an agenda and generally making his presence well and truly felt – had made her decide to just sit tight. Then within minutes of Peter's arrival, the spotlight had already found him.

"About our cross-platform strategy Peter," one of the company's editors had asked. "The way we're using content has vastly improved lately. I just wondered what we're doing differently?"

After a couple of false starts from Peter while he struggled for an answer, the growing awkwardness in the room had been so excruciating that Grace had felt compelled to jump in. "It is looking good isn't it? When we work with brands on promotions, we now expect them to provide some relevant video content for us to use socially which is much more impactful. The picture desk has also been amazing, making sure we get our own news footage as well as pictures. That's down to Sam really but it's also why we've been working so closely together to make sure we have lots of our own content to play with."

Grace had then stopped suddenly and was thanked warmly for her contribution. She had launched in believing she was actually helping and then panicked. This was why Peter had employed her wasn't it? For her knowledge of all things digital? For her ability to switch focus from one social media platform to another with perfect cyber grace? Why then could she feel the heat of his stare? She tried her best not to be over dramatic but just as she was trying to convince herself he was in fact glowing with pride and not anger, the sales director butted in and sounded her death knell.

"And there we have it in a nutshell ladies and gents. The dinosaur of the past," he said as he nodded at Peter, "and the bright young star of the future," with a nod and a smile to Grace.

Grace hadn't known where to look. Other than definitely not at Peter. She had managed to avoid him for the rest of the day and had then gratefully headed off for the weekend. It was really no wonder then that he'd been so pumped up this morning, wound up like a clockwork toy and then released the minute she'd walked through the door. She'd done her best not to think about it over the weekend. Peter, on the other hand, had clearly been stewing with his blood on a low simmer ever since.

Peter had already moved on to his next victim by the time Grace sat back down at her desk. While of course she felt for whichever colleague was now in the hot seat, she was glad to be reminded that at least he didn't save all his vitriol just for her. Peter's default position was that everyone around him was useless and equally deserving of daily abusive ear-bashings which was both tragic and comforting in equal measure.

When Peter decided to go out for a while later that day, Grace hesitated for just a second then grabbed her phone and stepped into the corridor to find a quiet corner. Once she was happy there was no one in earshot she dialled a number and waited.

"Hi, Anna? My name's Grace. I wondered if I could arrange a time to come to see you?"

"Of course. Let me just grab my diary."

Grace's first thought was that she liked the sound of Anna's voice; a thought that was followed by a roll of the eyes as the tougher Grace immediately recognised the desperation to believe this woman was indeed the person who could turn things around for her. She smiled, if for no other reason than to celebrate the fact that the tough her still existed.

"How are you fixed next week?" Anna asked, her strong velvety tone melting into Grace's ear.

"Tuesday would be great. A rare day off so whenever suits you." It would mean a special trip into the centre of town but Grace felt it would be worth it not to feel rushed.

"Okay, let's go for ten. I'd normally ask you a few questions but I'm waiting for a client so can I send you a brief questionnaire? I'll include the address so you know where to find me."

Grace gave her a personal email address and returned to her desk with a renewed sense of optimism which, in turn, inspired some well-needed motivation. She duly set about annihilating her to-do list, one satisfying tick after another.

Periodically, the door to the department opened and one of her colleagues would come in, a face taut with tension that would immediately relax the moment a quick glance to the right confirmed Peter was absent. Grace smiled. Clearly there was nothing funny at all about this shared terror but in her current state of mild euphoria she chose to see it all as vaguely ridiculous, even comical, that a group of intelligent, normally confident individuals could allow themselves to be reduced to what looked on any average day like a group of extras from a low-budget zombie movie. But of course no one wanted to admit they found it difficult to cope with. This was the heady world of national newspapers! No room for delicate flowers here! So instead, they moved around each other in a beautifully choreographed daily dance of fake smiles and forced jollity. Grace wondered for a moment if it was time to take action and then she quickly shook her head to dislodge the idea. She might be zipping through her list with a rare and hugely enjoyable sense of enthusiasm but bringing the extended team together for some joint therapy was definitely a step too far, even today.

Grace was so energised that it was nine o'clock before she left the office but she had achieved plenty and felt suitably uplifted as a result. Adrenaline was still coursing through her veins as she jumped in her car and headed for home, so much so that the thought of going back to an empty flat suddenly held little attraction. With a quick change of direction, she headed instead for the café. She was greeted by the sound of laughter and general merriment, the coffee duly substituted in line with the hour with bottles of beer, wine and cocktails. She wound her way through to an empty table and enjoyed the feeling of melting into the general mêlée, signalling for a beer as she went from a waiter she didn't recognise.

When the beer arrived a few moments later, it was icy cold and the first few gulps brought with them an immediate and very welcome fuzziness. Grace caught sight of Warren and watched him expertly moving amongst the crowds, laughing with people, occasionally stopping to chat but always aware of who was waiting to be served. When he finally flipped the open sign to closed, the café was almost empty. The last hour had been so busy he hadn't even noticed Grace come in but he smiled as he saw her and wandered over.

"Don't often see you in here so late," he said as he pulled up a chair and sat down.

"Oh you know, just one of those days when only a beer will do." There was a pause and Grace felt her eyes avert and her cheeks flush. She frowned, wondering how blatant her unexpected awkwardness was.

"Fancy going on somewhere for one last drink? I could do with a change of scenery."

Grace struggled to hide her surprise, immediately in danger of overthinking the invitation. "You mean there's no date tonight?"

"Only a casual arrangement with some friends. But it's been a long day. It won't matter if I don't show."

And then Grace wasn't sure what to say. She had one of those strange relationships with Warren where she had sort of known him for years but didn't really know him at all. Turned out the snatched conversations over a coffee now and then and her scanty observations of him didn't actually add up to much. Before she had time to process the fact that she was actually quite flattered by his offer, or maybe even a little excited at the suggestion of a drink, Warren chose to accept her hesitation as a no.

"Another time maybe," he said and, before she could correct him, he was standing up and heading behind the bar for his jacket. As he put it on, he turned back to Grace who was now getting herself ready to leave. "Come on," he shouted over to her, "I'll walk out with you."

"My car's right outside."

He smiled. "Even better! You can make up for knocking me back with a lift home."

They chatted easily as they got into Grace's car with Grace forced to let go of the disappointment that she hadn't been quicker to say yes to him. Warren threw in directions as they talked and all too quickly, they were pulling up outside his building. Warren unbuckled his seat belt and then with his hand on the door, he turned back to look at her.

"Thanks for the lift."

"No problem."

He hesitated for a moment. "You're welcome to come in. If you want to?"

Grace smiled. "I don't think so."

"I am capable of polite conversation you know. Women have been known to visit my flat and leave untouched by these two fair hands!" His eyes sparkled as he waved his hands in the air. He was teasing her.

"Maybe that's what I'm afraid of."

Grace's expression gave nothing away, despite having surprised herself with what she saw as an uncharacteristically provocative response. Warren looked at her, his eyes suddenly wide, his expression a little confused. She knew he was wondering what she meant but, deciding it was probably best left unchallenged, he got out of the car and shut the door.

Grace studied him in the rear view mirror as she pulled away, standing motionless as he watched her go. She wondered what he was thinking, hoping just a little that he was wishing she had stayed.

7

Anna

"So, tell me about yourself Grace."

Anna watched Grace take a deep breath, clearly wondering where she should start. Grace's response to Anna's questionnaire had given her a good idea of why she was there but it was always good to hear it all first-hand. She liked to give someone the chance to start with a mammoth off-loading of all the woes and troubles, the challenges and dilemmas. Some responded with an initial hour of rambling, switching from one thing to another as one problem triggered something else and they then bounced from topic to topic in an exhausting fashion with barely a breath drawn. Others found it harder to open up and needed constant probing before Anna could get a sense of what was really going on, picking away slowly but surely to get to the core of their issues.

"Okay, here goes." Grace smiled and then she started, slowly and deliberately. Anna could see she was working really hard to maintain a calm pace, despite her obvious desperation to just spit it all out. Anna had become an expert at picking out the important stuff and letting the rest just wash over her so, for now, she sat quietly and just listened.

"I've always worked hard and done well. I was always the annoying one who actually looked forward to going into work every day. Until my current job that is. Everything moves so incredibly fast it's ridiculous. The environment's tough, really tough and the people even tougher and you want to think you can survive and cope with it all and then you wonder why? Why would anyone choose to be like some of the maniacs I work with? But the alternative is to admit defeat and watch everyone look at me with even more pity than they do already, thinking that I just wasn't up to it. And then there's Peter, my boss. As if it isn't all pressured enough without some bullying egomaniac verbally battering me on a daily basis. When someone tells you constantly that you're useless, after a while it's hard not to believe there must be some truth in it. So I'm constantly knackered, I feel beaten, trapped and then it becomes so all-consuming you realise there's no time or energy left for anything else, until life just feels like it's all about work. One failed relationship after another until you just feel like there's no point even trying."

And then she stopped, momentarily out of steam, her little speech delivered more in the style of a runaway train than the slow and clear oration she had been hoping for. Grace's eyes were watery and her bottom lip quivered ever so slightly which, for Anna, was not unexpected. This first meeting could often be quite emotional. While Grace had been talking, Anna was able to watch her carefully as she spoke very articulately and with real passion despite the rapidity. Even dressed casually as she was today, there was something very striking about her. Her dark hair was shiny and fell in natural waves to her shoulders. Anna quietly chastised herself for instinctively touching her own short, slightly brittle hair, the result of a multitude of dyes and treatments regularly administered over the years. Today, it was a kind of dull blonde. She had long since forgotten what her natural colour was. Grace's brown eyes were full of expression, her defined cheekbones perfectly highlighted with just the right amount of make-up (it was a natural and subtle look that Anna had never been able to achieve) and she had an understated air of confidence, despite her current situation. She had a significant job that most likely meant financial independence (Anna couldn't see the labels in Grace's clothes but was in no doubt the jeans, jacket, shirt and trainers would all have come at a considerable price) and while she obviously had ambition, there was nothing to suggest Grace was ruthless in her pursuit of greatness. Yes she wanted appreciation but not to fuel ego – she simply wanted people to be pleased with her. Anna studied her for a moment. How very touching, she thought.

"Tell me more about Peter."

"He shouts all the time and swears like no one I've ever met. He doesn't listen. I can't remember the last time I actually managed to complete a sentence, never mind put forward a sensible solution to something or pitch a new idea. But it's the way he constantly undermines me that's just so demoralising. And when he tears into me in front of colleagues, it's just so humiliating."

Anna watched Grace lost in thought for a moment, the pained look in her eyes suggesting she was reliving examples of this behaviour as she talked.

"What are you afraid of?" Anna asked, her voice a well-practised tone that was low and calm.

"That I won't be good enough. That he'll fire me." Grace's answer came without hesitation.

"So is it the job that's the problem or is it Peter? I'm just trying to establish if the root of the career frustration is the role or the boss?"

"It's hard to separate them but I suppose the pressure would be easier to bear without Peter. But I do wonder sometimes that if I'd been more strategic about my career choices, if I would ever have ended up where I am. Or if I just got swept along, taking opportunities as they came up rather than sitting down and working out what I really wanted to do next."

"And your personal life fits in where?"

Grace smiled but not from a place of happiness. Anna waited. A massive hole of silence was opening up but she wouldn't be the one to fall into it. She watched as Grace's expression morphed from pained to anxious to embarrassed as she struggled to find a way to tell Anna and then their eyes engaged. "I was in a relationship until recently. He was arrogant and controlling and it turned out he was also a serial cheat. Just when I thought it couldn't get any worse, I found out I was pregnant. I couldn't have brought his child into the world so I had a termination. And then I finished it." She shrugged, her eyes blurred now with tears, and then forced a smile. "But I do have the best friends in the world so it's not all bad."

Anna gently probed, challenging Grace to look at her own behaviour as they talked through various moments from her relationships with both Peter and John and then she glanced up at the large clock on the wall and smiled. "That's our hour almost up. Let's keep the focus on Peter next time. We'll talk through some specific examples of how he behaves towards you and start to look at ways to rebuild your confidence so you're better equipped to deal with him. Once we have that cracked it will be easier to work out whether or not the job itself is right for you. How does that sound?"

"That sounds great."

Anna stood up and Grace immediately followed suit, picking up her bag and jacket as Anna opened the door and then she followed her out into the corridor.

Anna offered Grace her hand as they reached the lift which Grace took firmly. "Thank you. It feels really good to finally be dealing with this stuff," Grace said as the lift doors opened.

They said their polite goodbyes and Grace disappeared inside. Anna lowered her head slightly in a well-practiced move to avoid any awkward last-minute eye contact while they waited for the doors to close. As she then turned around, she immediately stopped in her tracks at the sight of Matthew sitting very comfortably on a sofa, one arm spread across its back, the other casually flicking through a magazine.

"Matthew! What brings you up here?"

"I thought I'd take a walk on the wild side! Coffee?" Before Anna could answer, Matthew was up and making them both a drink. Anna stood, shifting her weight from one foot to the other while she waited. After a few moments, he handed Anna a mug and then sat down again, nodding to a seat opposite him that she obediently dropped into.

"So," he said slowly, "life coaching. Tell me again exactly how it works?"

Anna smiled. "Are you interested in some sessions?" Matthew raised his eyebrows in response and Anna felt a rush of heat to her cheeks. Slightly embarrassed at his reaction, she took a deep breath and carried on. "It's about helping people to attain their goals in life. So one might encourage someone to think about what's important to them. Think about where they want to be, what they want to do, what makes them feel fulfilled, and empower them along the way to be able to make the changes necessary to achieve those goals."

"So you tell people what to do with their lives?"

"No. There's no 'telling'. What I do is assist people to help themselves." Anna watched Matthew digest this, convinced that he was struggling to see the difference.

"But if you know the answer to someone's problems, why not just tell them?"

"Because life coaching is about long-term change and that has to come from the person themselves." Anna waited while Matthew mulled this over. She started to feel slightly hot again, aware of an uncomfortable burning sensation around her neck, a feeling that immediately increased as Matthew slowly leaned forward towards her.

"But how would someone know? How would they know if you chose to…" he stopped for a moment, taking time to make sure he used the right words, "…to guide someone in a certain direction?"

"I'm not sure I know what you mean?" Anna shifted in her seat.

"Then let me explain. I'm working with a research company whose work focuses on human behaviour. As part of a wider and very significant piece of work, we're looking at the role that trust plays in someone's decision-making process and then, more specifically, how people in different jobs inspire different levels of trust. So to what degree could a life coach, for example, change the course of a client's decision making based purely on the trust developed with him or her?"

"Which would surely mean abusing that trust?"

Matthew shrugged. "A small sacrifice for the positive impact the results of the overall study will have. It will investigate the impact of an extensive range of emotional states so what you and I are talking about is just a tiny part of the overall picture. And it would be very subtle. If you were interested in getting involved, it would be as simple as getting a client to make contact with me. You would be asked to provide as little explanation as possible as to why they should do this so that we can confidently surmise their decision is based primarily on trust. Or maybe they won't do it. Either way, it all counts." Matthew looked at her and smiled. "I would really like you to be involved, Anna. You would be credited amongst a highly esteemed group of contributors. We may even hold some events to present the findings so there could be opportunities to speak about the role of trust in both personal and professional relationships. Such high level exposure could be good for business. And you would of course be generously compensated for your contribution to the study." He paused for a moment. "So what do you think?"

"I think it's a no," Anna said, without waiting a beat. "I appreciate you considering me but it feels unethical and the money would be no compensation for that, so I'm afraid it's definitely a no."

Anna stood up and Matthew followed suit, stepping forward as he did so. She immediately felt uncomfortably close to him, his breath warm on her face as he spoke. "I'll tell you what. Let's have lunch or a drink next week sometime and talk about it some more." He handed her a business card which she instinctively accepted. "Give me a call and we'll set something up."

Anna was about to tell him that he shouldn't expect to hear from her but he had already walked away. Her body shivered as the intense flush of heat she had felt in his company started to fade, leaving her feeling momentarily chilled. She wondered for a moment if she'd understood him correctly; that she should basically work in direct contradiction to the principles of her profession and abuse the well-earned trust of a client. She shook her head in disbelief. Not a chance.

Anna was still standing where Matthew had left her when the lift pinged and her next client emerged. Instinctively she smiled, forced to relegate any thought of Matthew and his nonsensical proposition to the back of her mind. She made a silent pact with herself not to give him, or his ridiculous study, another thought.

8

Grace

The revolving doors spilled Grace out into the cold. She felt a little light-headed and emotionally drained, numb almost. She hadn't been sure what to expect but she definitely hadn't imagined feeling so vulnerable which now seemed a tad naive. This wasn't therapy after all. Or was it? Grace had assumed a professional, business-like approach to sorting out her work problems but even as she thought this, she knew it wasn't really true. Her problems were clearly nothing to do with her ability to do her job. It was all the emotional rubbish that got in the way. Grace steadied herself with a slow, deep breath. She had no idea what to make of it all so quickly decided the best course of action was to just park it for now and head for the nearest department store. An hour and three bags later – mascara, nail varnish and a lip gloss in one, none of which she needed, a jumper in the second that she didn't need and a pair of black trousers in the third, that she definitely didn't need, and she slowly started to feel better.

Lunch arrived in the shape of a glass of wine and a posh sandwich, consumed at a table outside under the warmth of a heater that left her cheeks flushed and her eyes stinging. It was a joy not to be in work and her leisurely pit stop was in stark contrast to the constant stream of people hurrying past, heads down, expressions fixed, all desperate not to waste a single moment of their precious lunch hour.

The sandwich quickly polished off, Grace relaxed with her wine and, with no further distractions, she felt ready to think about her session with Anna. Before she focused in on the specifics of their conversation, she wondered for a moment if she should have taken the leap and opted for actual full-on counselling. She smiled ruefully wondering if she had, how long it would have taken for the conversation to turn to her mother.

* *

Before

A glance at the clothes neatly laid out for her confirmed it was Friday. It was the one day of the week that Grace's mother felt required a slightly more casual look, the normal colour-coded outfits substituted by a simple pair of jeans and a jumper. Grace eased herself out of bed and immediately straightened the duvet behind her, taking a moment to smooth it with her small hands, pulling gently on the corners to make sure it was as neat as was expected. But her eyes were barely open. She knew the drill without needing to be fully awake yet.

When she wandered into the kitchen a few moments later, Isobel was already placing items carefully into Grace's lunchbox. Isobel had been around for as long as Grace could remember. She wasn't sure how old she was but Grace liked to think of her as a much older sister. As they spent so much time together, it somehow felt better to imagine her as a bonafide member of the family rather than the hired help that she knew she really was.

Grace watched Isobel expertly fit some fruit and a healthy snack in the gaps around her sandwich. She had asked her mother many times if she could just have school lunches like her friends, her ears immediately tuning out at the familiar speech about the necessity of a balanced midday meal which the school was apparently incapable of providing. It was the same with her clothes. When she had turned ten she had asked if she could start choosing for herself. Her mother had looked confused. "What's wrong with what I pick out for you?" she had asked. Grace hadn't had the verbal dexterity to explain that wasn't really the point. Never mind. She was eleven now and in September would be off to big school with its strict uniform. Then no one would get to choose.

Grace sat down at the kitchen table where her breakfast was waiting for her. A bowl of porridge, a dollop of Isobel's home-made jam, a glass of milk on the right and a neatly ironed checked napkin to the left. She quietly sniffed the air and felt her mouth flood with saliva. Toast! She knew that Isobel often had a few sneaky slices in between Grace's parents leaving for work at some ungodly hour and the moment when Grace would appear. What Grace wouldn't do for a thick piece of lightly toasted bread smothered in butter. She looked down at the porridge which elicited no such sensation of joyful anticipation. She then dutifully picked up her spoon and tentatively set about eating it. It wouldn't do to head to school without a healthy breakfast inside her. So she'd been told.

Half an hour later, with a gentle shove from Isobel to propel her through the school gates, Grace's eyes were drawn to the gaggle of mums, chatting and laughing as they did every morning, their charges released with a selection of hugs and kisses, their faces warm and loving. She knew her mother frowned upon them. "I like to be a positive role model for my daughter," she would often announce loudly to anyone in the vicinity. "Important for her to see a working mum in action." Often followed by, "Off for a coffee? Oh to have time for such indulgences!" Grace had no idea what point she was trying to make but the look on the other women's faces whenever they saw her mother (which thankfully was almost never) suggested her words were deemed unkind.

Grace hurried on to catch up with her friends, a smile simultaneously spreading across her face as she felt herself relax in preparation for the day ahead.

"Don't forget you're going to Emily's house after school! I'll pick you up at six," Isobel shouted after her. Grace raised a hand and waved her acknowledgement, her smile widening even further in response to the very welcome reminder.

Grace loved school. Her parents had high expectations but she was naturally clever so what could have been a constant pressure had become a means of earning otherwise elusive praise and approval that she was doing so well. Not that they didn't push. Achieving eighty percent in a test meant a goal of eighty-five or more for the next one; coming second in the class meant striving for first; and when that target was regularly hit, the focus quickly became smashing any existing school record for attainment. Grace constantly rose to the challenge. Her parents weren't demonstrative types so if working hard and doing well were the only ways to warrant attention or affection of any kind, Grace was well and truly on board with it.

The day passed uneventfully and Grace felt the excitement building as the end of the school day neared. "Come on, Mum'll be waiting," Emily said, grabbing Grace's hand and pulling her through the playground.

"Hi girls!" Jo was already rummaging in her bag. "Here you go. Cookies as it's Friday." She held out two large homemade biscuits, loaded with over-sized chunks of chocolate. Emily's younger brother, Harry, was already half way through his, one chocolatey hand hooked around his mum's thigh.

"Thanks Mrs Davidson. They look delicious."

"You're welcome, Grace. And it's Jo. You make me sound like my mother-in-law." She smiled warmly at Grace, knowing her frequent request to drop the formality was futile but, as always, she felt it was worth a try. "Right, come on. Let's get home."

The girls walked on ahead, deep in conversation. It was only a short walk and the minute they were through the front door, bags, shoes and coats were discarded, with only Grace stopping to make sure she had left hers as tidily as possible, and then they disappeared off to Emily's bedroom, desperate to get the door firmly closed before Harry tried to join them.

Grace loved spending time at Emily's house. Every radiator was typically covered in damp clothes with every room infused with the smell of fresh washing as a result.

There were piles of stuff on the stairs to be taken back to whichever room the random collection of items had come from that everyone, except Emily's mum, repeatedly ignored. She was never without something in her hands, on a mission to return something to its rightful place, only for it to be picked up again and abandoned moments later for her to pick up again. It was that wonderful sense of organised chaos, that sense of family life happening loudly and messily right now, that Grace couldn't get enough of. It of course bore no resemblance to her own home where everything had its place. Here, Grace was sure that was also true, it just wasn't so immediately obvious. And she would get to eat fish fingers and chunky chips for tea, smothered in ketchup with ice cream and every kind of sprinkle you could imagine for pudding. Heaven.

When the time came, they ate their tea in the kitchen at a large wooden table that occupied around a third of the space. The middle third was dominated by a huge fruit bowl that had also become home to stray keys, a ball of elastic bands, a tape measure, a pot of glitter and a random selection of pens. The end of the table played host to various stacks of papers, school notices, books and magazines, all held on to for a reason. Or maybe not. But the overall sense of the room was one of shared moments, of love and warmth, of making plans and lots of animated family meals.

"We're going to the cinema tomorrow," Emily announced to Grace. "Mum, can Grace come?"

"If it's okay with her mum, then of course she can."

"We're busy I think." Grace would love nothing more than a trip to the cinema but knew her Saturday was to be spent pounding the halls of the Science Museum. They were studying the key inventions that shaped modern society at school this term so her mum had already decided a family outing to support Grace's learning was the perfect way to spend their weekend. It was a nice thought but it would be dull and boring. Like a school trip but without her friends to have a quiet giggle with. There would be no laughter of any kind and Grace knew her father would be just as disappointed to be on the outing as her so, while her mother marched from one exhibit to another reading aloud the cultural significance of each, they would reluctantly trail along behind her with Grace at least, doing her best to look like she was glad to be there. It was a look she had learnt to perfect over the years.

Before Grace was required to elaborate on her family's plans, the doorbell rang. "That'll be Isobel," Jo said as she headed for the door. Grace quickly cleared away her bowl before following on to retrieve her things. Jo and Isobel were already chatting away as Grace walked into the hallway. Grace knew it would be very different if it had been her mum at the door. The relaxed conversation that Jo and Isobel were enjoying would be replaced by a few awkward pleasantries with Jo doing her best to engage her mother in conversation and her mother resisting, shutting down every question with a short, closed reply. Grace let the thought drift through her mind unchallenged and bent down to put on her shoes. With the front door still open, she then heard more voices and looked out to see Emily's dad and her older brother, Richard, walking up the path. Harry heard them too and came bounding past her, throwing himself into his father's open arms.

"Careful buddy!" he said, hurling Harry over his shoulder as he squeezed his way down the crowded hallway, with Richard following closely behind. Richard had been playing in a football match and was now dropping large chunks of mud with every step he took into the house.

"Hey Grace."

"Hi Mr Davidson." Grace blushed as she answered but wasn't sure why and then she smiled, loving the immediate chaos around her – Jo and Isobel still chatting away, Harry squealing, Emily pushing his wayward legs out of her way as she now joined them, Richard doing his best to squeeze through the bedlam, his eyes fixed firmly on the kitchen and finding something to eat, their father beaming from ear to ear.

"Thanks for having me," Grace said as she pulled on her coat.

"You're welcome here any time, my love."

And then with a final flurry, the door was closed and Grace and Isobel started their walk home. Grace hung on to the noise of the cheerful banter and laughter for as long as she could until the distance between them swallowed it up, their echoey footsteps on the pavement the only remaining sound.

"Is Mum home yet?"

"She's hoping to be back before bedtime." Grace glanced at Isobel. The slight edge to Isobel's voice was impossible to miss causing Grace to wonder if, yet again, she'd been forced to make a snatched call to her boyfriend or to one of her friends, letting them know that she was working late and therefore wouldn't be joining them that night despite best laid plans. She'd heard her mother tell Isobel on numerous occasions that she was required to stay late. She had never once heard her ask if Isobel was actually free to do so.

Isobel slipped her arm around Grace's slim shoulders and gave her a squeeze. "I've made some banana cake for you. I won't tell if you don't." Grace smiled and nodded and then quickly looked away to avoid Isobel seeing her smile disappear. She knew Isobel was trying to make her feel better and she really wanted her to believe it was working but it was hard to look happy when her head was full of the love and laughter she'd just left behind, and the harsh reality of the cold empty home that lay ahead.

"We could watch a film if you like? Or what about a game of Junior Monopoly? You might have to go easy on me though. You know I'm not the best."

Isobel continued to chat as they walked but Grace was no longer listening.

9

Grace

Now

Grace contemplated a second glass of wine and then instead opted for the bill. She was determined to make the most of what was left of her day off, leaving all thoughts of the session with Anna to one side to be dissected at some point later. She spent a rare hour browsing around a bookshop before whiling away the rest of the afternoon watching street performers in Covent Garden. Time passed in perfect harmony with the beautiful sounds of a string quartet and then it was time to head home. Or at least to the café that was almost like home.

Within minutes of arriving, Grace and her bags were comfortably settled at a table with a large cappuccino and an even larger cinnamon swirl. Not her normal pastry of choice but the change felt befitting to the day. She sat back in her chair, her hands cupping the warm mug of coffee and then with a conscious effort, she let her shoulders drop and her neck lengthen and, with a smile, she felt herself relax.

As she took the first delicious bite of her pastry, she was suddenly distracted by Warren, his expression alarmingly stern, angry almost, as he moved from table to counter and back again. As she searched for an explanation, her eyes fell on a smart, older man, sitting alone, his expression not dissimilar to Warren's.

"Can you wipe the table please?" Grace heard the man ask Warren who obliged in silence. "And I'll have another coffee. Hot this time if it's not too much trouble."

Warren visibly bit his tongue as he retreated to the counter and dutifully made another coffee. He placed it on the table in front of the man who then managed to make it last for a further forty-three painstaking minutes – in between looking at the news on her phone and checking emails for anything urgent, Grace felt so engaged she did actually time him – and then he finally stood up. Warren was immediately in front of him and as he picked up the empty cup, their eyes met for a split second and Grace actually felt quite anxious, fearing some kind of altercation but the man just sighed and slowly headed for the door. Warren watched him go and then as he turned around he saw Grace and she smiled, trying, unconvincingly she was sure, to look like she had only just noticed him as he had her. To think she had come in today wondering if there would be any awkwardness after their last encounter, an event that suddenly felt somewhat insignificant in comparison to what she had just witnessed, whatever that was.

Grace gestured for Warren to come over and he sat down, elbows immediately on the table, his head falling heavily into his hands.

"You okay?" she asked.

Warren lifted his head ever so slightly and looked up at her, his eyes tired and sorrowful. Grace waited as his mouth fought the weight of his saddened face and slowly curled into the meekest of smiles. "I'll survive."

"Who was that?"

And then he pushed back his chair and stood up again, clearly agitated. "My dad," he said quietly and then he walked away. Grace was relieved he missed her jaw dropping and her eyebrows simultaneously rising in what she imagined was a very unattractive manner although she was desperate for him to come back and explain what on earth had been going on.

Before Grace had the chance to call Warren back, Emily arrived, talking long before she actually reached the table. "I'm so glad you're around today. An hour to kill and nerves already taking over," she said at speed as she sat down, her head immediately looking behind her for a waiter and, more importantly, a drink. "You drinking?" she asked with a quick glance back towards Grace and then her head whipped around again.

"I'll have a glass of wine if you are," Grace replied to the back of her head.

"Warren!" She gave up waiting to catch his eye. "Two glasses of red please."

And then she was fussing in her bag for something while in between hitching at her skirt and generally flapping so efficiently Grace swore she was creating a breeze. "Emily stop it! You're literally unravelling before my eyes."

Emily immediately stopped, her expression pained. "I know. Why do I do this?"

Grace raised her eyebrows. It was a question she would love to know the answer to. On any average day, Emily was totally together and comfortable in her own skin until, that was, the subject of relationships was raised and then her confidence simply evaporated. With a date looming, Grace was faced with someone who looked like Emily on the outside but who was nothing more than a bundle of nervous energy on the inside. It would be infuriating if it wasn't so desperately sad. No, Grace thought, it actually was infuriating.

"Emily, do you want someone in your life?" Emily hesitated. "Do you?" Grace asked again, her tone making it clear she was deadly serious.

"Yes, I do," Emily said, her words quiet and tentative.

"Well you don't sound very convincing."

"Yes, yes I do," Emily said again, louder this time with a very welcome strength slowly returning to her voice.

"Do you need someone in your life at any cost?"

"No, I absolutely do not need that."

"And how do you make sure you attract the right person? By being yourself and believing in yourself or by trying to be anyone *but* yourself?"

"Definitely the former."

Grace reached across the table and took hold of Emily's hand. "Anyone, and I do mean anyone, would be so lucky to have you in their life. Why can't I get you to believe that?"

"I promise to try. Just don't make me say it out loud."

Grace smiled. "So remind me who he is?" Thankfully the question at least made Emily sit still for a moment.

"Jim. A teacher." She shrugged. "He seems perfect but then so did Brian." And then finally the twinkle in her eye returned as she silently relived the edited highlights of the

68

disastrous date she'd had with Brian. Her beautiful face broke into an enormous smile which Grace mirrored. And then they were laughing, Grace with relief that Emily was finally seeing the funny side, Emily slightly hysterically if truth be told, perhaps not quite as ready to see the funny side as Grace.

"Your drinks ladies." Warren put the glasses of wine down and then looked at Emily. "You okay Em?"

She pulled herself together and nodded with a tight smile and for a moment, Grace thought she might cry and her heart contracted in response to Emily's obvious pain. And then Warren looked at Grace and she could only hope her smile was more convincing. "She's fine. Honestly."

He looked at Emily again and then back at Grace and then back at Emily one last time before he decided to leave them to it.

Grace leaned in a little closer. "This bit's supposed to be the fun part Em." Emily looked at her, eyebrows raised, eyes wide and slightly desperate looking. It was clearly anything but. "How can you possibly just be yourself when you get into such a state?"

Emily's head lowered. It was clearly a question she simply couldn't, or wouldn't, answer so instead she opted for the classic brush off. She pulled herself up with a swift shake of her head. "I'll be fine. Honestly. It's just a bit of stage fright. Nothing to worry about."

Grace looked at her and for a moment she wondered whether or not to challenge her further before deciding to focus on the positive. Emily was pushing herself way out of her comfort zone and getting on with her life and that was clearly to be celebrated.

Before she could think about it further, her eyes were drawn to Warren. He was standing very still, staring at nothing in particular, his eyes glazed. His whole demeanour looked heavy. He looked beaten. She wondered if she should invite him over but, while she hesitated, she watched him disappear for a moment and then return with his jacket. She opened her mouth to call out to him but he was out of the door and striding quickly away before she had time to find her voice.

10

Anna

"Let's talk about Peter." It was a week after their first session and Anna wasn't about to waste a single moment. She watched Grace shift in her chair, her eyes clouding at the mention of her nemesis. Anna found herself feeling mildly irritated. There was no point coming at this with any sense of reluctance. This was why Grace was here, wasn't it? To let Anna help her make things better? Anna took a deep breath and forced a smile. "Okay, let's start with other work relationships. How are they?"

Grace immediately perked up. "Good. Really good."

"How would your colleagues describe you?"

"Supportive, loyal, hard-working."

"Competent? Good at what you do?"

"Yes I think so."

"So what does that suggest to you?"

Anna waited, happy to sit tight for as long as necessary for Grace to loosen her pursed lips and say what she needed to for them to really get things moving. Come on, Anna thought, spit it out!

"I know. Of course I know. The problem is his not mine. But then it is mine! I'm the one who's suffering. I'm the one whose confidence is on the floor. I don't see him suffering in any way. Anything but."

"Nevertheless the problem is fundamentally his," Anna said, her words slow and deliberate. "So what role do you play?"

"Should I be more aware of why he does it? Is that what you mean?" Grace was clearly struggling. "Perhaps he suffered abuse as a child or was bullied?"

"I'm not interested in why he does it. He's not my client, you are. I'm only interested in why you let him behave so badly towards you."

"But what choice do I have?" Grace shifted uncomfortably in her seat. Anna could see the distress in her face and hear the confusion and frustration in her voice but she remained undeterred.

"So you accept you do have a choice?" Grace said nothing as Anna watched her grapple with the idea that this might actually be the case. "We can't do anything to change Peter's behaviour," Anna continued, "but we can work on changing how you respond to him. So let's concentrate on that."

For the next half an hour or so, Anna worked hard with Grace, slowly helping her to work out various different strategies for how she might better cope with Peter, alongside some exercises designed to build her self-esteem. Then a sudden and loud knock at the door came as such a surprise to Anna that, for a moment, she froze despite having been in full flow. Her clients knew to take a seat by the lifts and wait to be collected which meant she was unable to think of another occasion when one of her sessions had been interrupted. "Just give me a minute," she said, getting up to see who on earth it could be.

"Hello Anna. Am I interrupting?"

"Yes Matthew, you are." Anna held on tightly to the door, keeping the opening as narrow as possible. "I have a client with me."

"I just thought I'd see if you were free on the off chance but perhaps we can speak later?" he said as he started to back away. "You'll call me?"

Anna's response was to simply close the door.

She allowed herself the briefest of moments and then she turned to face Grace. "Well I think that's us done for today Grace. I'll see you next week."

For a moment Grace didn't move and just looked blankly back at her but Anna needed only to raise her eyebrows and Grace was immediately grabbing her things and heading for the door.

11

Grace

Grace stood for a moment in front of the door that had quietly closed behind her, feeling like she had been unceremoniously dismissed. The tone of the whole session had been very different to the first one and she certainly hadn't expected it to be quite so challenging. But despite that, she had a strong sense that Anna might actually be able to help which was a really good feeling. She was certainly a very direct and forceful woman, until the end of course, when her eyes had been full of nothing but a raw anger. Grace made a mental note never to knock on her door without very good reason.

As Grace walked back into her own office half an hour later, she was relieved to find it empty, the silence broken only by the sound of her phone ringing."Hello?"

"Grace, it's John."

Grace hung up. John was now withholding his number which was incredibly annoying but as Grace took so many work calls on her mobile, she had neither the time nor the energy to constantly ditch calls just in case it was him. Almost immediately the phone rang again. Grace hesitated for just a second knowing this was something that had to stop.

"What do you want?"

"Please don't hang up! I just want to talk to you. We can't just leave things the way they are."

"I think we can."

"No, we can't! Can't I just see you, even for an hour?"

"No," she said again, as firmly as possible.

"Grace, please!"

Okay, she thought. Enough is well and truly enough. "Listen to me, you complete and utter bastard," she hissed, her voice low and firm. "I will not see you. I don't even want to talk to you. I hate you with a passion that scares me and you are a part of my life I intend to bury so deeply, it can only be found with the help of a team of bloody archaeologists. There is no room for the word 'us'. Do you understand?"

"I don't understand why we can't at least be friends?"

Grace threw her arm into the air, holding her phone aloft and for a second she came dangerously close to hurling it against the wall. Thinking better of it, she instead let out a sharp yell, whether the result of frustration, anger or regret or a toxic cocktail of all three, was immaterial. Whatever it was, she needed to let it out before she burst. And then she put the phone back to her ear.

"You just won't listen will you? Are you really that insensitive? What does it fucking take?" Grace was suddenly aware of other people in the room. She hadn't noticed them quietly creep back in. Moving to sit down at her desk and turning to face the wall, she continued in an angry whisper. "I don't want to hear from you again, is that understood?"

Silence.

"Is that understood John?"

"Yes," was all he could manage, in a barely audible whisper.

"Then consider this our final goodbye."

As Grace turned back to face the room, she jumped violently in her seat. Peter was standing over her desk, smirking. "Problem Grace?"

"Nothing I can't handle thank you."

"Well, if you need any advice, do feel free to ask. Looks like you handle your personal life with the same degree of ineptitude as you do your job." Amused by himself, he then disappeared into his office, tapping a colleague on the shoulder as he went and beckoning him to follow.

Within minutes, the yelling from beyond Peter's door had started. Grace quickly gathered her stuff together and headed for the door. She wasn't ready to start practising her newly-explored techniques just yet, opting instead for the tried and tested speedy getaway. As she walked through the editorial floor, her eyes were drawn towards raised voices. The unmistakable boom of the advertising manager loomed large as the daily fight for colour pages took place, the features editor on one side of the editor, Sebastian, arguing how her material would be severely damaged by the loss of yet another colour page; the ad man on the other side arguing that without more colour ads, there simply wouldn't be the extra pages for the feature in question to run at all. One of many vicious circles that spun on a daily basis.

Grace moved on, passed the serious faces of the news desk and surrounding reporters, passed a burst of laughter from the showbiz office, passed the corridor that led to the online team and then she slipped into Sam's office where she sat down and finally set to work.

"I thought you might be here." Sam appeared a few moments later and put a coffee down in front of her. Grace smiled, immediately picking up the drink and taking a welcome sip.

"Thank you. You're too kind."

"I do my best."

Grace immediately felt herself relax. She loved the buzz of the editorial floor and the little sanctuary she had found with Sam. Everything about her job felt different from here and, thanks to Anna, for the first time she actually felt it might be possible to cope better with Peter. She smiled as she realised the strange feeling she was experiencing was a very welcome sense of hope.

As Grace headed out of the office that night, her phone started to ring. She thought about ignoring it until she saw Emily's name. "Hi Em."

"Meet me in the café for a drink. It's been one of those days and I need to vent."

Grace smiled. "Put like that how could I possibly refuse?"

When Grace arrived, there was typically no sign of Emily so she settled herself at a table and ordered herself a glass of wine.

"Well if it isn't my favourite customer!" Warren appeared with his jacket on and sat down beside her.

"You done for the day?"

"I am indeed. You waiting for someone?"

"Emily."

"Could be a while then," he said with a smile. "Do you want some company while you wait?"

"Sure." Grace felt the warmth of his smile flush her cheeks as he headed for the bar and helped himself to a beer. And then he was back, sitting beside her again.

"So what's the occasion?"

"Oh you know us. We don't need an excuse."

"And long may that continue otherwise I'd very quickly be out of job! And the only person who'd be happy about that would be my father and I'm not in the habit of doing anything to please him. At least not intentionally!"

"Things looked a little strained between you both the other day."

Warren hesitated. "Let's just say he struggles with my career choice. It was only meant to be temporary while I worked out what I wanted to do. Turns out knowing how much it annoys him has made it hard to move on." He rolled his eyes with a smile. "God that makes me sound like such a child!"

"Sounds like your mum needs to bang your heads together."

"I'm sure she would if she were still with us."

"Oh no, I'm so sorry Warren. I had no idea."

He smiled warmly but there was an unmistakable sadness in his eyes. "No need to apologise. She died a very long time ago now. You'd think my dad and I would be close as a result but...." He stopped suddenly. "How on earth did we end up talking about all this?!" He downed his beer. "Fancy another?"

Before she could answer Grace's phone buzzed with a text message. As she read it, her body language clearly gave away her frustration.

"Is there a problem?"

"Bloody Emily's bailed."

"Why don't we grab a bite somewhere instead then?"

"Yeah, why not," Grace said without waiting a beat. She wasn't about to lose out to hesitation a second time.

They chose a nearby Italian restaurant and were soon settled at a small cosy table, separated only by two large glasses of red wine and two generous bowls of pasta. The conversation continued to flow easily as they ate.

"That was quite a break up you went through."

Grace felt her eyes narrow as she smiled. "You don't miss much do you?"

Warren shrugged. "I don't mean to listen but sometimes it's hard not to. He sounded like a complete arse so I'm glad you're rid of him."

"Yes, me too. It's funny how little time it takes to be able to look back and think 'what was I thinking?' Or not thinking. He treated me so badly but it's the fact I let him that's so hard to reconcile."

"Don't beat yourself up about it. I know only too well how easy it is to get sucked in by someone."

"Do you?" Grace watched as Warren shifted slightly in his chair. "You don't have to tell me if you don't want to."

"It's not a big deal now. Just a relationship from years back that went way off course. She was a few years older than me and it was really intense. We worked together but she was

79

more senior, more experienced and used to getting her own way. My friends didn't get her at all which I totally understand now but, in the moment, I was simply hypnotised by it all. And then her behaviour started to change. Nothing major initially, just lots of little things that eventually added up to something quite suffocating. So I finished it." He stopped for a moment as if remembering. "And that was when the fun really started."

Grace waited and then couldn't resist nudging him. "Why? What happened?"

"Let's just say she found the break-up difficult to accept. I ended up going travelling then working abroad for a while just to get away from her." And then he bit down on his lip which Grace read as a sign he'd said all he was going to on the subject.

"It's been a really lovely evening," Grace then said with a smile, keen to put an end to the threat of their first awkward silence.

"It has, hasn't it?" he said, immediately smiling back. "Do you want another drink?"

"No, I've had more than enough thanks." She looked at her watch. "In fact, I think it's probably time to go."

As they stepped out into the cool night air a few minutes later, they decided to walk for a while and Warren laid his arm casually around Grace's shoulder. As they approached a crossroads, they were brought to a temporary halt while they waited for the lights to change. Grace smiled up at Warren and instinctively, he bent down to kiss her. It felt like an eternity before his lips finally reached hers and when at last contact was made, she closed her eyes and let the warmth of his kiss spread through her body. And then his arms were around her and Grace felt herself melt against him.

She wasn't sure how much time had passed before they finally pulled apart but she was suddenly aware of people moving around them. The illuminated red man had been dutifully replaced by a green one and obediently the waiting crowd had restarted its journey. Warren took hold of Grace's hand and they took their place amongst the flow of people.

Grace waited until the throng started to thin out and then she stopped. "Why don't you leave me here? It's silly for you to go out of your way. You'll be home in five minutes and I can get a cab from here."

She watched Warren wrestle with her words. "If you're sure you'll be okay?" he said, with an unmistakable reluctance.

"I'll be fine, really."

Warren smiled at her and then put out his arm to an approaching taxi. Grace gave him one final kiss before she climbed into the waiting car and as soon as she closed the door, it merged seamlessly back into the evening traffic.

Grace settled back into the seat with a contented smile, feeling more at ease and relaxed than she had for a very long time.

12

Anna

Anna had been completely thrown by Matthew's unexpected visit. She found few things more annoying than people who didn't listen and, as far as she was concerned, she'd made it quite clear that she wasn't interested in his little project. Pointless, therefore, to just turn up without warning. She knew she'd brought her session with Grace to an abrupt end but Grace's bemusement as she left was matched only by Anna's indifference to any discomfort she may have caused.

It was lunchtime and Anna made her way down to the café. As she stood in the queue, she felt her phone vibrating in her bag and instinctively reached for it. It was a text from Matthew. 'We should talk. I'll look out for you'. Anna took in the words and felt her cheeks flush. Why was he deliberately choosing to ignore her decline? She quickly typed a reply. 'I appreciate your interest but as I said I'm not interested. No more conversation needed.'

She stuffed her phone back in her back and bristled as her foot started to tap. She willed the people in front of her to do less chatting and more choosing, her eyes flitting this way and that, determined to spot Matthew if he was around before he saw her. When finally it was her turn, she grabbed a sandwich and a drink and then for the first time ever, hurried back to her office. She had no intention of talking to him. She didn't have to justify her decision and she absolutely would not be coerced into doing so.

Anna quietly ate her lunch and then she quickly scanned her emails before her next session was due to start. In amongst the unopened mail she found a reminder from a friend about drinks planned for that evening. Or perhaps 'friend' was too strong a word? She felt more comfortable with the idea of acquaintances, liking the lack of intimacy that the title suggested.

She felt her shoulders sink slightly. She wasn't one for girls' nights out as a rule. The date had been fixed weeks ago as a chance to catch up with some old work colleagues who continuously berated her for never joining them for a chat and a gossip over a bottle of wine or two. She cast her mind back and vaguely remembered pulling out the last time they were due to get together. She sighed. She would have to go, trying to convince herself that going along would at least mean she would be off the hook for a while. She only ever went to remind them where she was and what she was doing, using the catch-ups as a means of seeking out referrals. Perhaps she could secure herself a couple of recommendations to follow up on? That would at least make it worth her while.

After a couple of really good sessions and two trips to the coffee machine without bumping into Matthew, Anna started to feel more like herself. Back in control, her tough exterior slowly resealed itself around her like a security blanket of iron. It was six o'clock before she knew it and, as she bade farewell to her last client of the day, there was just enough time to touch up her make-up before heading out.

When half an hour later Anna emerged from the tube station, she was on unfamiliar territory. She gave herself a moment or two to find her bearings and then headed off to the bar where her friends were waiting.

"Anna you made it!" A cheer rippled around the small group as Anna approached.

"Only because I couldn't think of an excuse not to."

More laughter and scraping of chairs as everyone shoved up to make room for her. "Here, have some wine," said Olivia, thrusting a large glass into Anna's hand as she sat down. "Kate was just telling us about the latest sexual harassment complaint at her place. It's rife! You've missed Sophie's news – she's been promoted again already. Bitch!" (Laughter at her own joke). "And Lucinda's bursting to tell us something so no doubt she'll be next. Then we need all your news!"

Anna raised her eyebrows and did her best to look interested, determined to ensure from the outset that the spotlight stayed as far away from her as possible. Not that it was hard when everyone else was so eager to take their turn centre stage.

The chat continued, growing ever louder and more animated with each fresh bottle of wine. Anna found herself getting slowly drawn in and eventually gave herself permission to relax, choosing her moment to plug some recent successes that were pertinent to the conversation.

"Give me a few of your business cards," Kate said, her hand immediately outstretched. "I need to get you connected with at least three people I know who definitely need your help."

"Me too," Sophie agreed, her own outstretched hand now waiting in line.

Anna duly handed out her cards with a concerned smile. "Of course, ladies. You know I'm always happy to help if I can."

The conversation quickly moved on again and Anna took a quick glance at her watch. She was amazed to see it was already past eleven and immediately started to put on her jacket.

"Sorry ladies but I have to go," she said at the next pause. "Early start tomorrow."

There was of course a flurry of objections – the night was yet young, they were planning on moving on somewhere else, it was so rare to have her with them that she simply had to stay for just one more drink – but she stuck to her guns. With a flurry of goodbyes, Anna left them to it and, despite having had a reasonably pleasant few hours, she couldn't help but feel like she'd escaped the moment she stepped outside. She relished for a moment the immediate sense of relief as the door to the bar slowly closed behind her and the buzz of conversation and noisy background music finally faded away to a more bearable hum.

Without further delay, she started walking before taking stock of exactly where she was, weaving her way through the usual bursts of revellers as they rolled passed her in erratic waves. After a few moments, a quick look around confirmed she had no idea where she was. She stopped for a moment, looking this way and that, hoping to see something she recognised and then she gasped. A painfully sharp intake of breath that burnt her throat and scorched her heart that now pounded uncontrollably. She desperately wanted to look away and believe she was mistaken but her eyes were wide and locked, the noise and bustle around her forgotten, sucked way into the background as if she was suddenly in some kind of vacuum with all sound replaced by an eerie yet deafening silence. Her hand was locked to her mouth, terrified that she might actually release a blood-curdling scream as she watched Warren, her beautiful Warren, tenderly lean in to kiss not just any woman, but Grace! In a heartbeat, she was transported back to a time when she had tried desperately to convince Warren to give their relationship another chance. She had begged, she had pleaded, she had tried to be calm and level-headed and then she had cried uncontrollably, she had got angry, so very very angry, until he had simply vanished. His phone disconnected, his flat empty, his friends mute. It was like he'd never existed. Try as she might she'd been unable to find out what had happened to him and eventually she had been forced to accept that he really had gone.

The hole he'd left behind was immense, the pain as real today as it had ever been, a catalogue of disastrous relationships and a broken marriage now behind her as she'd desperately tried to move on. But it had been impossible. She had endured over a decade of misery and now Grace, poor bullied little Grace, was standing right where she should be, wrapped in strong arms that belonged around her, feeling the touch of lips that only her own lips should ever know.

As Anna watched them gaze into each other's eyes, their smiles wide and content, their kisses intense and intimate, she had only one thought. She needed to make them stop. She needed Grace as far away from him as possible so she could reclaim her rightful place beside the only man she had ever loved and had continued to love year after year after miserable year. She needed to take Grace on a new direction and ensure she left Warren behind.

Anna was suddenly rummaging in her bag, never taking her eyes off them. When she found what she was looking for, she reached for her phone and dialled.

"Matthew, it's Anna. Yes, I know it's late but I wanted to let you know I'll do it. Your research project. Whatever you want, I'll do it."

And then she abruptly ended the call and slowly walked away.

13

Grace

When Grace walked into the office the next day her heart felt light. So inflated was she with joy that she felt as if she was floating, gliding through the busy foyer then sweeping in and out of the lift. It was an unusual feeling for her and one she liked enormously. She paused for a moment as she approached the marketing department, closed her eyes and took a slow, deep breath. It's not about me, she said to herself, it's not about me, it's really not about me. It was time to start putting Anna's advice into play.

She walked in, consciously holding her head up, a broad smile across her face. As she took off her coat and sat down, Peter burst out of his office, his eyes darting from one person to another. Grace looked around at the lowered heads, aware of the collective sharp intake of breath as Peter's door had swung open. They needn't have worried though as his steely gaze quickly fell on her. And then he was the one who stopped suddenly as he realised Grace was not only looking directly at him but smiling at him too.

"Morning Peter," she said with her newly-discovered lightness. "What can I do for you?"

Grace held his eye until he was the one forced to look away and then, without saying a word, he turned around and went back into his office. Grace's smile widened. Game on.

Game on indeed. Grace opened a new document on her computer and started to type. Her fingers could barely keep up with the flood of memories of the endless occasions Peter had shouted at her, humiliated her, rubbished her and verbally trampled on her very soul. Keep notes, Anna had said. Write it all down. When she felt she had captured enough, she clicked on the document to close it and was immediately prompted to give it a name. She sat back for a moment. What should she call it? Retribution? Ultimate revenge? Diary of a spineless bully? Probably not the best route to go down. It wouldn't do for the document to leap out should anyone access her files. Unlikely as that was, Grace wanted the file to blend in so she sat forward and typed, 'Planning Notes Old'. That would do it. Innocuous sounding and both irrelevant and dated thanks to the addition of the word 'old'. Feeling the need to be just a little more cautious, she saved it into a work folder called 'Archive', well away from any personal stuff and then set about getting on with her day which was harder than it sounded when all she could think about was Warren's arms wrapped around her, that incredible feeling just before he kissed her for the first time, that glow that had warmed her all night like the softest of blankets. She had checked her phone first thing and then realised they didn't even have each other's numbers. Annoying as that was, at least she didn't have to spend the day wondering if he would be in touch.

A loud ping from her computer jolted Grace from her daydreaming. She was due in a meeting which was just the prompt she needed. There was no avoiding it now. She had to get on with some work.

A few hours later and with a couple of meetings under her belt, Grace decided to venture out to pick up some lunch. As she headed for her favourite sandwich bar, she took several large breaths of London's finest petrol-soaked air which was surprisingly refreshing after the stale air she had been forced to inhale all morning. The pavement was busy so it was a moment or two before she realised someone was walking alongside her.

As she looked up, she gasped, her cheeks immediately hot and flushed. "Warren! What are you doing here?"

"I heard a rumour you'd been drinking someone else's coffee. Tell me it's not true!"

Grace smiled. "Seriously, what are you doing here?"

"I didn't have your number and I didn't want it to look, I don't know, like it didn't mean anything. Not wanting to jump the gun or anything," he added quickly. "I just sometimes think you see me as a bit…" Warren struggled for a moment as he searched for the right words and then he changed tack. "It's just I'm going away for a few days and didn't want you coming to the café and thinking I was hiding from you."

"Well that's very lovely of you. Going somewhere nice?"

"I've got some stuff I need to sort out with my dad. It's long overdue." He hesitated for a moment then shrugged. "I suddenly have a renewed sense of purpose. Like anything's possible."

Warren smiled at her and Grace felt a repeat of the previous night's glow sweep around her body, bringing with it a rush of warmth. "Glad to be of service."

"Oh no, nothing to do with you. I won on a football bet and I'm feeling lucky." Warren immediately laughed as Grace gasped. "Of course it's because of you!" he said, nudging her with his shoulder.

Warren then slipped his arm around Grace who was suddenly so overwhelmed by the surprise of him just appearing beside her, by the relaxed and flirtatious banter, by the ease of his hand on her shoulder, she feared she might actually be hot to the touch. Warren certainly didn't seem to notice as they headed off to the sandwich bar together.

Taking her order as they arrived, Warren left Grace to grab one of the small tables outside. She felt herself relax and smiled, still struggling with the idea that Warren and his warped sense of humour had come all this way on the off-chance of bumping into her. Wow.

They chatted and laughed together as they enjoyed their lunch, voices animated, eyes bright and alive and then Grace glanced at her watch. "Shit. Fuck!" She leapt up and grabbed her bag, a look of real panic in her eyes. "I have to go."

"Sorry, I've kept you too long," Warren said as he stood up too, swept up in the sudden sense of unease and urgency.

"No, it's fine." It really wasn't. "But I do have to go."

Warren searched for his phone. "Just give me your number so I can call you when I get back."

Grace quickly reeled off her number and then Warren kissed her, rooting her to the spot until she could no longer ignore the alarm bell ringing in her head with ever increasing volume. She pulled herself away and smiled. "I really have to go. Thanks so much for coming over and have a good trip. I really hope you can work things out with you dad. Call me when you get back."

By the time the last words were out, she was already running, as fast as was physically possible in three and a half inch heels and a neat-fitting pencil skirt, aware how ridiculous she must look but without the time to care.

When Grace flew into the marketing department just a few moments later, she immediately stopped as if she had quite literally run into the wall of silence that greeted her. Peter had been mid flow, tearing a strip off one of her colleagues with the rest of them forced to act is if they weren't actually there. It was a clumsy attempt to save the victim's blushes which was pointless, obviously. But Peter's attention was immediately diverted and all eyes were suddenly on Grace.

"Grace. How nice of you to join us."

Grace struggled to find some composure determined that as soon as she did, she would cling on to it for dear life. She had done nothing wrong after all, just popped out for some lunch. She quickly reminded herself she was considered management which should mean she didn't have to account for every single minute of her day. Perspective, that's what was needed. She had done nothing wrong.

"Hi Peter," she smiled. "Just grabbed a quick sandwich in between meetings." Grace did her best to appear calm and relaxed as she shrugged off her coat and headed for her desk. "Did anyone see Sebastian on breakfast telly this morning talking about the results of the political survey the paper ran? He was amazing." Wasn't diversion in her armoury of tactics? She struggled to remember, looking around the room at the wide stares, the unblinking eyes. It was clear no one else was about to join in. Grace felt beads of sweat start to break out on her forehead, her palms suddenly coated with a thin film of unpleasant clamminess. She picked up her notebook. "Well, lovely talking to you all. I have a meeting," she said as she headed back towards the door.

"You'll have five minutes with me first."

It's not about me, she repeated to herself, it's not about me. And then she smiled at Peter before following him into his office. As he shut the door behind him, Grace leapt in.

"I've been meaning to ask how your United Radio meeting went?"

"What?" Peter looked genuinely confused. Or bemused possibly. Grace wasn't sure but he wasn't shouting which encouraged her to keep going.

"I'd really like to hear about it. Perhaps I could come to the next meeting, if there is one?"

"If there's what?"

"Another meeting. With United. I'd really like to get involved. Happy to get some promotional pages and a social media campaign mocked up to show them what we can do, if that would help?"

"What would help is you shutting up. Jesus Christ Grace!"

Grace stopped. Peter's voice was rising but he had clearly forgotten what he was going to bawl her out over. She watched him struggle for a moment, his footing well and truly lost. "Oh just get out."

Grace swiftly left with a discreet smile. Advantage me, she thought, as she headed back to her desk to send an email to Anna (she had promised her an update today) and then she quickly left the office before Peter reappeared for round two.

On the way back from her meeting, Grace wandered on to the editorial floor in search of her favourite sub-editor to check how the promotion was shaping up for the next day's paper. Jack was old school. He had been a hack for a hundred years and was just quietly biding his time as he coasted towards retirement. He was old-fashioned in his views and attitudes and Grace absolutely loved him for it. His chivalry and politeness flashed like a lone beacon that Grace was happily drawn to on a daily basis. She placed a large blueberry muffin down on his desk.

"Hi Jack."

"Darling Grace. Looking radiant as always. And bearing gifts!" He smiled as he picked up the cake. "Your page is all done. Go and loiter by the printer, there's a good girl."

Grace smiled. If anyone else spoke to her the way Jack did she would feel immediately patronised but, bizarrely, it just made her love him more. "Thanks Jack. I really don't know what I'd do without you."

Grace left Jack with a satisfied smile as he tucked into his muffin and headed for the printer. As she lifted her page, she started to read the copy as she slowly moved away and walked straight into Sam. His eyes immediately brightened and Grace felt her spirits lift. Two warm smiles within ten minutes. This was turning into quite an exceptional day.

"I was starting to think you'd found a new hang out?"

They walked together back towards his office. "As if that would ever happen. I'm just trying out a new approach on Peter."

Sam raised his eyebrows. "Tell me more."

Grace shrugged. "Oh you know, classic distractions, simple things like looking him in the eye and melting him with my dazzling smile!"

Sam looked at her, his expression a little confused. "That's great," he said, trying to sound enthusiastic. "Is it working?"

"Early days but I've managed to avoid being yelled at so far today so let's just say at the very least, he's been temporarily disarmed."

Sam stopped as they reached his office and Grace immediately started backing away. "Gotta get on. See you later."

"Don't be a stranger," Sam shouted after her, unsure if Grace had heard him as she strode off across the open office.

Grace still had a spring in her step when she left the office for the day and headed out for dinner. She was the first to arrive as always but had learned to relish the quiet few moments she always had as a result, enjoying the chance to slowly transition from frantic daytime Grace to the more mellow evening Grace, a simple enough process with the help of a large gin and tonic. She was happy people watching as she waited, straining to hear the conversations going on nearby and inventing her own backgrounds for the diners around her. The table to her left was definitely a man with his mistress. His eyes kept darting around the room, no doubt checking for familiar faces. She was dripping in jewellery. The price of her silence was obviously high. Either that or he had been letting her down a lot recently. To the right was a couple who Grace quickly decided were first daters as she watched them gaze continuously into each other's eyes. By contrast, next to them was a couple who had clearly been together for some time. They were relaxed and looked content, speaking only when there was something to say, their conversation seamlessly alternating with a perfectly comfortable silence. In the far corner was a large group of women, all talking over each other, each one eager to be the focus and have their say.

As she saw Phil approaching, she watched several pairs of eyes follow him to his seat with frantic whispering behind hands, some people immediately recognising him, others believing he was someone they knew but were unsure why. And of course many remained totally oblivious. Such was the reward for being a radio personality – a kind of bizarre intermittent anonymity. Phil successfully avoided catching anyone's eyes as he navigated his way towards Grace, stopping for a quick kiss and a squeeze before he sat down. As he looked for a waiter to order himself a drink, Emily appeared beside him.

"Great timing, Em. What are you having?" he asked.

"Just get a bottle if everyone's drinking wine?"

"Works for me," said Grace. "Glad to see you've actually made it tonight," she levelled at Emily as her friend sat down. "What happened to you last night?"

Emily's eyes went down and she suddenly became very busy laying her napkin perfectly across her lap, running her hands over it repeatedly until there was not a crease to be seen. Slightly bemused, Grace watched her fidget and then she turned to Phil who looked equally sheepish.

"What?" Grace asked them both, continuing to look from one to the other. "What is it?" she said again. And then she gasped. "You set me up?" She looked at Emily who was still avoiding her gaze and then she turned back to Phil. "And you were in on it too? You're supposed to be on my side!" She turned again to Emily who finally dared to look up. "You're supposed to be on my side!" she said again, this time to Emily. "Just don't tell me Warren was involved too?" Frantic looks from one to the other. "He was?" Desperation was now seeping into her voice. "You have got to be kidding me?"

"Don't be cross with Warren. He just wanted a helping hand, that's all," Emily said, her cheeks flushed.

"And don't be cross with Emily," Phil interjected. "She asked me what I thought and it felt like the perfect way to get John well and truly out of your system."

"So I should just be cross with you then should I?" Grace said to Phil, raising her eyebrows to further emphasise her clipped words.

Phil went to object and then he shrugged. "Fine, be cross with me. But I'm not sorry. Emily said he's a good guy and I thought you deserved to be taken out and treated well for a change. And you didn't have to go out with him. You could have said no."

Grace sat back in her seat with a sigh. She felt hot and agitated and was struggling to work out if she was right to be angry or if she should just be saying thank you.

Phil put his hand on her arm. "You didn't say no did you?"

Grace looked at him and smiled in defeat. "No I didn't. And we had a really lovely evening."

Phil smiled. "Well in that case, you are welcome!" He and Emily looked at each other and grinned, their eyes full of delight as they congratulated each other on their good work with the satisfying slap of a high five.

"Alright, that's quite enough," Grace said sharply, but not unkindly. "You got what you wanted, now let's move on."

"Just tell us if you'll be seeing him again then we'll drop it, I promise." Emily looked at Grace, her eyes full of expectation.

"He surprised me at lunchtime today to let me know he'll be away now for a few days but we're going out again next week when he's back."

Emily let out a tiny little "Yay!" and then happily picked up the menu.

They ordered some food and another bottle of wine which was followed several animated conversations later by dessert and another bottle of wine. When that was polished off, Grace asked for the bill and when it arrived a few moments later, Phil immediately swept it up.

"Dinner's on me tonight." Grace and Emily were quick to protest but Phil put his hand up to stop them. "The station's using me to front a teenage anti-drug campaign which means an unexpected pay cheque. So my treat."

"That's great Phil," Grace said with a smile.

"Yeah, well done you!" Emily added, raising her glass.

"Thanks. I am pretty chuffed if truth be told. Most of what I do is pretty vacuous. Feels good to have the chance to make a real difference."

Grace struggled through the next day with a slightly fuzzy head. Typically, it was as the last person left the marketing department that the fog finally lifted and she found herself feeling surprisingly motivated. She was quickly lost in thought, totally immersed in her marketing plans for the next few months, moving promotions and advertising campaigns around, dropping anything that didn't feel inspiring or original enough and working out where the gaps were. And then she literally jumped out of her seat, her heart in her mouth as she did so, as Peter slammed a report down in front of her with such force that the magazines and print-outs that covered her desk jumped along with her, a pile of documents immediately sliding on to the floor in a waterfall of paper. Her eyes shot up and she shrank back as Peter leaned over her desk, his eyes full of a whole new level of anger that she had never seen before. It was terrifying.

"What the fuck is this?" he yelled, waving the report centimetres from her face. Clearly she had no idea but, as her eyes struggled to see what was in front her, Grace quickly realised the report was merely for effect, it's weight required for maximum impact. What Peter was now jabbing at her was actually just a couple of sheets of paper. She pulled her head back further and slowly the words started to swim into focus and her heart stopped. As any colour left in her cheeks melted away, it was replaced by a rising heat that prickled her skin. Somehow, Peter had found the diary notes she had started writing about him and his appalling behaviour.

"Where did you get this?" she stuttered. "How did you get this?"

"Who the fuck do you think you are? You really think you can make trouble for me? Who the fuck do you think you are?"

Grace was so overcome with fear and so deafened by the growing ferocity of Peter's shouting, his venomous words coated in saliva as he spat each word at her, that she simply couldn't speak. "I…it was…I just…"

"You just what?" Peter growled.

"Everything alright here?" Neither Peter or Grace had heard Sam come in, their heads shooting round to see who had dared to interrupt. Peter immediately stepped back and for a moment, he and Sam locked eyes. It was impossible to determine who despised the other more, Peter oozing professional jealousy, Sam about to burst with loathing for someone he saw as a weak but dangerous bully but, for now, Sam was only interested in Grace.

"You okay Grace?" Sam walked towards her, his eyes full of concern. She didn't move. "Grace?" he said again, more gently. Slowly her eyes found him and immediately filled with tears. Sam picked up her bag and gently took her arm.

"Come on, time to go."

"Actually Sam, Grace and I were just in the middle of something."

"Whatever it is, I'm sure it can wait," Sam said, his voice icy cold as he helped Grace into her coat. "Have a good evening Peter," he added in a tone that dared Peter to say another word and then, with his arm protectively around her, Sam led Grace out of the office.

They were well clear of the large imposing building before Sam stopped. Grace had said nothing as they walked, Sam's arm still firmly around her until they reached the car park at which point Sam stopped and gently lifted her face, damp with tears, her eyes still firmly down.

"Grace?" She slowly looked up at him. "What the hell happened?"

Grace sniffed and wiped a hand across her face, desperately trying to compose herself. "It's fine," she managed. "You know what he's like."

"Yes I do. But I've never seen him like that before. What happened?"

Grace hesitated for a moment. "I did something he didn't like." She shrugged, desperate on one hand to tell him everything but equally keen to shut it all away and bury it. It was just too huge to deal with. How was she going to walk back in tomorrow? How could she face him? And how the hell did he find her notes? A violent shudder ripped down her spine as she thought about some of the language she had used, enjoying the chance to be brutally descriptive about how terribly he had behaved. She felt fresh tears flood her eyes and immediately squeezed them shut.

"Let me help you Grace, please!"

Grace managed a smile. "You have helped. More than you realise." They stood in silence for a moment and then Grace squeezed his arm. "Thanks for the rescue."

"That's just the point," said Sam, struggling to contain his exasperation. "You shouldn't need rescuing!"

Grace looked at him, her eyes fixed and tired. There was simply no response to that. Instead she touched his arm again briefly and said, "Think that's enough for one day. I'll see you tomorrow."

"You'll be okay?"

"Me? Of course I will!" Grace forced an unconvincing smile. "Made of pure rubber me. I'm the original bounce-back kid." She could sense Sam was still reluctant to let her go so she simply raised her hand in a wave and then turned and walked away.

Sam watched her go and then with a renewed sense of purpose, he turned around and headed back to his office.

14

Anna

Anna was sitting staring at her computer screen but it was a long time since she had really looked at it. The words in front of her were nothing more than a blur, her eyes fixed and glazed. She had been sitting in the same position for such a long time that the light outside was already dissolving and the buzz of people moving around the corridors and surrounding offices had long since faded to nothing. Eventually she blinked and slowly brought herself back to the moment. She shivered as a cold wisp of early evening air whispered past her from the open window. She lifted the cardigan from the back of her chair, slipped her arms inside and pulled it tightly around her.

She was surprised to see it was already past eight. She really had been frozen in time for hours and yet she still didn't feel suitably motivated to move, other than to close the window behind her and turn on a desk lamp. The instant beam of light made her start, as if she had been hiding and was now visible to the world.

Her subsequent conversation with Matthew, following her late night call to tell him she was on board, had been surprisingly short. She had not been surprised to find him waiting for her as she stepped out of the lift first thing the next morning.

"Anna!" he had said as he stood up, sounding like someone greeting an old friend. "Welcome to the team! Do you have a few minutes?" He had then sat down again as Anna had dutifully taken the seat opposite him.

"I do only have a few minutes though," she had said.

"Then I'll get straight to it. I'll email you something more detailed later today but, in summary, you need to select a client, without too much thought if possible, note down how long you've been acquainted and then see at what point you can make them call me without explaining why. If you're asked, your only response should be the words, 'trust me'. You should also note down what it was about the behaviour of your client at that point that made you believe they would make the call. Then we just see what happens next. And that's it." And then he had smiled at her. "Money for virtually nothing!"

There had been no further conversation. He had simply stood up, wished her luck and left her to get on with the rest of her day.

Anna had expected him to ask what had made her change her mind and was hugely relieved that he hadn't, having given no thought at all to how she would justify her sudden willingness to participate. The truth was, Anna had no interest at all in whatever nonsense Matthew was orchestrating but, since the moment she'd seen Warren, all she could think about was clearing the path that would lead her back into his life, quickly convincing herself that simply meant getting Grace well and truly out of the way.

Anna was aware of the stillness outside her office door as she continued to sit where she was. The thought of Grace made her skin crawl and instinctively, she started to scratch her forearm, her skin prickly and uncomfortable. Seeing Warren and Grace together had left her determined to render Grace emotionally exposed. In fact, so vulnerable that she would take any advice and guidance Anna cared to proffer which would be to escape to somewhere far away for a completely fresh start with the first task on her exit strategy being to cut all ties with Warren.

What Matthew had done was give her a legitimate excuse to throw the rule book out and interfere in Grace's life to get her the hell away from Warren as quickly as possible. How dare she be with him! The thought of them together, being intimate together, made Anna shudder and then she winced, suddenly aware of skin beneath her finger nails and the sight of blood on her fingertips. For a moment she just stared at the deep bloody grooves she'd carved into her arm and then she felt her jaw tighten. She would get Grace to make the call to Matthew but not until she had destabilised her to such an extent that she could remould her in any way she chose.

Anna had been eagerly waiting to hear Grace had started documenting Peter's behaviour towards her. They'd discussed how Grace would do this – either online or maybe in a notebook – and Grace had decided online would be easier. She could then sit at her desk and happily vent away without raising any suspicion. This had, of course, led to a discussion about where she would save the document and Grace had been confident that storing it discreetly on her work computer would be absolutely fine.

"I know I work in a strange place with unprecedented rules and more than the average quota of maniacs," Grace had told her, "but to believe anyone has time to trawl through everyone's online files would be ludicrous."

Anna had agreed. "Of course, you're right," she had replied with a smile, amazed how easy Grace was making this for her. They had agreed Grace would tell her what the document was called just as a sense check, with Anna making her interest look like concern, like she wanted to be certain it couldn't be innocently stumbled across despite how confident Grace was that this would never happen. What a silly, silly girl.

It had been easy to find an email address for Peter. Anna had then waited for the call from Grace for confirmation of the name she'd given the document before alerting Peter to the shameful trouble-making member of his team, anonymously obviously, and how he could find proof of her imminent betrayal.

Peter had of course emailed her back wanting to know who she was. She had hoped he would, for no other reason than she would then know he'd read it all. She'd expected him to react immediately, imagining him pacing like a caged animal, waiting for the moment Grace was alone, convinced such a delay would only heighten his anger and make his pounce all the more lethal.

She pulled her cardigan even tighter around her and wondered how it had all played out. It wouldn't have been pretty, that much she was sure about. Knowing the little she did about Peter, how insecure he obviously was, there was only one way it could have gone. Boom! She smiled, relishing the very idea. But, for now, she had no choice but to wait. Wait for the moment when Grace walked back in to tell her exactly what had happened. How there was no possible way she could stay in her job for a single moment longer. How she needed Anna's guidance and support more than ever. Then it would be time to help her to find the courage to move on, in whatever direction Anna chose. She was already convinced that poor frightened little Grace would do exactly what she was told.

And then her smile widened. Bringing Grace down was going to be her greatest achievement, and getting Warren back would be her most coveted prize.

15

Grace

Grace was sitting in the dark too. She had slumped into a chair the moment she'd got home and had then stayed there. Coat on, bag dropped by her side, lights off, the silence heavy with the despair that settled on her shoulders, its pressure keeping her perfectly in place. Her mind felt strangely empty. She wasn't going over and over the horrific experience with Peter. She wasn't trying to work out what on earth she should do next. She wasn't wallowing in self-pity. She wasn't thinking or feeling anything. She was numb, her eyes fixed and staring blankly at nothing in particular, her breathing slow and steady, the rhythmic inflating and deflating of her chest the only sign that she was actually still of this world.

If there was one thing Grace did feel it was exhaustion. She felt beaten, physically and mentally. Her eyelids became heavy and she simply didn't have the strength to keep forcing them upwards and so, unable to fight it, she eventually let them close.

It felt like only moments later when her eyes started to sting as the early morning light slowly strengthened its hold and then burst through the open window. She reluctantly opened them, squinting against the sudden brightness as she painfully stretched her stiff body and then stood up. A glance at a clock revealed it was just after half past six. Amazed that she'd slept for so long, Grace headed for the kitchen, finally taking off her coat as she did so. She turned on her beloved coffee machine and then, taking a deep breath, nervously switched on her mobile. In a matter of seconds it leapt into life with a series of beeps and whistles as messages and emails flooded forward, the dam of silence blown to smithereens in one tuneless eruption.

"You have six new messages," her phone politely informed her. She put it on speaker and laid it down so she could make herself a coffee. There was a beep and then the disembodied voice continued with a time-check, "Yesterday, 8.53pm," in preparation for the first message.

"Grace, it's Sam. Just wanted to make sure you got home okay. Give me a call or just send me a text and let me know." There was a moment's hesitation. "I'd really like you to call me if you feel up to it. Okay, bye."

Another beep. "Yesterday, 9.47pm," and then, "Hey, me again. Totally get you not wanting to talk but I'm worried about you. Let me know you're okay. Bye."

A beep. "Yesterday, 10.14pm." A pause. "Babe. Call me back." It was Phil.

Another beep. "Yesterday, 10.53pm." Another pause. "Okay, I give in." Back to Sam. "Get some rest and call me in the morning. Unless you do want to talk tonight in which case I'm here. Whatever time. Night."

Grace was surprised to find she was smiling. Well, the corners of her mouth were twitching in an upward direction. It was close enough under the circumstances. She sipped the coffee she had made as she listened, comforted by the knowledge that she had Sam on her side. Not that she was dismissing Phil. He was always on her side. He just didn't know it yet on this occasion.

"5.58am." Someone was up early.

"Grace it's Peter." Grace froze. "Look, things got a little out of hand. But we're okay, aren't we." It was a statement of fact rather than a question. "Anyway, I'll see you in a couple of hours."

Grace suddenly felt very cold as the final beep blasted and she waited for the last message. "6.17am." Grace felt herself twitch in preparation. "Grace, it's Sam. Hope you're okay. Listen, don't come in this morning. I'll explain later but just trust me on this. Head in after lunch and come and find me. Okay, I'll see you later."

Silence. Grace continued to slowly sip her coffee, feeling the warmth of the drink slowly circulate through her body and then she put her mug down, switched off her phone again and headed to her bedroom, discarding clothes as she went. She crawled under her duvet. Right under, until she was totally covered from head to toe and, closing her eyes, she was immediately drawn back into sleep.

Again, Grace slept surprisingly soundly and woke just after eleven. She had expected to lie awake, hidden from the world beneath the covers, caffeine coursing through her veins and keeping her eyes wide open. At the very least, she had resigned herself to fitful sleep, interspersed with tortuous anxiety-fuelled nightmares. Doing a quick calculation of the hours spent asleep in her lounge plus a few more in her bed, she didn't remember the last time she had actually slept for as long. She could only assume she had reached a point of such exhaustion that it was almost like passing out. Whatever it was, she was hugely grateful for the rest. She stretched herself awake and then headed for the bathroom and ran herself a hot bath. She was on autopilot, simply not allowing herself to think. She would relax in the soothing water, get herself dressed and then head to work. She wasn't ready to consider what would happen when she got there. One step at a time.

It was just over two hours later when Grace walked the long corridor towards the editorial floor. Her phone was still switched off. She'd found it easier to head into the office in complete ignorance to whatever was going on but now, as she got closer, she kept her eyes fixed and facing forward, quickening her step past the marketing department. She needed to speak to Sam before she ventured in there and then she literally jumped out of her skin as the door flew open and a slightly hysterical colleague burst towards her.

"Grace! Where've you been? We've been calling you all morning. Quick, come in here." Before she had a chance to react, she was being pulled into the office. As the door shut behind her, she struggled to take in the laughter, the animated chatter, the smiling faces. She had clearly stepped into some kind of parallel universe. Suddenly noticing her, someone else rushed over, hardly recognisable with such wide eyes and a huge, beaming grin.

"He's gone! He's gone!" he yelled at her.

"We're free!" shouted another. She could hear someone saying they felt so relieved they could cry while a voice in the background was proclaiming the rush of euphoria she was experiencing was better than any drug-induced high.

Grace stood with her mouth open, waiting for the initial wave of excitement to subside. When it was clear that wasn't about to happen any time soon, she decided she couldn't wait any longer to find out what on earth had happened.

"Just hang on a minute," she shouted above the noise and then waited for quiet. "Will someone just calmly tell me what's going on? Robert," she said, turning to the person closest to her. "You tell me."

"It's Peter. He came in this morning as usual and then got summoned by the MD. An hour later he returned looking like he was about to explode at any minute, all red and slightly dazed looking, with a security guard hot on his heels. He packed up his things with the guard standing over his shoulder and without a word he was then accompanied from the building."

Grace was struggling to take it all in. "I don't understand. Why?"

"Well we haven't heard the official line yet but you know how efficient the old grapevine is in this place. The rumours are rife already. Apparently he's been taking back-handers for years on all sorts of things. He's fixed competitions, chosen suppliers based on the personal benefits he could negotiate and a million other equally dodgy things. I think you can rest assured that anytime you were forced to do something exclusively with a company, it was because Peter had negotiated a big fat cash 'thank you' or a holiday in the sun somewhere. I don't expect us minions will ever know exactly what went on but it must have been bad to provoke this kind of reaction. I always knew he was a crook."

"But how did they find out?" Grace was completely lost.

"Nobody seems to know. Apparently there's been a suspicion for some time and then suddenly, it seems indisputable evidence was anonymously put forward that simply couldn't be ignored. Whoever was responsible, I'd love to find them and give them a huge sloppy kiss!"

As the partying continued, Grace backed quietly out of the office and literally ran the short distance to the editorial floor. She slowed to a fast walk as she dodged her way through desks and people and then stopped, slightly breathless, at Sam's door. He smiled as he saw her. "Hi," was all he could manage as he got up and walked towards her and then he gently touched her arm. "You okay?"

"Emotionally bruised and confused just about covers it. What's happened?"

Sam smiled. "So you heard already?"

"I heard Peter's been escorted from the building."

Sam gestured for Grace to sit down and then returned to his desk, pulling his chair towards her until they sat face to face. For a moment he said nothing, clearly trying to decide how much to tell her.

"Sam?"

He looked up. "Okay, hear me out before you say anything. I know I shouldn't have interfered but it's been really hard watching what he does to you. Watching the life being literally sucked out of you. So, a while back I did a bit of tentative digging and you can't really be surprised to hear that it wasn't long before I found evidence of…" he hesitated for a moment, "let's just call it 'wrong-doing'."

"We've all thought it but how did you prove it?"

113

Sam picked up his phone and held it aloft by way of an answer.

Grace gasped. "You tapped his phone? How do you even know how to do that?"

Sam smiled. "We all know how to. It's just that most of us choose not to."

"Bloody hell," she said. It was too much to take in.

"Indeed. I've just been sitting on bits of information and recorded messages, not sure how to talk to you about it and work out what to do. And then yesterday happened." He shrugged. "Game over, I'm afraid."

Grace sat for a moment and tried to process what it all meant. "So he's really gone?"

Sam nodded. "But no one knows it was me. And I'd like to keep it that way."

"Of course. I certainly won't be talking about it." And then she smiled. "Although if it ever does get out you might want to give Robert a wide berth. And if you're not sure who he is, he'll be the one rushing at you lips first!"

Sam pulled a face. "Not quite the reward I was hoping for."

And then they sat in contemplative silence for a moment. Grace's head was swimming. She didn't know what to say next or what to do next and then instinctively she got up and pulled Sam to a standing position. Putting her arms around him, she gave him a warm hug, squeezing him tightly as his arms then wrapped around her. "Thank you," she said quietly. "For everything. You've been the most amazing friend and I can't imagine what the last few months would have been like without your support, never mind the last twenty four hours." She hoped it was enough for him to know how truly grateful she was.

"You're welcome," he said as she slowly released him. "I have to admit it was a bit of a thrill catching him out."

Grace smiled at him. "Quite the super sleuth aren't you?"

"Sam Newman, PI." He pondered for a moment. "Has quite a ring to it don't you think?"

A tap on the door brought their conversation to a stop. "Sam, do you have a moment?"

Grace immediately headed for the door. "I'll see you later," she said as she walked past the waiting journalist, leaving Sam to do some proper work.

The following days were an absolute joy. To say there was a distinct change in the atmosphere would be the ultimate in dramatic understatements. It was like the department had been colourised, taken from bleak black and white to glorious technicolor in one beautifully choreographed move. Productivity shot through the roof and suddenly everyone looked ten years younger. Without any encouragement, and in the absence of any directive from above, the team instinctively looked to Grace for advice and direction and she somehow became the adopted leader of the pack. Then, just as she was about to pack up and draw a line under what had been one of the most surreal weeks in living memory, Grace got a call to say the MD wanted to see her. Now what? She thought as she dropped everything and headed for his office. Wouldn't do to keep the top man waiting.

As she walked into the austere office of Zac Hawthorne, she did her best to disguise the terror that she knew was lurking in her eyes. She wasn't sure she had ever had an actual conversation with him before, just the odd comment here and there. She had likened him to royalty – you didn't speak unless you were spoken to, such was the intimidating aura that surrounded him.

The man before her still managed to look huge despite the enormous desk that separated them. He smiled as he saw her enter and immediately instructed his secretary to hold all calls. "Come in Grace and sit down. Coffee?"

"No, I'm fine thank you." Grace did as she was told and sat down in front of him.

"So, how are things?"

"Fine thank you. Going really well I think."

"Well there's no doubt about that. The last few days could have been very unsettling. Perhaps unfairly, we deliberately sat back for a moment. I wanted to see how things panned out and I hear everything is well on track. And I believe I have you to thank for that?"

"I don't understand?"

"Well I hear you have natural leadership qualities and the executive team all speak very highly of you. So the marketing director role is yours if you want it," he said in such a way that not wanting it was, of course, inconceivable.

Grace was convinced she heard a crash as her heart hit the floor. She felt her mouth threaten to drop open unattractively and so closed it again immediately.

"I don't know what to say."

"How about 'I'd be delighted to accept' or maybe just 'thank you'?"

Grace sat up very straight. "I would of cou
to accept and I'm very grateful for the opp
thank you very much indeed." Is this what sl
hadn't even given herself a moment to t
Hesitation just didn't seem appropriate.

"It will of course mean a substantial pay rise and all sorts of benefits. I trust you won't abuse them?"

"Oh no, absolutely not sir, no."

"Good. I'll get the necessary paperwork drawn up and you get yourself settled in Peter's old office. I'll send a note out to everyone but I thought you might like to tell your bunch."

"Yes sir, I would, thank you."

"Great, that's sorted then."

Grace realised the meeting was now over and she stood up. She offered her hand as she left and Zac took it firmly. "Thank you sir. I won't let you down."

"I'm sure you won't. Let's have lunch soon. I'd like to get to know you better. I'll get Vanessa to let you know when and where."

"Yes, thank you sir."

Grace turned to leave. "One more thing Grace." She duly stopped and turned around to face him again. "Zac will do just fine."

With a slightly embarrassed smile and a nod, Grace left the office, tempted to pinch herself just to be sure this wasn't all some kind of crazy dream.

16

Anna

Anna sat back in her chair with a well-practiced smile on her face that she hoped more than at any other time was masking the abject horror she was actually feeling. She swallowed slowly and deliberately as she tried to dislodge the bile that had risen swiftly from her gut and was now burning the back of her throat. Could she possibly have heard that correctly? For days now she had delighted in trying to imagine just how desperate Grace must be feeling and yet here she was, sitting across from her, relaxed and buoyed, her eyes bright and alive, her smile almost too wide for her face, having just announced she had been promoted. What the fuck?

"I know," Grace gushed. A slightly unkind description of her delivery but that was how it felt to Anna. "I can hardly believe it myself. And just when it felt like your techniques were really starting to work. Not that I'm sorry not to need them anymore. The change has been quite remarkable. It's like getting to know the team all over again. They're all so different now that we're actually working as a team, listening to each other and supporting each other. We're the talk of the company. Our work's never been better or so appreciated. It's incredible."

Anna had zoned out. She knew Grace was still talking because she could see her mouth moving at an unnaturally rapid pace but she had stopped listening some minutes ago. It was too much. She couldn't listen to any more of this excited, happy bullshit. As the jabbering continued in the background she tried to regroup. What the hell was she going to do now? She was horribly aware of a crisp, white envelope on her desk. In it was a big fat cheque from Matthew to cover her time and expenses, he had said. While she had wondered if she should accept it, her hand had simultaneously stretched out and taken it. Why shouldn't she be paid? Anna tried to focus. She had to think of something. And fast. But first she had to stop Grace's incessant, annoying gabbling. Instinctively, she put up her hand.

"Okay Grace, let's take a moment."

Grace immediately stopped. "I'm sorry. I'm rambling."

Yes, thought Anna, you are. She managed a smile. "Understandably so, of course. What a turn of events!" She paused for a moment. "But let's just take a breath and try to find some perspective. You'll remember in our first meeting I asked you if Peter was the problem or if it was the job. You'll be tempted, now that he's out of the picture, to assume it was Peter but that may not turn out to be the case." Anna noticed Grace deflate a little, a pin suddenly pressed dangerously against her bubble of euphoria, ready to completely burst it at any moment. "I just don't want you to assume everything will now be perfect, only to end up back where we started." She watched Grace for a moment as she took this on board.

"But Peter leaving has to be the end of it all?"

"Maybe it is," replied Anna quickly, not wanting to depress Grace so thoroughly that she never came back again. "We just have to be open to the possibility that the role itself was playing a part in your unhappiness, in your lack of fulfilment. Let's see how things are when I see you next and discuss it more then."

Grace nodded her reluctant agreement and Anna decided to stop there. There was nothing to gain from completely crushing her. Not yet, anyway. Not without taking time to regroup and to carefully plan her next move which would be key if she was to achieve her goal.

"And what of John?"

Grace immediately perked up again. "I've stopped counting the days since I last heard from him so I'm tempted to say he's finally got the message. Moving on from such a destructive and toxic relationship is far more significant than anything going on at work. I feel strangely light as a result." She smiled at Anna. "It's a good feeling. And then out of the blue, I've started a new relationship which feels even better."

Anna clamped her teeth together and fixed her eyes. She must not react. This may have sounded relatively straightforward if it wasn't for the feeling of nausea that immediately started to churn in her stomach and the intense pressure she suddenly felt on her heart. Her fists clenched in her lap and every muscle in her body tightened. In fact, so powerful were the physical reactions that for a moment, Anna felt genuinely scared. She felt dangerously close to completely losing control, so all-consuming was this totally overwhelming hatred for Grace at the slightest thought of her with Warren. With all the effort she could muster, she took a deep breath and urged herself to channel every ounce of emotion she was feeling into slowly and painfully ripping Grace's life apart.

"Sounds interesting?" she managed, posed as a question and then she braced herself.

"I've actually known him for a while," Grace began, clearly happy to be recounting the tale of her blossoming romance. "Well, sort of known him without really knowing him, if you know what I mean?" Anna remained silent and motionless. "And then a friend set us up and that was that. Connection made. Then he surprised me at work and bought me lunch. How thoughtful was that? It's all a million miles from what I'm used to." Grace paused for a moment and when Anna said nothing, she took this as a cue to just keep going. "He's away for a few days now but there's been lots of contact. He's trying to sort out a very damaged relationship with his father. He said he suddenly felt ready to tackle it after letting it fester for years."

No, no, no, no, NO! Anna suddenly understood what it meant for your blood to boil. The sudden heat was immense, the bubbling in her veins unmistakable. How many times had she tried to get Warren to talk to his father? How many times had she pleaded with him to lift his head and be the one to offer an olive branch? Nothing. Not so much as a phone call. And five minutes with this feeble, eternal victim of a woman and he's off like a shot to right the wrongs of the past. Un-fucking-believable.

Anna took a moment and then there was that professional smile again. She took a slow breath and reconnected with her steady coaching voice, delivering her words carefully and calmly. "Have you ever wondered Grace, why you end up in bad situations? There's a pattern emerging if you stop to consider for a moment. I don't know the circumstances of how you and John got together but you certainly said you took your current job without really giving it the careful consideration it needed. And then the promotion. Again, you accepted in a heartbeat, without taking even a moment to think about whether or not it's actually what you want for yourself. And now this new chap, conveniently on the edge of your circle until a friend nudges you in his direction and bam!" Grace jumped as Anna clapped her hands together for maximum effect. Anna waited for a moment to be sure it was all sinking in. "The whole point of our sessions is about you fulfilling your potential. About you digging deep to find some self-belief and then nurturing it until you rightly believe you can have whatever you want. And then believe that you deserve it." Anna was giving the performance of her life but she wasn't done yet. However, she knew her trademark professionalism had been replaced by a fiery passion that had no place in her consulting room. It was time to rein it in. Anna sat back and took an exaggerated, deep breath and then smiled at Grace, her face full of apology. "I'm sorry Grace. I'm sensing very clearly that this is not what you were expecting. Or hoping for. But everything's suddenly moving so quickly. I just want you to stop. To breathe. To stop grabbing at whatever presents itself to you and start thinking about what it is that will really make you happy."

Anna lent forward. "Are you ready to start listening to me Grace?"

17

Grace

Well that was unexpected. For the first time, Grace had gone into see Anna feeling on top of the world and come out feeling vaguely suicidal. Normally it was the other way around. She had no idea what had just happened but instead of feeling like life was well and truly on track, she felt thoroughly derailed. Devastated in fact. And humiliated too. Or was she embarrassed? How could Anna seriously think she just took what life decided to throw her way without even the slightest consideration? That was definitely humiliating. But embarrassing too if Grace had just been rumbled. Anna had certainly seemed convinced, and she spoke with such authority and clarity of thought that it was hard not to just accept everything she said without question. Grace groaned inwardly. If she was prepared to just accept what Anna said unchallenged, perhaps she really was as weak-willed as Anna suggested? Or, if she was prepared to really face up to an unpleasant truth, perhaps this was the moment to admit that Anna had just unwittingly exposed the defective chink in Grace's armour.

* *

Before

Grace sat at the dining room table with her parents, Gillian and Oliver. Grace had immediately felt the physical distance between each of them, the imposing table and large intricately carved chairs making it impossible to achieve any sense of togetherness. This would only be a problem, of course, if there was any desire to create an inclusive environment which of course there was not. Instead, they sat as a small group of individuals, the air thick with tension, the silence suffocating. Oliver's phone periodically vibrated and Grace knew he was itching to pick it up. She also knew even he wasn't so stupid that he would risk angering her mother further. If that was actually possible. She had turned a kind of puce pink and looked like she might, quite literally, explode. The silence deepened, shaping into a cavernous hole, then waiting patiently for someone to risk life and limb and dive in. Turned out only Gillian was brave enough.

"The decision's made Grace." Gillian folded her arms to emphasise the subject was closed, her face fixed with a look that dared any further discussion. Not that there had really been any. Grace had been presented with a shortlist of four universities, the visits to their respective open days already confirmed. She would study English and maybe History, but definitely English, and the universities had been chosen because firstly, they were the best for Gillian's chosen subjects and secondly, because they were a suitable distance from their home in leafy Buckinghamshire so that a visit for lunch would be just about possible without the inconvenience of having to plan overnight stays. So you are intending to visit then? Grace had thought, not sure if she was more surprised or disappointed at the prospect and then she had desperately tried to imagine her parents spending more than half a day either on a train or trapped together in the car. It was a scenario she was simply unable to picture. But whether or not they decided to come and see her wasn't really what mattered right now. What mattered was that the plans for the next stage of her life had once again been neatly laid out for her and presented like some kind of non-refundable gift.

"But I want to study journalism or media studies."

"They're not degree subjects!" Gillian scoffed. "Good grief, you can do a degree in anything these days! It's quite ridiculous."

Grace's head went down. It was moments like this that reminded her how different her family dynamic was to everyone else she knew. Not that she either needed or wanted to be reminded. The very thought sent her plunging into an all too familiar depression.

Grace had never been sure if her parents really loved her but, whatever affection they did feel for her, there was nothing unconditional about it. Quite the opposite. She'd had to work really hard to earn every inch of praise and every morsel of fondness. Yes, that was it. They were fond of her at best. Or trying to turn her into someone they could be fond of. She definitely wasn't there yet. She'd spent more time feeling like an inconvenient visitor than a daughter they could be proud of.

"How was school today Grace?" Gillian would ask on the rare occasion they might spend time together in an evening.

"Good thank you," Grace would reply with an eager smile, searching for something remarkable to share that might just earn her a glimmer of warmth. "I got an A for my history project."

"But you got an A star for the last one," said with a look of horror. "What happened? Do I need to speak to your teacher? You clearly didn't work hard enough. I'll certainly be speaking to Isobel in the morning about your after school study time." And then the head would shake, the lips would purse, the face forming an all too familiar look of disappointment.

"But I...."

The immediate glare was enough to stop Grace going any further. It was a look that only got more threatening over time until she simply stopped trying to defend herself at all.

"Can I have Emily over for tea?"

"No."

She would wait. And then for a moment more. Nothing. Clearly no explanation was required.

"I've been invited to Alexa's party."

"No you can't go. That girl is totally unsuitable."

"Everyone's walking to school on their own now."

"Isobel will take you as normal."

"My friends are meeting in the park on Saturday."

"What on earth for?"

"Can I go to the cinema?"

"Emily's having a sleepover."

"Can I have these boots? Everyone else has them."

Eventually Grace was forced to accept there was no point even asking.

But the worst part had been the lack of affection. No hugs or kisses delivered just because. No involuntary words of encouragement, no warmth, no endearing nicknames, just a constant formality that now left Grace cold.

As Grace had got older, her attitude started to change. She could just about cope with a childhood where she had been manipulated like some kind of remote controlled toy but she was heading for adulthood now and having major decisions made without her input was simply no longer acceptable. Decisions significant enough that they would have a lasting impact on the rest of her life. This was the moment when she should be spreading her wings and she refused to accept that hers had been clipped before she had experienced even a whiff of independence.

Grace ran her hands across the smooth shiny dining table and then she stole a look at her father. His eyes were down too. Not through defeat, which weighed heavily on Grace's shoulders, but more a determination to avoid eye contact and be drawn into the conversation. Grace wanted to believe that he might support her. That he might actually celebrate her sense of vocation and the fact that she wanted to use her degree to move her closer to a job which was the point after all, wasn't it? Or was it just to be able to tell your friends that your daughter was studying the classics at one of the country's most esteemed academic institutions? Grace sighed. After all the rules and the endless micro-managing, the idea of breaking away was becoming more and more thrilling. Naively and foolishly, she now realised, she had made the mistake of thinking it would be on her terms.

"Maybe we could add in a couple of other universities to visit? Just to check out some media-based courses?" Grace carefully suggested.

"And what would be the point of that?"

Grace dared a look at Gillian and did her best to appear confident, tempting as it was to just shrivel under her stare. "Well what if any of the universities you've selected offer media courses? We could take a look at them while we're there?" Gillian's expression remained fixed and impervious. "Please Mum. What harm would it do?"

"Are we really still talking about this? I have to say I find your persistence as unattractive as it is insulting."

"I just want to take advantage of the fact I already know where my passions lie."

"Or you're just trying to annoy and frustrate me which, I have to say, you are achieving with great proficiency."

"I just want to make my own decision. It is my future we're discussing."

Gillian stiffened, causing her back to straighten and her neck to elongate, her presence growing as a result. "That's just the point, isn't it Grace?" she eventually said, each word delivered slowly and deliberately. "We're *not* discussing it."

Grace felt her resolve weaken. At least she had tried. "What you're proposing is fine. Of course you're right," Grace said as she pushed her chair back and stood up. "You always know what's best for me."

For a moment she thought her father was about to say something and then as he saw the satisfied look on his wife's face, he squeezed his lips tightly shut. Grace watched him grab his phone and make his getaway. The chance to escape was clearly greater than any desire to fight her corner. Stupid to have thought otherwise.

Half an hour later, Grace had swapped her formal dining table for Emily's warm and welcoming kitchen version. They sat opposite each other, separated by a large pile of prospectuses from a range of universities and colleges. Emily was planning on a graphic design course but, unlike Grace, she was doing so with the full support and encouragement of her parents. Grace could feel the sense of excitement radiating from her friend and she swallowed hard in an attempt to dislodge a growing lump of bitterness that was suddenly threatening to choke her. Sometimes it was hard not to really hate her mother.

"London looks like the best bet. There's loads of media and graphic design courses. We could get a flat! How cool would that be?" Emily asked, the rhythmic beat of her words increasing with every syllable.

Grace sat very still, unable to ride Emily's growing wave of enthusiasm. "London's not an option I'm afraid."

Emily looked at the glossy brochure in her hand and without hesitation, tossed it to one side. She didn't need to ask why. The objection would be Gillian's and that meant London was simply off the list.

"What about heading for the coast then? I'd love to live by the sea! There's loads of courses for you at Bournemouth and I could try for Portsmouth?"

"I'm not doing media studies. I'm doing English."

"Oh." Grace watched as Emily's bubble of excitement slowly started to deflate. They had been looking forward to this moment for months; the chance to plan the next stage of their lives while working out a way to be as close to each other as possible. Grace knew she didn't need to explain her unexpected sombre mood. Emily would know she had been well and truly Gillianed.

"So where are you going?" Emily asked.

"We're seeing a few but probably Durham. Which is kind of ironic on the basis Gillian said it was important she could visit without having to make an overnight stay. I guess that means she won't be visiting at all." Grace attempted a smile. "Every cloud."

Emily was already flicking through the brochures. "I don't have one for Durham. But then I doubt it's the kind of university that offers a graphic design course." She smiled reassuringly at Grace. "I don't suppose…"

"No. It's a done deal." Grace shook her head. There was no point pretending otherwise.

"My mum could talk to her?"

Grace simply raised her eyebrows. No words were necessary. "You should stick with London Em. Don't compromise because of me. I'll just feel guilty on top of everything else. Durham's only three or four hours on the train. We can still do weekends."

Emily slumped back in her chair leaving Grace feeling wretched. She felt like Gillian had taken her enthusiasm in one large bite, brutally chewed it to nothing and then spat it out again as if it were poisonous. After all the build-up, this was definitely not how she had imagined their plans would turn out. Although now that they were actually talking about it, it seemed churlish to have expected anything else.

Several months later, the A Level results were in and Grace and Emily had cause to celebrate. Grace had studied hard and achieved the straight As of her mother's dreams and was rewarded with the gift of a beautiful Tiffany necklace. Opening the iconic blue box at a celebratory dinner with her parents, which in itself was totally unexpected, Grace had been unable to stop a gasp of disbelief escaping at the extravagance of it all. There on the end of a delicate chain was a perfect silver heart, exactly what Grace would have chosen for herself. It was, without doubt, the most significant gift ever bestowed on her. Her father had been more animated than she had seen him in years, offering to help her put it on, telling her over and over again how proud he was. Her mother, meanwhile, had sat quietly, saying very little, but Grace had hoped it was pride she could see in her eyes too, eyes that seemed unusually bright and alive. The necklace was perfect and to Grace, said everything her mother couldn't. Or perhaps, simply wouldn't.

Emily achieved more than enough to secure her place in Brighton, having decided London might be a little too intimidating without her best friend by her side, and now the two were ready to toast their success. A huge party had been organised in a nearby pub for all those about to finish school, many of whom were now set to move away. It would be the last time they would all be together and not being there was simply unthinkable. Grace had subsequently left home before Gillian was around to raise any last-minute objections and headed for Emily's house to get ready. She had mentioned to Gillian months ago that the party was taking place and then deliberately, she had not mentioned it again since. If she had, there was every chance Gillian would have stopped her going and there was no way she was going to miss out. She had therefore decided she would prefer to have a difficult conversation about it after the event rather than risk not making it at all.

There had been no time to eat anything substantial and the party was already in full swing when they arrived. The alcohol was flowing freely, the lightness of mood and excited chatter enough to lose track almost immediately of exactly how much was being consumed. Everyone had arrived with a plain white t-shirt in hand which were now all doing the rounds with a selection of permanent marker pens and being signed and drawn on. As Grace moved from one group to another, she felt like she was seeing many of her peers for the first time. There was a sense of maturity suddenly, a feeling that this unruly bunch of kids was slowly realising they could now legitimately call themselves adults which further fuelled the general sense of celebration.

Grace vaguely remembered the passing of midnight and then, nothing.

The next morning, despite the fact that her head was pounding and she'd had to painfully rip her tongue from the roof of her extraordinarily dry mouth, Grace's over-riding feeling was one of huge relief that she'd managed to make it home in one piece. A quick glance under the duvet revealed she had even managed to remove her clothes and had slept in her underwear. She carefully placed her head back on the pillow and then she must have drifted back off to sleep because the next thing she knew, her curtains were being violently whipped open and the bright daylight that flooded in threatened to burn her eyes. She immediately lifted the duvet over her head as an act of self-preservation rather than objection. When the duvet was then swiftly removed too, Grace was suddenly wide awake, lying semi-naked and vulnerable, under the intense stare of Gillian.

"Yes, you should look ashamed," she had almost spat at Grace. "You're an utter disgrace. I thought we were being burgled when you came crashing in at goodness knows what time last night. Your father had to practically carry you upstairs and I had to undress you. You were virtually unconscious."

Grace curled herself into the foetal position. She felt herself shiver and desperately wanted some water but was simply not equipped, or brave enough, to ask.

"And your necklace. Where is it?"

That was enough to have Grace immediately sitting bolt upright, one hand grasping at her bare neck, the other covering her mouth, partly in shock and partly in an attempt to stop herself throwing up.

"That was a gift to say well done. Something I had hoped you would cherish, but no. You're selfish and ungrateful and I couldn't be more disappointed in you." There was a brief pause as Grace's frantic eyes flitted from her dressing table to her bed and then scanned the carpet, desperately hoping she would suddenly spot the silver heart buried in the soft pile.

Gillian's harsh words hung heavily in the stale air until she was ready to continue. "Do you have any idea how dangerous it is to lose control like that? Anything could have happened to you."

For the briefest of moments, Grace was overwhelmed by the belief that this outburst was testament to how much her mother actually cared which made the verbal bashing slightly more palatable. But, just as she thought Gillian was about to soften, she turned her back.

"I'm appalled and disgusted. I can't even look at you."

As Gillian strode out of the room, Grace pulled the duvet tightly under her chin and could do nothing more than stare crestfallen at the ceiling.

Grace had tried everything she could think of to find the necklace. She called the party venue several times, put up posters around the immediate vicinity and called as many people as she had numbers for, all of which had been fruitless. She had walked the route backwards and forwards from her home to the pub, constantly giving it one more try just in case she got lucky. But there was simply no sign of it anywhere. Eventually, she had been forced to give up and accept it was lost.

If her mother noticed her efforts, she chose to ignore them and it was never mentioned again but the repercussions lingered unpleasantly. Irreparable damage had been done and there was nothing Grace could do to redeem herself. The atmosphere at home remained strained and a couple of difficult months followed until Grace finally made the move to Durham.

It was with immeasurable relief that Grace sat in her new bedroom in one of the campus accommodation blocks. She could hear laughter in the corridor and voices growing then shrinking away as people moved past her door but, within her own four walls, everything seemed eerily quiet. Her parents had left half an hour before, her mother suddenly fussing about the long car journey home. She doubted she would see them again until she went home for the Christmas holidays.

They had said a formal goodbye and Grace hadn't really moved since. Her eyes slowly took in every inch of the space around her. A wardrobe, a desk, a few shelves as yet unfilled, a television (a present from her father; his one single act of bravery that Grace was extremely grateful for), a kettle with a couple of mugs and a small fridge (a gift from her mother to make sure she knew her milk, butter and any other small chilled essentials were fresh and untouched by others). In the middle of the room were two large suitcases which, once emptied, would be stored under the bed she sat on. Next to them were four boxes, packed with her books and various other mementos to help to create a home from home. To the right of the bedroom door was her own bathroom and then elsewhere, there was a large shared kitchen and general hanging out space and a study area. She had even heard talk of a gym.

Grace felt a shiver of anxiety ripple down her spine and then she smiled, choosing to morph the feeling into a tiny seed of excitement that slowly expanded until she gasped as it pushed its way out. Looking around the room again, she did so this time with a growing sense of appreciation as the realisation suddenly hit her like a smack in the face.

This was her space. She could finally play by her own rules.

18

Grace

Grace hurriedly left Anna's building, desperate to leave her confused thoughts behind her as she headed towards Soho. Feeling the need for some fresh air, she decided to walk and set off at quite a pace, keen to put as much distance between herself and Anna as quickly as was humanly possible. She had been looking forward to this for days and hated the fact that her heart now felt heavy in her chest, physically dragging her down and her mood along with it. As she hurried along the pavement, she was aware of a cool breeze in her face and she willed it to blow away the doubts she was now feeling. She was more than capable of making her own decisions and to suggest otherwise was frankly absurd.

A brisk twenty minutes later, Grace arrived at their chosen bar. With a final shake of the head to dislodge any remaining negativity, she closed her eyes and focused hard, visualising the beautiful butterflies that she knew were deep within her somewhere and willed them to wake up. And then she smiled as she felt it. That wonderful sensation of anticipation and excitement, mixed with a slight dash of fear, that came together in a rush of adrenaline. It made her heart beat just a little bit faster and brought a glow to her cheeks and a sparkle to her eyes that she now slowly opened. And then she pushed on the heavy door, her eyes immediately searching for Warren until there he was, standing up as he saw her. Grace felt a swell of warmth rush through her body at the sight of him, at the smile that lit up his whole face, at his strong arms folding around her as she reached him and the brush of his lips on her cheek. She wrapped her arms around his neck, immediately asking herself what on earth Anna was talking about and then she felt everything stop at the mere silent mention of Anna's name, the memory of her words suddenly suffocating every last butterfly and crushing the hope in her heart.

Oblivious to this inner conflict, Warren took over. "So how are you? What can I get you to drink?"

Grace sat down next to him. "Red wine please." She would stick with the easy question first. "A large one."

Warren disappeared for a moment and returned with a bottle of wine and two glasses and then turned his attention back to Grace as he poured. "So how's your week been?" he said, handing her a glass.

Grace smiled. "No, you first. I want to hear everything about what happened with your dad."

Grace relaxed as Warren launched into a detailed account of his last few days, eager and happy to share what had been a sometimes difficult but ultimately successful visit.

"It started with a fight, obviously. And then once all the anger and frustration was finally out of the way, we talked properly for the first time in I don't know how many years, possibly ever."

As Grace listened, she tried to imagine what it must have been like for this terrified little boy and his equally terrified father when they lost the most important woman in their lives. Having seen Warren's father in the café, Grace could only assume that Warren looked more like his mother. She wondered for a moment if that meant that every time he had looked at Warren over the years, his father was reminded of the woman he had loved and lost. If every time he looked at his son, he saw his beautiful wife looking back at him from deep within those piercing blue eyes. Grace felt her own eyes fill with tears at the tragedy of the situation, knowing at the same time that the sadness she felt was the perfect cover for her own emotions which had been looking for an excuse to show themselves ever since she had left Anna.

"Hey don't look so sad!" Warren took hold of her hand. "It's all good. Better than good in fact."

"I know," Grace replied through a large sniff. "I was just trying to imagine while you were talking what you've both been through."

"Yes it's been pretty shitty but I'm in a place with my dad I never thought I'd get to. Then this afternoon, I contacted a charity supporting children who've lost parents and arranged to chat about how I could use my own experiences to help. Something else I've been meaning to do for a very long time. And now I'm here with you."

Grace smiled and something changed in her eyes. Bollocks to Anna and her 'grabbing anything that came her way' nonsense. Too right she was going to jump right in with both feet and why shouldn't she? It was way too long since she'd looked into a face full of such kindness and she was buggered if she was going to ruin it all on the opinion of someone who barely knew her. And then Warren kissed her and Grace felt so alive, so full of joy that every thought of Anna finally dissolved.

They decided to stay where they were to eat. They were far too comfortable to consider moving on somewhere and as they skipped from one conversation to another, laughing at everything and nothing, a flirtatious eyelash flutter here, the casual touch of a hand there, Grace felt flooded with pure joy. It was a feeling that started deep in her core and then, as the evening progressed, she felt it slowly infuse every inch of her body. It was intoxicating.

"Is it time to move on?" Warren asked, suddenly needing to raise his voice slightly to be heard above the growing swell of chatter. Grace had been so focused on him she hadn't noticed the bar filling up with an early Friday crowd, eager to welcome in the weekend. She smiled and nodded and grabbing their things, they squeezed their way through to the door.

"I hadn't realised how hot it was in there," she gasped as they stepped outside, breathing in the cool evening air.

"Let's walk for a bit." Warren took hold of her hand as they headed off, wrapped in a comfortable silence. Occasionally, Grace stole a glance in Warren's direction and was surprised to see a look of intense concentration, his eyes scanning from left to right and back again, with an occasional backwards glance when he clearly thought her attention was elsewhere. She let it go the first time but when it persisted, she started to feel a sense of unease.

"You okay?"

Her words snapped him back to the moment and he immediately smiled. "I'm great. Why?"

"No reason," she said, smiling back. She must have been mistaken.

"So are you going to invite me back to yours or do I have to invite myself?" he asked, any hint of tension already forgotten.

When Grace woke the next morning, there was a split second while she pulled herself out of sleep before her mind played her the most perfect recap of the evening before. Her head was flooded with a series of images from the bar to her flat to her bedroom and every beautiful moment in between. And then she smiled as Warren slipped his arms around her waist and kissed her head.

"Good morning," he whispered.

"What time is it?" she asked.

"Time for some of us to go to work I'm afraid. Much as I'd love to stay here I have a café to open up."

"But it's Saturday," she objected. "We could get some coffee and breakfast somewhere?"

"And it's exactly because of people like you that I have to go to work!" He kissed her gently. "Pop in and see me later. Now go back to sleep."

Grace did just that for a couple of hours and then dragged herself out of bed to go to meet Phil. By the time he arrived, the table was already adorned with coffee and a selection of delicious looking pastries.

"Heaven!" he said as he sat down, immediately knocking back the espresso that was waiting for him as if it was a shot of tequila. He gave his head a quick shake as the caffeine raced through his veins and then he grinned. "That's better!"

"You look as shattered as I feel," Grace said as she watched him use his best sign language to order another coffee.

"If that's your way of saying I look shagged then thanks for nothing. And if that's how you feel too then...bloody hell you've had sex!"

"Shhhhhhh!" Grace frantically flapped her hands as if she could somehow retrospectively dull the words that seemed deafening to her ears, as she tried to temper a now annoyingly animated Phil.

"How was he?" he asked, his eyes wide with delight.

"I'm not answering that."

"By the look on your face I'd say pretty good. Well thank fuck for that. Literally!"

Phil laughed and Grace could feel her face redden with every chuckle. Thank goodness she hadn't met him at Warren's café, something she had come dangerously close to suggesting. The very thought just made her face flush even more.

"I'm sorry," Phil said, finally composing himself. "You know I'm just excited for you. I'm really pleased it's all going so well."

"Yes it is," Grace said, relaxing back into her chair, the colour in her cheeks slowly returning to normal.

"But?" Grace could feel the intensity of Phil's stare as he immediately picked up on the doubt in her voice.

"No buts," she said with a smile. "It is going really well. It just sometimes feels like he's holding something back. Like he's not quite opening up. Or like he's just a bit distracted." She shook her head. "I can't quite put my finger on it."

"Don't over think it. It's still early days. And how are you sleeping?"

Grace forced a smile. "Not bad. Only the occasional nightmare."

Phil waited. Grace knew he would be waging the constant battle he regularly had with himself about whether or not to push her on the subject of John, the termination and the resulting recurring nightmares, or just trust her to talk if and when she felt ready. "So what else is new?" he then asked, choosing to assume the growing silence meant Grace wasn't about to elaborate. Glad of the opportunity to move the conversation on, she immediately filled him in on her most recent meeting with Anna.

"Do you think she's right?" she asked. "That I just accept what life throws my way without question?"

"No, I don't," he said without the slightest hesitation. "But I do think it's slightly ironic that the woman you chose to help to boost your confidence is actually causing you self-doubt. That's what I'd be worrying about."

Grace sat back and let his words sink in for a moment and then she allowed herself a wry smile. It suddenly seemed slightly hilarious that she might be paying someone to make her fell even worse about herself that she did already.

"So you're done with her surely?"

"No, I don't think I am." Grace thought about it for a moment more. "I need to be challenged. I know I didn't really get the chance to put her coping mechanisms into play with Peter but for at least a couple of days, I actually walked into the office with a smile on my face, honestly believing I was equipped to rebuff him and that was huge for me." Phil look unconvinced and she smiled at him. "Two more sessions and then I've done what I originally agreed with her. Then I'll happily walk away."

19

Anna

When Grace left their session, Anna had been just a few moments behind her. The first few minutes had been the most challenging, trying to get out of the building without Grace seeing her but after that, it had been relatively easy to follow her from a comfortable distance. Grace had set off at quite a pace but was so focused on where she was headed with her eyes permanently forward that Anna was convinced she could have danced along naked behind her and Grace would have been totally oblivious. She smiled. Everything about Grace's clipped body language, her brisk strides and unnaturally straight arms made it clear Anna had rattled her.

As Grace had finally disappeared inside a bar, Anna had waited for as long as she could before walking up to the side of the building where she'd stood for a moment, a bank of windows to her right. She'd slowly leant in just enough to be able to peek inside, her eyes quickly covering every inch of the place until she'd gasped, her eyes now frozen on Warren. She'd held her breath as she watched him, looking relaxed and happy, his eyes bright, his smile wide and for a moment, Anna allowed herself to believe it was because of her. And then Grace suddenly eclipsed her view and the world went dark again. Anna had exhaled loudly. It was as if Grace was taunting her. As if she was guarding Warren from

145

her, turning herself into a literal physical barrier. Well not for much longer.

Anna knew she was taking a risk but she had simply been unable to wait to find out more about the life Warren was now living. She moved herself a safe distance away from the window and then waited as the bar slowly filled up. Once the crowd inside was suitably dense, she had slipped in, ordered herself a drink and sat at the edge of the bar, well out of sight but confident that she would be able to see them leave.

Time limped by and then finally she'd seen them stand up and head for the door. She'd turned her back for a moment, not wanting to take any chances and then slipped out after them. She felt her heart start to pound as she followed them, knowing that any minute they would either disappear into the underground or jump in a cab and she'd have no choice but to go home alone. She could already see herself lying in bed, torturing herself imagining what they would be up to and then she stopped. She'd been so busy tormenting herself she'd lost concentration for a moment and was suddenly aware of Warren looking over his shoulder. Could he have seen her? She ducked into a doorway for a moment and then, as she watched him once again flip his head around with a quick scan of the crowds, she slowly started walking backwards, letting them slip away from her. Holding back was the hardest thing she'd ever done but she wasn't ready for him to know she'd found him.

By the time Warren left Grace's flat the next morning, Anna was already outside in her car. She'd assumed they would end up back here and thanks to the information Grace had provided before their first session, she knew where she lived. With her boys at her ex-husband's for the weekend, she was free to do as she pleased and more than anything, she wanted to know where the café was that Warren worked. In fact, it was more than that. She needed to know where he was.

She watched him climb into the back of a waiting minicab and felt a real buzz as she slowly pulled out behind them. The excitement at being so close to him, to just know he was alive and well, was still almost too much to bear. She was suddenly aware of herself smiling and then a laugh escaped, the swell of emotion simply too much to contain.

She didn't take her eyes off the car for even a second, frightened to even blink in case she lost sight of it. The roads were quiet at this time on a Saturday morning but as a passenger in the back of the car, and therefore with no rearview mirror to check behind him, she felt it was pretty unlikely she would be noticed. But as the car pulled in and Warren stepped out, she was sure she sensed him looking around quickly before he unlocked the door to the café and disappeared inside. She couldn't decide if she was imagining it or if she'd made him a little paranoid after getting too close the night before. She would need to be more careful but despite acknowledging this, here she was, sitting directly opposite the café and unable to leave. She watched as the lights flickered on and saw Warren busy himself behind the counter in preparation for the day ahead. A short time later a couple of teenagers arrived, one male, one female, who Anna assumed were the cheap weekend help. She was transfixed as she watched Warren chat with them, his face so beautifully animated, his eyes full of a gentleness that she had once known, her memory of which had been buried so deeply that to see it again left her immediately light-headed.

* *

Before

Anna sat on a large chair in the corner of the room. Her feet didn't touch the ground as she swung her legs slowly back and forth, her eyes glued to her shiny new black patent shoes. She was very proud of them but the tights she'd been told to wear were making her hot and the new black dress was itchy. She had made her discomfort known but hadn't been able to find anyone who cared, a constant stream of hands shooing her away all morning with nothing more than a tut or a dismissive shake of the head.

Anna looked around the room. Her eyes were met with a sea of black and a blur of very serious looking faces. Everyone was talking very quietly and occasionally, someone would glance over at her, a look of pity in their eyes. Each time this happened Anna stared back with what she hoped was her most fierce expression and then she smiled to herself as, without exception, the worried eyes would dilate and then quickly look away.

The only noise was coming from her mother. She was drunk, her body anaesthetised to such an extent that her legs didn't seem to be working very well. She had subsequently slumped in a chair, occasionally shouting an unintelligible bundle of words, all slurred into a series of long excruciating yells. Various people fussed over her but she batted each of them away with a floppy arm, her head lolling from left to right and back again. Anna winced, her cheeks flushing with embarrassment and making her hot which just made her even more itchy and uncomfortable. She continued to swing her feet as if marking time until the torture was over.

When time didn't pass quickly enough, she slipped off the chair and wound her way through one small group to another then on to the next, listening carefully to snippets of conversation along the way. Everyone was of course talking about her father. She'd been told it was a car accident that had killed him but she knew his car had never left the garage. She'd heard her mother scream from the garage that day too in a way that was so chilling it had sent her au pair, Helen, racing to her aide. Anna had stayed where she was. Her mother seemed to limp from one alcohol-fuelled drama to another so she wasn't overly concerned until she had seen an ambulance arrive and then a police car. By the time she tried to leave her bedroom the door had been locked, leaving her with no option but to watch the scene unfold from her bedroom window. It felt like she had to wait hours before she heard the sound of a key turning in the lock. She was half way across the room when Helen appeared in the doorway, her face blotchy and swollen from crying.

"What is it?" Anna had asked.

"It's your father," she had stammered in reply. "There's been a terrible accident." Then a pause. "A car accident." She had sounded unconvincing even then. Clearly troubled, she had continue to fluster and hesitate as if unsure how to continue.

"What Helen?" Anna had shouted. "What's happened to him?"

"I'm afraid he's dead."

Anna had frozen. So many emotions to process. So many questions. And an unexpected surge of anger that she had struggled to get control of. It was all way too much for her eight year old brain to cope with. Anna was aware of Helen staring at her, eyebrows raised as she waited, Anna imagined, for her to say something.

"Oh," was eventually all she had managed.

Over the coming weeks, Anna kept herself to herself. She refused the offer to stay off school and would disappear off to her room the minute she got home. She came downstairs to eat dinner with Helen and then went straight back to her room, not resurfacing until it was morning when she would appear for breakfast which she again ate with only Helen for company. Getting herself to bed was the loneliest moment but she powered through and soon it just became another functional part of the day. As young as she was, she quickly realised the sooner she learned to look after herself and got used to being on her own, the better.

Occasionally, her mother would sweep into the room, a glass of something in one hand, a lit cigarette in the other, moving precariously on unstable legs. She would look at Anna and smile with eyes full of pity and nod at her in a knowing way as if she understood how Anna was feeling. Which of course she didn't. Anna had loved her father. Her mother had not. Anna had soaked up the man's warmth and kindness. Her mother had not. Anna felt lost without him. Her mother felt nothing.

There was a steady flow of visitors in those weeks after the funeral and Anna would listen at the door of the study when anyone came to talk to her mother. She would then marvel at the stellar performance her mother would give, rebuffing any offers of help as unnecessary and strongly opposing any suggestion that Anna might be struggling. It was impressive to listen to and mental notes were taken. Occasionally Anna would see a guest leave and look in disbelief at how reassured they looked, how relaxed they were as they said their goodbyes amid constant declarations of 'you know where I am if you need me.' They'd done their bit. They'd shown willing and Anna soon worked out they wouldn't be back.

When Anna's mother died of heart failure ten years later no one batted an eyelid. It was the day after Anna's eighteenth birthday. Helen, who was no longer needed as an au pair but had stayed on in the capacity of general housekeeper, had found her. By the time Anna was told and had returned home from school, her mother's body had already been taken away, leaving behind a sobbing Helen whom Anna consoled as best she could before dispatching her home in a taxi.

As soon as she was alone, Anna poured herself a large glass of wine, something she'd been doing since the age of fourteen when her mother had first badgered her to loosen up and just 'bloody well have a drink'. She took the drink and chose to sit in the lounge, a room barely used. The soulless house was eerily quiet but Anna felt calm. In fact, she felt relaxed in a way she didn't recognise. She thought for a moment, likening the sensation to begin unshackled after years of imprisonment. She felt light. She felt free.

The next day she met with the family lawyer. She knew there was plenty of money but even she was surprised when she was told exactly how much. There were properties she knew nothing about, endless investments and a majority share in the company her father had built from nothing.

"I'd like you to sell everything," she told him calmly. "Send someone to the house who can pick out anything of value to be sold. The rest can go to the local charity shop. I've got an estate agent coming tomorrow so I want everything done as soon as possible." Anna waited but the lawyer said nothing. "Mr Edgar?"

"Maybe you should wait a while and then see how you feel?"

"I'll feel exactly the same as I do now."

"Your father hoped you might take over his business one day. You should meet with the chief exec and talk to him."

"I have no interest in his business," she said without hesitation, "and if my father really wanted me involved he should have stayed around to make it happen instead of electing to take his own life. So please sell his shares and all the investments. Sell the properties, sell anything valuable in the house and that includes my mother's jewellery."

"Surely you want to keep that?"

Anna felt her brow furrow. "I don't want any of it. Am I not making myself clear enough for you?"

"I've seen this many, many times Anna. You're grieving. Just give yourself some time."

Anna looked at him for a moment. "Is there any legal reason for you not to do what I'm asking?"

"Well no, but..."

"Then please just do as I've asked." She stood up. "Thank you for your time."

Three years later, Anna had sailed through university with her head down, coming out the other side with a number of connections but no real friends. Exactly how she liked it. With the help of an astute financial adviser, her money had all been reinvested and although she lived a comfortable life, it certainly wasn't obvious that she was an incredibly wealthy young woman. Explaining her fortune would mean talking about her past, and that was something she was always keen to avoid.

By the time she and two of her 'connections' were packing up their flat, Anna had already secured a job in London with a large financial PR firm. She was joining as a trainee but the company was one of the best with an impressive client list so there was plenty of scope to develop. When she'd headed for London for her second interview, she factored in some flat hunting and found herself a stunning one bedroom flat in an old factory just south of the river. The rent was extortionate but she felt she'd more than earned the right to be extravagant for a few months until she found herself the perfect place to buy. And to top it off, she hired someone to get the place ready for her. With her usual impeccable brief, furniture and kitchen essentials were bought and the subsequent deliveries supervised with a variety of soft furnishings then suitably placed and scattered accordingly. The bathroom was filled with all her preferred products and the fridge and cupboards packed full of all her favourite foods. When she walked in three weeks later, she was able to go straight to the kitchen and make herself a cup of tea, relax in front of the huge, wall-mounted TV on her beautiful new sofa and then fall into a perfectly made bed.

Over the next few years, the promotions came thick and fast.

"I've never met anyone as organised as you Anna. Your work ethic is outstanding and your ability to keep cool in a crisis is exceptional," she was told.

"Your results and achievements put you streaks ahead of the pack," came next.

"Your lack of emotion when faced with a problem gives you a real edge Anna," her current boss enthused.

"Her lack of emotion is unnerving," her colleagues whispered at the water cooler.

Anna knew what her peers said about her and cared not. Presenting a company's financial updates to the world at large, explaining gains and losses along the way, the hirings and firings, justifying everything from working conditions to positions on the environment and diversity, often required nerves of steel. Anna saw it as a huge advantage that her own nervous system was made of pure metal. Not that she couldn't be charming when required if it meant she got what she wanted.

By the time she hit thirty, Anna had been made a director of the company and was living comfortably in her own home. Loving the distinctive features of the old building where she'd been renting, she waited until a three-bedroom flat came up for sale and leapt at it. There were people she could call on if she felt like being sociable but most of the time she chose her own company. She developed a taste for fine wine, her walls were decked with a careful selection of original art and she had a wardrobe full of expensive clothes. Life was working out pretty well.

Shut away in her own office, Anna was rarely distracted by the office hubbub, despite the glass wall that separated her from the daily comings and goings. Until the day Warren came in for an interview. She looked up to see him walking across the office floor with one of her colleagues, relaxed and chatting as he passed. She was unable to take her eyes off him, her mind and body immediately flooded with alien feelings that unnerved her enormously but were simply too powerful to be ignored.

It was three days before Anna was able to get more information. For some reason, she felt unable to just ask the small number of direct questions required to establish who Warren was and if he would be joining the company which was also totally incongruous to her normal straight-talking self. So it was a relief to finally discover that the events management team was indeed taking him on.

"Can I make you a coffee while I'm here?"

"If you don't mind, that would be great, thank you. Just black for me."

Anna smiled as she set about making another coffee. It had taken her less than a week to work out Warren's routine so engineering a little moment to introduce herself had subsequently been easy.

"I'm Anna, by the way."

"Warren," he replied. "This is my first week."

"And how's it going?"

"It's a bit overwhelming trying to get up to speed but I'm really enjoying it."

Anna found his smile quite hypnotising which was making it hard for her to concentrate. She turned her attention back to making coffee for a moment, giving her the chance to refocus. She needed to make sure she kept to her plan. "Well feel free to pop by my office if you need any client background. No one knows them better than me."

"Wow. Coffee and a generous offer of help. This is turning into quite a morning."

Anna felt herself blush. If his smile was hypnotic then Warren's perfectly pitched confidence was thoroughly intoxicating.

"Enjoy your coffee," she said as she handed it over. "And if you want to know the really good stuff, you'll have to buy me a drink."

Anna was walking away before Warren had the chance to answer. She was desperate to look back to see his expression, to get even a tiny glimpse of how likely it was that he'd bite but she kept her head high and firmly forward, her heart beating hard in her chest. She smiled. This was going to be fun.

20

Anna

Now

Anna sat at the kitchen table with a coffee and some paperwork and listened to the conversation in the hallway.

"Do you have your homework book Eddie?" she heard their nanny, Marta, ask her youngest son, her voice as calm and gentle as always. There was no reply but she heard the footsteps of her eight year old as he ran off and up the stairs to retrieve the missing book. She rolled her eyes. It was the same every morning and it annoyed her enormously. Almost as much as it did hearing her son's name shortened. How many times had she told Marta his name was Edward? Heavier footsteps announced the arrival of Charles.

"Hey Charlie." Anna heard Marta greet him and bristled at the second hypocorism in as many minutes. "Have you got everything?" Again, there was no reply. "You need your PE kit today and the consent form for next week's trip. Did you get your mum to sign it?"

Anna glanced along to the end of the table and saw the envelope waiting for collection. He was ten years old now. Those double figures should surely mean he could organise himself sufficiently? She shook her head, remembering how independent she was at his age. The kid didn't know he was born. A moment later, Charles appeared. He looked at her

157

with a completely blank face. There was nothing rude or disrespectful about his demeanour. It was more a complete indifference to her, as if he hadn't even seen her. He picked up the envelope and left the room again. Anna watched him go and, for a moment, she thought about calling after him but quickly realised she had no idea for what purpose or what she might say so instead, she went back to reading the report in front of her.

"Got it," she heard Edward say as he came running back down the stairs. There then followed a variety of rustling noises, zips opening and closing and arms slipping into coats. And then it went very still. She listened intently and heard Marta's gentle whisper, making her usual desperate plea to the two boys to at least say goodbye to their mother. Not for the first time, Anna wondered if she should put her out of her misery and tell her that she was well aware what she was trying to do and that she shouldn't bother. A forced farewell would make little difference to her day. Anna waited then heard the front door open.

"See you tonight Anna!" Marta shouted.

And then they were gone.

An hour or so later, Anna was slumped on the sofa in her office, coat still on and bags still in hand. She'd sat down the minute she'd come through the door, feeling the need to gather herself for a moment and then she'd stayed there, her mood making her feel heavy and unable to move.

She didn't think about it often but today, with her emotions pushed uncomfortably close to the surface since the moment she'd seen Warren, she found herself picking over the start to her day, musing over the fact that she had no relationship with her children at all. Any sense of connection or attachment was entirely absent.

She closed her eyes, squeezing them tightly shut as if to hold in the toxic cocktail of guilt, resentment and regret that brewed deep within her every time she found herself questioning her maternal instincts, or total lack thereof. Of course she blamed her ex-husband for her current pain. One son was looking increasingly like him; the other gradually adopting all of his most irritating personality traits. It was surely no wonder she struggled. She thought about it for a moment and then forced herself to accept that it wasn't the boys' fault they had been born to the wrong father.

It was a thought powerful enough to make her finally sit up, her head immediately full of thoughts of Warren and how different life might have been. Finally taking her coat off, Anna moved to her desk, a steely determination back in her eyes. Enough self-indulgence. There was work to be done.

Anna opened her notebook and started scouring the pages full of notes from her sessions with Grace. She knew she should be concentrating on Matthew's brief but right now, all she wanted – no *needed* to do – was hurt her. Really hurt her. She'd spent the weekend forced to watch Warren from a painful distance when all she wanted to do was feel the strength and warmth of his arms around her, to be close enough to breath in the intoxicating smell of him. Her feelings towards Grace, as the one obstacle she saw between them, were becoming more and more extreme as a result, a primal jealousy suffocating any sense of perspective or professionalism. She needed Grace to feel some of the immense pain she'd been forced to endure when she lost Warren. To know how it had felt to feel alone and totally helpless. What it felt like to face a future that would always be, at best, second rate and, at worst, nothing more than pointless.

When after a few moments she realised she'd been through her complete set of notes, she immediately went back to the beginning and started again, her eyes urgently flitting from one line to the next, the pages quickly becoming curled and creased as she hurriedly turned them backwards and forwards, backwards and forwards. There had to be something here. A point of vulnerability that she could latch on to. She continued to flip and scan, scan and flip and then she stopped, momentarily amazed it had taken her so long to spot the very obvious Achilles heel. A smile slowly crept across her face.

"Gotcha," she whispered.

21

Grace

Despite the fact she had only just buzzed him into the building, Grace still jumped out of her skin when Phil burst into her flat, arms waving, the air around him toxic from a string of expletives that continued to spill from his angry mouth as he strode straight for the window. His eyes were full of a raw fury as he scoured the parking area below, muttering under his breath a complete jumble of unintelligible words. Grace chose to watch and wait, seeing no point in trying to talk to him until whatever it was that was consuming him had waned. Right now, he was like a man possessed and one who didn't look like he would appreciate any interruption or any attempt to calm him down. Grace headed for the kitchen to make coffee. She might as well do something useful while she waited.

When she returned a few moments later, a mug of coffee in each hand, Phil was still at the window. "Okay, enough now. You're freaking me out. What's going on?"

Phil's eyes remained firmly on the cars below. "Some bastard's following me."

"Really?"

"Yes, really." Phil glared at her, clearly angry that she would doubt him. "It's a photographer, I'm sure of it. He's been following me for days now and it's really starting to get on my nerves."

Grace raised her eyebrows. She definitely wasn't going to argue with that. "Come away from the window. Staring at him isn't going to help."

Grace put the coffees down and slowly pulled Phil away, gently encouraging him onto the sofa and then handed him his drink. She sat in a chair opposite him and for a moment they remained in silence, the only sound the occasional slurp. "Do you want a biscuit?"

"No I don't want a fucking biscuit." Phil checked himself as Grace visibly flinched. "Thanks all the same," he added less aggressively. Grace said nothing. The silence that followed was awkward and uncomfortable but it was still preferable to having Phil snap at her. She watched as he hung his head for a moment, rubbing the back of his neck with his free hand in an attempt to relieve some tension. Eventually he looked up. "I'm sorry. It's just really unnerving. What's he after? What's so interesting about me?"

A week later, Grace, Phil and Emily were back in their favourite restaurant, the wine and conversation flowing.

"So how's the dating going Em?" Phil asked.

Emily rolled her eyes. "I don't know if I'm just too fussy or my expectations are too high or if I just haven't quite worked out yet how to negotiate my way through the minefield that is online dating, but suffice to say the progress is slow."

"Oh well. Few more frogs and it'll be your turn I'm sure."

She smiled at him. "If only you were straight my search would be over."

"If he was straight he'd be going out with me!" Grace leapt in. "Wouldn't you Phil?"

As Phil looked from one to the other, his phone rang. "Saved by the bell!" he said with a huge smile, picking up his phone and excusing himself to take the call.

When he came back to the table a few moments later, his eyes were watery, his complexion pale.

"What's happened? Who was that?" Grace said, taking hold of his hand.

"It was my agent. There's a story running tomorrow saying I'm a fucking addict. And we just did a press conference a few days ago announcing the huge anti-drug campaign I told you about. It'll be ruined. And I'll lose my job."

"But it's not true!" Emily shouted. She turned to Grace. "No one's allowed to make stuff like that up are they Grace?"

"Absolutely not," Grace said. "Get your agent to threaten them with a law suit."

Phil sat with his head down. "They have pictures of me with lines of coke."

"How is that possible?" Grace was aghast.

"I have no idea but apparently they've been authenticated, whatever the fuck that means."

"But that's ridiculous!" Emily cried. "They can't just print something that's a blatant lie!"

Phil and Emily looked at Grace. "If they think they have proof the pictures are real they can," she said, and then she thought for a moment. "We need to do something." She looked at Phil. "You need to speak to your boss and warn him. And someone in your press office too."

Phil's eyes had glazed over. It was all too much to take in and he looked like he'd just shut down. "Phil!" Grace said and then again a little louder. "Phil!" She squeezed his arm. "I'm going to speak to Sam and see what he can find out. You need to make the calls!"

Phil slowly got up and went in search of a quiet spot to make the difficult call to his boss as Grace searched her phone for Sam's number. She quickly brought him up to speed and then left him to make some calls of his own.

Grace and Emily sat in silence while they waited, Emily folding and refolding her napkin over and over again; Grace tapping her foot at great speed as was her wont, her eyes fixed on a picture on the wall opposite, studying it intently but seeing nothing.

Just as Phil headed back towards them, Grace's phone rang. It was Sam. She put him on speaker and put her phone down in the middle of the table.

"So how do we prove it's all made up?" Grace asked him. "Could he get an injunction to stop it running?"

"I'm afraid it's too late," Sam said, his voice flat and grave. "It's already online."

22

Anna

After following Phil on and off for a few days, Anna had realised it was a pointless exercise. She'd tailed him to and from work and to Grace's flat and had taken a few pictures of him interacting with people along the way but it was nothing more than a bit of casual chat here and there, or a fan stopping him for a selfie. What a boring life he led, Anna had thought. The only saving grace was that as he worked in the evenings, she'd been able to fit her extracurricular activities around her normal work commitments. Despite that, she was still very aware she was wasting a lot of time. She would need to be more creative.

Anna had sat in her kitchen, the house around her still and quiet, scouring the internet for pictures of Phil. There were so many and in minutes, she had a folder full of shots of him in various social settings, out with friends, in clubs and parties and in countless different bars. And then she had experienced the most wondrous moment of clarity.

"I'm off now Anna." Anna had looked up to see Marta in the doorway, making her check her watch. It was eight thirty. "Edward's asleep and Charles is reading. So unless there's anything else?"

Anna had duly noted Marta's careful choice of words. It seemed her latest chat about name shortening had worked, for the time being at least. "Thank you Marta. Have a good evening."

Marta had nodded with a brief smile and then quietly let herself out. By the time she got home, they both knew there would be no evening left to enjoy, a fact Anna felt she more than made up for with an above average salary and a healthy Christmas bonus.

Anna had then continued her search for a while longer with a renewed sense of purpose and then she'd smiled as she reviewed her haul, marvelling at how frivolous Phil had been with his privacy online. She'd checked the time again and was surprised to see it was almost ten o'clock but she couldn't stop now. She picked up her phone, scrolled through her contacts until she found the name and number she was looking for, and hit dial.

"Hello?"

"Frank, it's Anna. It's been a while, how are you?" Anna waited. She could almost hear his brain whirring as it scanned back into his past and then finally, he spoke.

"Bloody hell, Anna! There's nothing wrong is there?"

She smiled, remembering. "No Frank, there's nothing wrong. But I do need your help."

Anna had found the world of finance an often unscrupulous place to inhabit. In her public relations role, the numbers spoke for themselves (most of the time) but Anna had found the people were rarely as straightforward. If she wanted to stay ahead of the game, she had quickly realised she needed to be all-knowing, from the intricate details of her clients' personal finances to the men and women they slept with, to everything about the key staff they surrounded themselves with. The same went for the journalists she dealt with, from their politics, to their personal and professional relationships and everything in between. Her colleagues had always thought it impossible to unnerve Anna and, although that was true, for the most part her sense of calm was often the result of being incredibly well-informed. Unwanted surprises were simply not something she was prepared to tolerate. And she had never had to, thanks to Frank, an investigator who lived in the shadows with the kind of contacts for whom no off-shore account was too remote, no secret too deep and no firewall too high. Frank had subsequently had a precarious relationship with the law so Anna wasn't surprised his first thought was that the past might finally have caught up with them.

"What do you need?"

"I need a picture doctored and something to convince a newspaper it's authentic."

"Consider it done."

"I'm going to send you a selection of pictures now with some notes," she said, never having doubted for a second that this would be beyond his capabilities and loving the fact he was so immediately focused. "Use whichever one will work best and let me know when they're ready. And I'm sure I don't need to ask for your discretion?"

"I'm insulted you even have to ask."

"Well thank you." Anna could sense the smile in his voice and she felt bizarrely nostalgic for a moment as her mind wandered off into the past to a time when Frank and his merry band had made her feel hugely empowered.

"I'm glad to be able to help," he said, waking her from her trip down memory lane. "And it was really good to hear from you. We should have a drink sometime and...."

Anna had already hung up before he had the chance to finish his sentence.

While Anna had waited for Frank to work his magic, she had been both surprised and delighted to discover that handing over her freshly doctored pictures for publication would be the easiest part of all. 'We pay for your stories!' had immediately leapt out at her from one of the tabloids when she'd looked online. She'd quickly scanned the copy that followed and as soon as she'd seen the line saying it was okay to remain anonymous, she hadn't felt the need to look any further.

When the picture arrived back just a few days later, Anna had been blown away. She'd sat at her desk and scrutinised every millimetre of it, after which she defied anyone not to immediately accept it as genuine. And if anyone dared to question its authenticity, she had a perfectly convincing report explaining the use of leading forensic software to determine that the picture was, beyond doubt, an unaltered original. She'd paid Frank a small fortune but my, it had been worth every zero.

As Anna now scrolled through the umpteenth online news report, praising herself for such a well-executed plan, she clasped her hands together to fully capture the feeling of pure glee that instantly overwhelmed her as she dared to imagine the fall-out. Grace had talked extensively about Phil, it was obvious how much she relied on him and how empty life would be without him if her worse fears were realised and he chose to further his career abroad. A move Anna felt was now inevitable as he'd been exposed as a fraud and would almost certainly lose his job as a result. For a split second, Anna felt badly for Phil and the pain the coverage would undoubtedly cause him but the feeling didn't last long. He was a necessary pawn in the game she found herself playing. A sacrificial lamb, if you will. And then she had quickly reminded herself that any blame lay entirely with Grace for spouting forth so unashamedly, and so unnecessarily, about the intimacies of their friendship.

Anna sat back in her chair with eyes wide and nerve ends tingling. There was no possible way this could backfire. Phil would leave the country and Anna would convince Grace to go with him. She couldn't possibly survive without her strongest source of support so surely the only course of action was for Grace to reward herself with a fresh start too? Anna smiled. It would be hard not to ask Grace if she'd like some help packing her bags. Perhaps a lift to the airport?

Anna jumped as the loud ring of her mobile shattered the silence. In her rush to answer it – anything to stop the dreadful, piercing noise – she only clocked Matthew's name at the exact moment she accepted the call. She felt her cheeks flush as she quickly tried to compose herself.

"Matthew, hello."

"Just wondering how you're getting on with our experiment, Anna?"

Anna had been so focused on her own agenda, she hadn't given Matthew's experiment any thought at all. "The appropriate seed has been planted," she said, grimacing at the sound of her clichéd words. "I'm just waiting for it to take hold. I'll know how that's going next week when she comes in again."

"Okay but let's try to get things moving a little faster can we? Important we keep any momentum going."

What was with all this 'we' business? Anna found him both patronising and incredibly irritating. She didn't like being caught out and that was how she felt. She forced a smile which she hoped would translate into her voice. "Of course. I'll be in touch next week."

Anna took a deep breath as she put down her phone and then she slowly exhaled. She would recommend Grace give Matthew a call as she bid her a happy and fulfilled life somewhere hot and sunny and then leave it in the hands of fate. Matthew had made it clear the result had meaning whether Grace made contact or not so she certainly wasn't going to concern herself with the outcome.

She sat back in her chair. She was almost there. Then she quickly sat forward again, opened her emails and hurriedly started typing. Just one last piece of insurance to put in play. Then she would be done.

23

Grace

Grace was sitting with Phil at his kitchen table. The air that surrounded them was thick with tension, the silence eating up oxygen and threatening to suffocate. The only sound came from Phil turning the pages of one newspaper after another while Grace sat quietly beside him, scouring the internet.

She wasn't sure what was more surprising – the sheer volume of coverage (she knew he was popular but had clearly underestimated just how much) or the countless comments left on articles and posted on social media. She thought she was pretty unshockable but bloody hell people could be cruel. There was clearly a huge contingent who loved nothing more than the chance to celebrate someone's downfall, lurking in virtual shadows and ready to pounce the moment there was any hint of a fall from grace. Suddenly awash with nostalgia, she longed for a time when a discussion over a pint or a glass of wine in the pub was the norm; a disposable exchange of views that today, with the touch of a 'send' or 'post' button, was immediately shared with hundreds, thousands, sometimes millions of people around the world. Grace shivered, relieved that Phil had opted for the more traditional media. She would come up with a plan later to try to keep him away from all this spiteful crap.

Grace had come straight home with Phil from the restaurant. She'd done a quick survey of the immediate online coverage and given him the edited highlights, urging him not to read it himself but instead to wait for the morning when he could review it with a clear head. Both had subsequently been up and awake early with Grace choosing to make the dash to the local newsagent to buy the morning's papers, leaving the important task of making a pot of extra strong coffee to Phil.

An hour or so later with more caffeine than could ever be considered healthy coursing through their veins, Phil closed the final newspaper he had been reading and tossed it onto a growing pile on the floor.

"Well it could have been worse," he said, his voice heavy. Grace looked at him, her eyebrows raised in challenge. "No seriously. It really could have been a lot worse," he said. "Thanks to Sam's advice, at least everyone's included a line from me saying it's not true and that I'm determined to clear my name. Without that, it would have been a total whitewash."

Grace watched as his head then fell forward. They both knew that whether he could prove falsehood or not, the damage was already done. He would be booted off the anti-drug campaign and the public humiliation would be forever part of his story.

"I'm just so angry it's happened at all," Grace said, reaching across the table to take hold of his hand.

Phil forced a smile. "Well there's nothing we can do about it now. You'll have noticed there's no credit for the source or the photographer? That's the major disappointment for me. The only thing that's kept me going in the last few hours is dreaming about what I would do to the fucking scumbag that's behind all this."

Grace let the comment go. She strongly believed the omission was a blessing in disguise. The last thing Phil needed was an assault charge on top of everything else. She drained the last of her coffee and shut her laptop. "So what now?"

"I'm going back to bed," Phil said through a very large yawn. "Need to look my best when I go into work later."

"There'll be photographers waiting, you know that don't you?"

"Don't worry. The press office are bringing in rent-a-crowd complete with banners protesting their love for me to show my fans are still behind me which should lighten the next round of pictures. Sneaky little buggers. And they look like such a harmless bunch!" He smiled and for the first time since the news broke, Grace saw a tiny glimpse of the sparkle she so loved in him. She felt her heart swell and her eyes glisten as she dared to believe he might not be totally broken after all.

Grace left Phil to sleep and headed to the office with the aim of immersing herself in work. There had been a text from Sam checking she and Phil were both okay and she had replied with her thanks again for his help. She'd resisted getting into a conversation about it all. Sam would ask about

Phil's next move, leaving Grace with no choice but to admit it was now highly likely Phil would decide it was time for a fresh start. And once that decision was made, he would be online in a flash, booking a one-way ticket to who knew where. She shivered at the very thought.

Grace was soon suitably distracted by the usual discussions of the day and the standard set of hurdles that required negotiating, causing Phil's text to sit unnoticed for forty-seven minutes. She held her breath as she read his message, the gist of which was that he'd been told by his boss to stay away for a few days while the next steps were discussed. He said nothing about how he felt as a result. It was just a calm statement of fact. She immediately called him but Phil had switched his phone off. He never did that. Ever. But then he'd never been in a situation quite like this one before. Next she tried Emily. Voicemail too. Grace sat back in her chair, her eyes staring but seeing nothing, the conversations around her suddenly muted. So much for focusing on work, her ability to do anything constructive now consumed by the tight ball of anxiety that sat grumbling low in her gut.

After a few absent moments, Grace stood up and headed to the editorial floor.

"I was just thinking about you. How you doing?" Grace imagined her face said it all as Sam's initial expression quickly changed from looking pleased to see her to sharing her obvious concern. "Sit down for a minute."

Grace ignored him, choosing instead to pace up and down. No mean feat in Sam's modest office.

"I just feel so helpless. I know it's not true but that doesn't seem to matter. We'll never turn this around."

"Did he show you this?" Sam handed her a piece of paper that she quickly realised was the full statement from the radio station. "I thought it was really fair. They've offered their support while he takes time to clear his name." Grace stopped and looked at him, eyebrows raised. "I know the idea of taking time off probably wasn't his idea," Sam continued, "but it's all about perception. And the perception is they're on his side and that really matters right now."

"But he's been dropped from the campaign and you and I both know he won't be able to clear his name so the next statement will say he's decided to quit – the supportive way of saying he's been ceremoniously fired."

Grace's tone made it clear there was no point disagreeing and Sam was way too smart for empty platitudes as a way of trying to make her feel better.

"How's he coping?" he asked instead.

"I don't know. He's switched his phone off."

"Well let me know if I can do anything."

If only there was something, Grace thought as she smiled her thanks and left him to it.

By eight o'clock, Grace was pushing open the door of the café. Warren had already finished his shift and was sitting waiting for her. He smiled as he saw her, immediately out of his seat and wrapping his arms around her as soon as she was close enough to do so. "Hello lovely lady."

Grace felt the tension of the day melt away, his body absorbing all the anxiety and madness leaving her feeling deliciously light-headed. Warren pulled back and looked at her. "Okay, I get it. You need food and wine as quickly as possible," he said, taking her hand as he led her back outside.

An hour later, Grace felt like a different woman. Her stomach bulged after a large bowl of comforting pasta and her cheeks glowed with the flush of red wine.

"Welcome back!" Warren smiled at her. "You look like you needed that."

"Yes I did. It's been a strange and challenging twenty-four hours."

"How's Phil?" Grace had left a series of rambling messages for Warren to let him know she was temporarily out of action while she supported her friend. "Has the storm passed?"

"He was okay when I last saw him but I haven't been able to get hold of him since."

"He'll be okay. And I'm sure it's made a huge difference to him having you by his side."

Grace had already zoned out and was vaguely aware of Warren gesturing to a waiter. And then he was chatting again but she wasn't listening, his words simply washing over her.

Grace wasn't sure how much time had passed but she was suddenly aware of a delightfully sweet smell tickling her nostrils. She inhaled deeply and then snapped back to the present. She looked down to see a hot sticky toffee pudding had been placed in front of her.

"Oooh, pudding!" she exclaimed, picking up a spoon and tucking in.

"I thought that might do the trick," Warren said with a grin. "Never underestimate the power of the pudding!"

"It's amazing! Do you want some?" Warren shook his head and then suddenly Grace stopped. "Oh shit, your meeting at the charity! I can't believe I haven't asked you yet. I'm so sorry. How did it go?"

"It was good. Really good. I'm going to do some basic training and then start helping with some of the support groups. And in the meantime, they run a youth club on a Friday so I'm going to start hanging out there when I can, just joining in the activities and looking out for any of the kids who might need to talk."

"Warren, that's amazing. I'm really proud of you."

Warren shrugged. "Maybe doing something positive will finally help my own healing process. Has to be worth a try."

"Don't sell yourself short. It's a wonderful thing to do."

"Well thank you. That means a lot." He smiled at her. "Come on. Let's go home."

Warren left early the next morning. It was Saturday and hard as it was to leave Grace in bed, he was glad to have pulled the early shift so he could be back in time to spend the evening with her.

Barely stirring when he headed out, it was a few hours before Grace finally surfaced. She showered and dressed and was just wondering what to do with her day when her thoughts were interrupted by the loud buzzing of the front door.

"Hello?" she said, picking up the phone that would let her speak to whoever was outside.

"Miss Davies?" said a male voice.

"Yes?"

"My name's Detective Sergeant Jacobs. Could I come in for a minute?"

"Sure." Grace pressed the button that released the building's front door then opened her own and waited. She listened to the sound of footsteps moving swiftly up the stairs until DS Jacobs was in front of her, a tall smart looking man in his mid-thirties. His face was friendly looking and Grace happily welcomed him in as he flashed his badge at her, reassuring her as he did so that there was nothing to worry about, obviously well used to people assuming something terrible had happened to a family member when he turned up unannounced.

Grace encouraged him to take a seat, eager to hear what this was all about.

"I'm sorry to bother you but I need to ask you some questions about the activities in the flat across the hall. Have you noticed anything strange going on?"

"I'm ashamed to say I don't even know who lives there. Someone new moved in a few weeks ago and I've been meaning to knock and say hello but just haven't got round to it."

"Well we have reason to believe there's a brothel in operation."

Grace gasped. "What? You're kidding?"

"We've been watching the place for a while now and there's at least three girls working there. They're advertising the place as a massage parlour but there's a great deal more on offer." Grace couldn't believe it. To think there was twenty-four hour sex going on just a few feet away and she hadn't even noticed! While she struggled to take it all on board, DS

Jacobs continued. "I'm afraid we need your help. You're perfectly within your rights to say no but while we can obviously see who's coming in and out of the building, the only way we can confirm the men are going into that particular flat is by watching through the spy hole in your front door. How would you feel about me hanging around for a few hours a day, just for a couple of days until I have enough proof?"

Grace thought for a moment. It couldn't do any harm. "Yeah sure, why not."

"Thank you. You won't know I'm here, I promise. And it's Dave," he said, putting his hand out to her.

"Hi Dave. I'm Grace," she said, taking his hand warmly. "I guess I'll see you tomorrow then?"

"Well if it's not inconvenient, I'd like to stay around for a bit now. If it's not too much trouble?"

Grace hesitated for just a moment. "No that's fine. Knock yourself out. I'll make some coffee." As Grace headed for the kitchen, Dave moved over to the window and positioned the curtain so he could watch what was going on outside without being too obvious. At least Grace guessed that was the plan. When she returned a few moments later with coffee and biscuits she was amazed to see how quickly he had got to work. Armed with some kind of log book, he seemed to be making a note of every car that pulled up in front of the building. As she set down his coffee, someone had clearly caught his eye and Grace watched him lean forward and then he was on his feet and heading to the front door, peering intently through the spy hole. She heard her neighbour's door open and then close. "And we're off!" he said with a smile, retaking his position at the window and thanking her for the coffee.

Grace looked at her watch. It was still only ten thirty. "What, they're at it already?"

From behind a magazine, she then watched him yo-yo from the window to the door. The girls were obviously in demand and business was clearly booming. In between each new arrival, they chatted easily. "So how did you hear about it?"

"We caught one of the girls a couple of months ago. It's never long before they start up again so we've been following her. It's the pimp we're really after and we're determined to get him this time."

"But how do you know what they're offering? I mean they could be measuring these men for new suits or something."

"One of the team's been in there and believe me, a new suit is definitely not on the menu."

"They've been in?" Grace was aghast but Dave merely shrugged with a smile.

"All in a day's work."

It wasn't long before Grace started to feel somewhat surplus to requirements. "Do you mind if I go out for a while?"

Dave was more than happy to be left to it. Grace urged him to help himself to more coffee and moved a chair to the window so he could make himself more comfortable and then she headed off to get some food with enough idle pottering to avoid an entire day of making polite conversation.

Warren returned just after six to find Dave still in situ. When Grace let him in, he came through the door and did an immediate double take as he walked into the lounge.

"Warren, this is Dave. Dave, Warren."

"Good to meet you Warren. I'll let Grace explain."

Warren was too confused to speak, unable to make any sense of the newly appointed window seat and this man sitting in it with his large pad and pen. Grace took his elbow and turned him around. "Go have a shower and then we'll go out. You are not going to believe it when I tell you about my day."

24

Anna

"So, how have the last few weeks been?"

Grace thought for a moment. Where to start? "Not without their fair share of drama."

Anna raised her eyebrows and waited as Grace hesitated, rummaging inwardly for the edited version. "Phil had a run-in with the press which was pretty unpleasant and as of this weekend, I have a brothel running in the flat opposite and the police holding a stakeout in my flat." Anna's eyebrows shot up even further and Grace smiled. "I know, you couldn't make it up. But works great and Warren's great, so it's not all bad."

Anna was momentarily thrown by the mention of Warren's name so was glad to have such an unexpected distraction. "What do you mean a brothel?"

"Just that. A group of prostitutes have set up next door and I'm doing my public duty to help the police make some arrests."

Anna was confident Grace hadn't clocked the flicker of excitement in her eyes. She immediately focused on keeping her voice and general demeanour neutral. "And how exactly are you helping?"

"I have a detective in residence, logging the men coming in and out of the building and then clocking who's ducking into the flat opposite. The spy hole in my front door is apparently the key to achieving justice."

Anna smiled. She had promised herself no more meddling but this was irresistible. When she had followed Phil to Grace's flat, she had taken pictures of him going into the building, for no other reason than to attempt to hide her face. Looking at the images, no one would know which flat he was visiting. She forced herself to focus. "Well of all the things I expected to hear today, that definitely wasn't one of them!" Anna allowed herself a brief smile and then took a breath. Enough niceties. It was time to get this done. "Let's talk about work. When I first met you, you talked about wanting to write features. Gritty, reportage type stuff. It was a pertinent moment because your whole body language changed as you spoke about it. It was the moment in that session when you seemed most alive." She stopped. Best not get carried away. "Where does that fit into your plans now?"

Grace laughed. "You really know how to knock the wind right out of my sails don't you?"

Anna didn't move a muscle. Not voluntarily at least. In the far corner of her left eyelid, a tiny little muscle twitched. A sporadic wave of annoying spasms to which Anna had reluctantly long since conceded control. "You came to me to be challenged. If that means making you uncomfortable on occasion then I make no apology for that. This isn't about just accepting that life at work has vastly improved. It's about empowering you to fulfil your potential. And that means identifying what it is that is going to make you feel most fulfilled. You told me what that dream was so we should be looking at how to help you to achieve it."

Anna watched Grace struggle, taking her time to blow out a long weighted breath. Bizarrely, under the circumstances what she had said to Grace was true. They could just accept that Grace's working life had been massively improved and that with Peter out of the picture, she could now achieve great things and actually enjoy her new role, although it massively irked Anna that she had inadvertently made that possible. This certainly hadn't been her planned outcome when she had encouraged Grace to keep notes on Peter and then told him where to find them. Regardless, she had always said they needed to work out if it was Peter or the job that was the problem and however improved the situation was, by her own earlier admission it wasn't what Grace really wanted to be doing. Anna checked herself. Fascinating as all this was, none of this really mattered unless she could use it to get Grace to make contact with Matthew.

"Maybe the whole feature-writing thing was a pipe dream rather than an actual ambition? I couldn't imagine a world at work without Peter so of course I was fantasising about a very different career."

"So you're telling me you now have no aspiration to write?"

"Yes. No. Well, maybe." Grace fidgeted, turning the ring on her finger round and round, scratching behind her ear then rubbing her hands along her thighs. A veritable feast of nervous tics in one fluid sequence. "I love the idea of researching and writing features but anything would have been better than suffering Peter's bullying. The last few weeks have been full of massive developments. Maybe I should just take stock, enjoy things as they are for a while?"

"You never struck me as someone who would ever be happy to just settle." Anna saw the shock in Grace's eyes but held her stare.

"You think I'm settling?"

"I think things have changed but not because you instigated it. It all just happened to you. You didn't learn to cope with Peter. He left. Your friends decided Warren was right for you and now you're in a relationship." Anna shrugged. "It might all be fine and the perfect outcome but, for me, you're still in the passenger seat. My job's to get you behind the wheel."

Anna looked at Grace, challenging her with every inch of her fibre.

"So what do you suggest I do?"

"Explore, question, challenge." Anna hesitated for just a second. If she didn't strike now, the moment would be lost. Reaching for the folder on the table beside her, she opened it and pulled out Matthew's card. She handed it to Grace. "Consider a call to Matthew to be the start of your exploration. He's very well connected and is always starting new projects and taking on protégées. I've sent a number of clients his way with great success, helping them with the idea of transitioning from one role to another or sometimes into a completely unrelated field. He'll blow your mind with possibilities. Give you a sense of the opportunity that's out there if you just take the time to look."

She watched Grace put the card in her bag. It was a clumsy act but they'd agreed a limited number of sessions and Anna was convinced Grace wouldn't be looking to extend their relationship further which meant clumsy was all she had. She needed to get this done so that the time they had left together could be spent getting Grace on a plane, chasing Phil to some far flung destination and out of Anna's way. Another round of unwanted publicity should be more than enough to set that ball rolling.

Anna looked at the clock on the wall. "That's us done. Make the call Grace. What have you got to lose?"

25

Grace

The next morning, Grace had only made it as far as the office canteen where she sat heavily, an untouched coffee in front of her. She felt hollow. As if the person who had comfortably inhabited this body just wasn't there anymore. Who was she? She was in a job she apparently didn't want; she was in a relationship because it was conveniently suggested to her; she had one friend who seemed to be ignoring her and she had no idea why (she had lost count of the number of messages she'd now left for Emily) and another who she was sure would be imminently announcing his departure to foreign climes. For a moment her spirits lifted as she wondered if she could pack up and go with Phil and then she slumped even further if that were possible, seeing an image of herself sitting in the passenger seat alongside Phil, resplendent in its vividness, taunting her and reminding her just how truly pathetic she was.

Grace reached into her bag and pulled out Matthew's card. Would calling him make her feel better? Make her feel like she was exploring and not just accepting her lot? Or would she just be doing as she was told? Doing what someone else thought was right for her? She dropped it on to the table. This was not the moment to make any kind of decision.

"You okay Grace?"

Grace forced herself to focus. It was her colleague, Robert. "Bit of a headache."

"Can I get you anything?"

His concern was so genuine it made Grace want to cry. She was horribly aware that her chin was starting to wobble and she smiled in an attempt to stabilise it. "I'll be alright in a moment but thank you."

He left her to it with an encouraging smile and Grace forced herself to sit up straight. Enough wallowing. She needed to pull herself together. If only she knew how.

The day soon passed and before she knew it, she was bidding farewell to one colleague after another until eventually she sat alone. The sudden stillness in the office was quite chilling and she felt her thoughts gathering, readying herself for another depressing onslaught, something she was desperate to stop before it started. Picking up her phone, she rummaged once again for Matthew's card. A little exploration couldn't hurt, she told herself. It might just prove that she did actually want to be exactly where she was. Then she could thank Anna for her time and for taking her on such a valuable journey to appreciate everything she already had. And if he had helped other people to work things out then why not give him the chance to help her too? And then as she dialled the number, it hit her that she hadn't done a single online search to find out anything about this man. For a split second she froze and then the call connected and his phone started to ring. Was it too late to hang up? Her number would now be showing on his phone. Did that matter? If she called back in a while after some quick research, would he even notice he'd seen the number already? She imagined herself stuttering out some garbled explanation as to why she'd aborted her first call and felt sweat breaking out on her forehead as she did so. Grace squeezed her eyes shut in an attempt to stop the increasingly panicked inner chatter. The truth was it didn't matter who he was. She just needed to be able to tell Anna she'd made the call which was infinitely preferable to having to come up with a reason why she had elected not to. And if she told herself calling Matthew was a positive move then that's exactly what it would be. A voice of experience and maturity, a father figure if you will. Grace felt her back stiffen at the very idea.

* *

Before

Of course being at university hadn't meant Grace was free at all. She was on a longer leash certainly, but she had quickly realised that Gillian didn't have to be in close proximity to have a negative and lasting impact. The years of being dangled on puppet strings had taken their psychological toll and Gillian's voice remained an uninvited guest in Grace's head. So much so that when Grace was faced with anything from what to wear on a night out to whether or not a piece of college work was indeed complete or needed a final edit, a bizarre process came into play. It was like she struggling to speak a foreign language that she wasn't yet fluent in, listening to the question, translating it, considering her answer and then translating it back before delivering a response. So she would think about the matter at hand, immediately come up with what she felt was the appropriate course of action and then, annoyingly, find the Gillian in her head chipping in her unfavourable opinions before settling on what to do. The resulting course of action was therefore never her own instinctive response. At best, she justified the consultation with her 'inner Gillian' as a shrewd sense check but, more often than not, she saw it as simply feeding her already well-established belief that she was incapable of thinking for herself.

So, for Grace, her three years at university were accompanied by a constant inner battle as she struggled to work out who she really was when left to her own devices. Turned out it was someone she actually quite liked. On good days, she believed she supported her new friends because she wanted to, not because she felt it was the only way to make them like her. And she happily accepted the flirtatious interest from her male peers, believing she had something genuine to offer. But on darker days, the voice in her head that no longer sounded like Gillian but clearly shared her domineering values, goaded her that she was still always on the lookout for opportunities to please, that the only men she was ever attracted to were always dominant characters and that she continued to just toe the line as a result. And there was a long list of behaviours she hadn't even tried to change. Her room was always the tidiest, she never missed a deadline and worked hard to maintain the highest possible grades and, while she had thrown herself into the vibrant social life that was available on tap, she had never once allowed herself to get so drunk that she couldn't remember how she got home.

When Grace and Emily went off on an extended holiday the minute their final exams were behind them, Grace had already secured her first job. After two nerve-racking interviews, she was beyond excited to be joining the marketing department of a local newspaper. Actually, that wasn't quite true. She was thrilled to be joining a newspaper but the marketing department was a cop out. What she really wanted was to be joining as a trainee journalist but there was no point dwelling on that. The look of pure disappointment when she had shared the news with Gillian had been devastating enough. She had been forced to listen to her endless diatribe about how she had wasted three years at a top university, how her obvious lack of ambition was a very personal blow and not reflective at all of the role model she had always been, blah, blah, blah. She had finished by saying that at least Grace hadn't set her sights on being a journalist, a career a million miles away from her idea of what constituted a proper job. It was mildly comforting to know, therefore, that if Grace had chosen to pursue her dream, Gillian's reaction would have been a whole lot worse.

The best part was that Emily had decided to stay on in Brighton so when the job had come up on the Brighton Argus, Grace had thrown everything at it. And having got the job, the minute Emily's college flatmate moved out, Grace had moved in.

Roll forward a few years and they had substituted Brighton for London, Grace moving to a bigger role with a business publisher and Emily taking her first full-time position with a design agency. They immediately loved the hustle and bustle of the city, taking as much advantage of the culture and entertainment on offer that their modest salaries would allow.

Another couple of years under their belts and Grace moved on again to a magazine publisher. She celebrated the move in tandem with her thirtieth birthday and with the new sense of maturity that came along with the milestone birthday, she finally felt like she was starting to find her feet. For the first time ever, she believed she was good at what she did, her confidence finally coming into bloom. Emily, meanwhile, had met James and Grace knew it was only a matter of time before a ring would appear and then a different kind of change would be afoot.

It was on a Friday afternoon, with the weekend almost within touching distance, when Grace got a call to say Gillian had collapsed and been rushed to hospital. Without hesitation, she had grabbed her bag and coat and raced for the door, shouting to anyone nearby that she wouldn't be back.

It had been an agonising journey, not knowing what would be waiting for her. She couldn't concentrate on a book or magazine and instead had simply gazed out of the window, letting her frantic thoughts run wild. Would Gillian already be sitting up complaining about the lack of service when she finally made it to the hospital? Or would she be unconscious? Would their relationship remain in limbo, unchallenged by Grace? Would she be dead? It was this final terrifying thought that made Grace realise just how badly she did actually need to challenge Gillian. She needed Gillian to explain herself. She needed her to know how she'd made Grace feel over the years, know about the irreparable mental scars that remained unseen but were there nonetheless.

When Grace finally made it to the hospital, Gillian was asleep with Grace's father, Oliver, sitting in a chair beside her bed. So she was alive at least. A private room had of course been negotiated already and Grace stood quietly in the doorway for a moment, trying to acclimatise to the sight of her mother looking so small and vulnerable and, at the same time, quash her immediate sense of anger at the sight of her father looking twitchy and disengaged.

"Grace, you're here," he said the second he saw her, immediately standing up and heading to greet her. As she stepped into the room, he took hold of her arm and kissed her briskly on the cheek.

"What happened?"

"She's had a stroke," he said, his voice a low whisper. "They're still doing tests but the doctors think it was pretty significant."

"Will she be okay?"

"They're still trying to establish the extent of the damage to her brain." He hesitated for a moment. "You're okay to sit with her for a while aren't you? I could do with a break."

He didn't wait for an answer. Grace sat down beside her mother and watched her sleep. She tried not to focus on the tubes and wires and the machinery that seemed to surround her and looked only at her pale face. She was so unnaturally still, with the only visible movement coming from her eyelids which flickered every now and again. Grace wondered if she was dreaming and if so, what thoughts her brain was trying to make sense of. Assuming she was still capable of such basic cognitive functions.

Grace sat back in her chair for a moment, feeling slightly nauseous. She had drunk way too much coffee and she'd had virtually nothing to eat. Since she'd got the call to drop everything, she had also been desperately trying to control a heightened sense of anxiety so it was no real surprise that she was feeling a little green around the edges. The knot in her stomach tightened as she dared to picture a world without Gillian. Should the idea make her feel sad? Or was it okay to imagine her loss would be met with an overwhelming sense of relief? Or even joy? The idea of celebrating the death of her own mother was enough to make her mind simply shut down and, closing her eyes, she subsequently thought of nothing, her full focus on the gentle rhythmic sound of Gillian's breathing. In, out. In, out.

Grace had lost all sense of time passing when an incoming text message jolted her back to the moment. It was from her father, letting her know he'd gone home and would see her there later 'when she'd had enough.' Grace put her hands up to her temples and slowly rubbed them in small circular movements. The man really was all heart.

It was several hours before she followed him home. He heard her come through the front door and his hollow words of apology for running out on her were already tumbling out of his mouth before she'd even reached him in the lounge where he sat in a large high-backed armchair, whisky in one hand, large cigar slowly burning in the other. Grace put up her hand to stop him.

"I'm going to bed," she said, then simply turned around and left the room.

A few days later, they were told the stroke had indeed been major and that recovery would be slow. Oliver made arrangements for Gillian to be moved to a private hospital where the volume of staff would ensure she had plenty of human interaction. He had looked surprised when Grace said she was heading back to London with no attempt at all made to hide his frustration that she wouldn't be available around the clock to sit at Gillian's bedside. Initially Grace had felt herself waver but Emily had quickly stepped in, reminding Grace how hard she had worked to build a life of her own. Gillian's condition was still being monitored and she was in no immediate danger so, as politely as she could, she had suggested to Grace that if Oliver felt Gillian needed someone permanently by her bedside then perhaps that responsibility should fall to him.

When, after a few weeks, Gillian was still finding speech a challenge and seemed to be almost permanently confused, Oliver and Grace were given the devastating news that the stroke had, most likely along with a series of smaller strokes leading up to it, caused vascular dementia. Grace found it hard to listen at that point, the words of the doctor merging together and washing over her in waves, each one more devastating than the last. All she heard was that Gillian's decline from this point would be unpredictable and the only thing they were certain about was that there would be decline. There was no realistic prospect of a meaningful recovery. Grace's eyes had immediately filled with tears, knowing how much Gillian would hate the idea of her demise being so haphazard and badly planned.

For Grace, slowly watching her mother lose control was incredibly distressing. She seemed too young and the decline was so fast. In the increasingly rare moments when she was suddenly lucid and so horribly aware of what was happening to her, Grace doubted she would ever be able to erase from memory the look she saw in her mother's eyes. The horror of what was happening to her, a look of what seemed to Grace to be shame that she could no longer see through a simple task or remember the most recent of conversations. Despite everything, it had all seemed so unjust, so cruel.

But there was guilt too. Grace was immediately reminded of all the times she had silently cursed her mother for taking her through childhood in a virtual straightjacket, for rendering her emotionally retarded, for constantly seeking acceptance from others, for mistaking control in relationships for love. It felt like Gillian was being punished for it all but this wasn't what Grace wanted! She hoped beyond hope that she hadn't somehow willed this devastating turn of events to happen, knowing that of course she couldn't be responsible but worrying all the same that in some way she just might be.

And lurking behind the guilt was anger. At times she was consumed with rage that her mother had claimed the last word and then retreated from the world before Grace could have her say. Before she could take the moment she had always thought would one day be hers and ask her mother if she had any idea what she had done to her? Ask her why she had stripped her of the ability to think independently, causing her years of angst as she struggled to find self-confidence and self-belief. Grace had played this conversation out in her head so many times, imagining her mother would listen, exclaim genuine shock and then explain that she had only ever been motivated by love. They would hug in a warm compassionate way like they never had before and their relationship would start again. They would be equals for the first time.

Well that would never happen now. However badly Grace wanted to purge herself of the years of hurt and frustration, she wouldn't risk it being the last lucid conversation she ever had with Gillian. If it went badly, which even she could see was almost inevitable despite the romantic version she played in her head, she would simply never forgive herself.

With a need for care around the clock, the only option for Gillian was a special residential home where she could be properly nursed and looked after. Work kept Oliver away a lot and her decline had been so swift that she now needed constant monitoring if she was to be kept safe. As the months slowly rolled by, Grace continued to make time to visit regularly sometimes enjoying lively conversation but, more often than not, Grace simply sat and held Gillian's hand, her heart breaking at the vacant expression looking back at her, at the eyes that couldn't find her, at the mind that no longer knew her.

When, out of the blue, Oliver invited Grace for dinner, she assumed it would be to discuss Gillian's ongoing care programme. They had had little contact and Grace felt as ready as possible to bat back any suggestion that she should be doing more when his response to date had simply been to throw money at whatever problem arose. He certainly hadn't made visiting Gillian a priority. Nothing even close.

When Grace dutifully arrived at the restaurant, what she definitely hadn't expected was to find her father looking nervous and distracted, necking a glass of wine like it was water as she approached. She slipped into the seat opposite as he put his glass back down on the table, a discreet nod to a nearby waiter prompting an immediate refill.

"Wine?"

Grace nodded and then watched her father twitch and fidget as her glass was slowly filled. His was already half empty by the time the waiter walked away. Grace watched him, unnerved but determined not to look it, her expression fixed as she waited to hear what he had to say.

"So the thing is," he started and then immediately stopped, taking another large mouthful of wine. "The thing is I'm leaving. For America. Washington to be more precise. With Davina."

Grace looked at him. She knew her eyes had widened with shock and she could feel an uncomfortable heat rising up her neck but she remained motionless. Inwardly, she was in turmoil. He was doing what? And who the hell was Davina?

"You're probably wondering who Davina is," Oliver continued, his voice slightly higher than normal, his delivery staccato. "No point hiding it now. We've been together for years. Your mother and I had, well, we were...." He hesitated for a moment. "She doesn't even know who I am any more so it's not like she'll miss me."

And then, to her absolute horror, Grace watched her father visibly relax in front of her. He'd said what he needed to and the relief was obvious. Job done. But not for Grace.

"What about me?"

Oliver looked startled, her words louder than even she had expected and shaped as an unmistakably heartfelt plea.

"What about me?" she asked again, her eyes searching for a sign that he had given her even the tiniest consideration in his planning. And then she sat back, shaking her head in disbelief, desperate not to accept what was blatantly obvious. "You didn't think about me at all did you?" Oliver's head went down. "Who are you?" she asked but his head remained firmly down. Grace sat forward, lowering her voice to an angry whisper. "You're a cold-hearted, selfish bastard who's been physically absent on and off for years and emotionally disengaged for way longer. Mum may have been cold and controlling but you? You are so much worse. And shall I tell you what you are not?" Grace waited for his eyes to come up to meet hers. "You are not a father. And you are not to call yourself my father."

"Are you ready to order?"

Neither had been aware of the waiter approaching and Oliver for one was glad of the interruption which only made Grace even more aware that she was wasting her time. She picked up her bag and stood up. "Nothing for me thank you," she said, never taking her eyes off Oliver and then she simply turned and walked away.

She ignored his calls over the following days until finally he had emailed her. It was brief and to the point. There was no apology just lots of reasons why the move made sense for him. She almost didn't read it but something compelled her to get to the end where he announced the deposit of a ridiculous amount of money into her bank account for her to buy a flat with enough left over to leave her without any money worries for some considerable time to come. He said he wanted her to feel secure, an irony that wasn't lost on her. Grace was under no illusion about his motivation. This was no act of generosity. It was a pay-off. The father daughter equivalent of a one-off divorce settlement.

Grace knew that Emily was itching to move in with James and that her loyalty to Grace was the only thing holding her back so Grace took the money and bought her flat, leaving herself sufficient funds to furnish it and still have enough to put away for treats and emergencies, whichever .

And that was that. Grace had never heard from him again.

26

Anna

Anna closed her eyes to fully embrace the wonderful fluttering in her chest, her hand still resting on her phone, the brief call from Matthew just concluded. She had started to worry about the amount of time she was spending at her desk without actually doing any work. There had been a great deal of soul-searching and scheming and very little coaching of late. Justified, she had reminded herself, to fulfil her promise to Matthew and at the same time find a path that would lead her back to Warren. But that was all done now. The Matthew part at least. So Grace had called him. And better than that, she had agreed to meet him. He'd thanked Anna for her time, hoped she'd enjoyed her part in the experiment and proclaimed firmly that she could leave the rest to him. If she hadn't been so relieved it was over she might have allowed herself a moment to consider the slight edge to his voice, dismissing it instead as imagined.

Anna opened her eyes and sat forward, feeling the need to take stock. Her work for Matthew was done. She felt her shoulders drop. Thank goodness. So now, at her next session with Grace, operation 'Get Grace the Hell Away' could be well and truly put into play. And away meant away. Right away. Out of sight, out of mind and then quickly forgotten, erased from memory as if she'd never even existed. She started to organise her thoughts as to how this could most efficiently be done and then physically jolted, immediately sitting up very straight as the answer came to her with such a surge of nervous energy that it shot through her body and propelled her upwards. It was suddenly so obvious! She didn't have to put Grace off Warren! All this time she had been desperately holding herself back, convinced that Grace needed to be removed from the equation to leave the path back to Warren obstacle free. But she could of course walk that path regardless. She had been so stupid! All she needed to do was go and see him. Surely as soon as he saw her, all the emotion, the longing, the love from their past would come flooding back, all the anger and bitterness immediately forgotten? How could his five minutes with Grace have any lasting significance when compared to what they had shared? She smiled. There was clearly only one way to find out.

* *

Before

It only took Warren twenty-four hours to ask Anna out for a drink. When his email flashed up on her screen she'd been unable to stop an immediate smile appearing, her eyes wide with expectation. Another twenty-four hours and they were sitting in a small pub, far enough away from the office to ensure they remained hidden from prying eyes. They'd talked about work for a while but the conversation quickly moved on, the flirtation becoming more blatant as alcohol slowly dissolved inhibition.

"Shall we go back to mine," Anna had said when last orders had been called. It wasn't a question and it certainly never crossed Anna's mind that Warren would do anything other than follow her as she stood up and headed for the door.

And so it began. Within weeks Anna had moved Warren into her flat. She did as much as was necessary to make him feel like it was his home too and as she'd never done very much with her third bedroom, he was delighted when she took him shopping and bought a selection of exercise equipment that was perfect for using at home. "No need to spend hours in the gym now," she had told him.

Anna was totally besotted and the more she fell in love, the further she encouraged Warren away from his close friends. Initially their relationship was quite quarrelsome while Anna slowly manipulated and reshaped him into the amenable and acquiescent man she wanted, one fight at a time. It was a subtle process that took place over many months and yet somehow, the relationship seemed to work. In fact it more than just worked. For a while it was all quite blissful. Playful flirtatious moments at work when no one was looking, hands held as they left the office in search of a quiet restaurant for dinner, watching endless movies cuddled together on the sofa and weekends spent in their own protective bubble that was perfectly made for two.

So all pretty idyllic until the moment Warren started to push back.

"I might be a little late home tonight," Warren said tentatively one morning. They were in the kitchen, moving perfectly around each other in a well-practiced breakfast routine with one preparing pots of fruit and muesli, the other filling travel mugs with coffee.

Anna immediately stopped what she was doing, forcing the kind of direct eye contact that Warren had clearly been hoping to avoid. "Why?" she asked, the tone of her voice igniting a look of apprehension in his eyes.

"Today's the last seminar in the series we've been hosting for PharmCo so we're having a celebratory team drink. It'll look strange if I don't go."

"I doubt it would matter to anyone if you're there or not," Anna quipped back.

"Well it would matter to me."

There was a momentary stand-off and then Anna shrugged. "If it means that much to you."

Anna spent the evening pacing around the flat in an eerie silence, the TV off and no music playing making Warren's absence all the more pronounced. By the time he came home, she had already gone to bed, locking the bedroom door behind her.

Anna then barely spoke to him for the next few days, hoping to make the atmosphere as unpalatable as possible to deter a repeat of such irreverent behaviour. But Warren had other ideas.

"It's Stacey's leaving party tonight. Do you fancy going?" he asked a week or so later as they walked into the office.

"I can't think of anything I'd like to do less."

"I said I'd show my face but I won't be late. Have a good day." Warren's parting words had been perfectly timed, delivered just as they parted company, leaving Anna no choice but to stand and watch him walk away. It wouldn't do to make a scene but her anger was screamingly obvious to anyone taking more than just a cursory glance in her direction.

Over the next two months, Warren could count on one hand the number of times he'd shared a bed with Anna. They bounced from loud vicious arguments to angry silences to desperately making-up until the potency of their promises to change or try harder evaporated away to nothing, leaving them with nothing more than a toxic existence on almost permanent mute.

But Anna was never going to admit defeat. She had invested way too much in this relationship and failing just wasn't part of her make-up. So, however bad things got, she chose to remain convinced that Warren would get whatever was bothering him out of his system and then everything would be perfect again.

"I want out!" Warren yelled at her after a particularly spiteful row. "You think you're worth more than me in this relationship, you never think about me or what I might want or need. Everything's great as long as I'm doing and saying exactly what you want!"

"Stop being such a child!" she had shouted back.

"I can't breathe!" he pleaded. "You've made me dependent on you for air. It's like I can't breathe on my own anymore!"

Anna rolled her eyes. Such drama! And then Warren grabbed a bag and started stuffing his things in it. "That's it!" he yelled. "I can't take any more. It's over Anna."

"No!" Anna screamed, desperately trying to grab the bag from his hands. "I won't let you leave!"

Warren refused to let go of the bag and a tug of war ensued. Eventually he pulled the bag free, his voice low and calm. "I'm leaving Anna. It's over."

"Please Warren, don't just walk out. Let's have some dinner. Let's go out to eat and just talk. We haven't done that in such a long time. We can work this out. I know we can."

Anna held her breath and then after what felt like a lifetime, Warren dropped the bag.

This became their new pattern with Warren desperately trying to find the courage to leave and Anna resolute that was never going to happen, her ability to manipulate his thinking reaching spectacular new heights. His bags were subsequently packed and unpacked with increasing efficiency.

Anna always text Warren to say she was leaving the office which was his cue to pack up and meet her in reception. She'd been waiting for ten minutes when a ripple of unease swept over her. She headed for his department but there was no one there. She checked the kitchen and any other communal area she could think of but it was already quite late and the place was virtually deserted. She called him but it went straight to voicemail.

Anna called him several more times during a tense cab ride home but his phone was clearly switched off. The traffic was terrible which wasn't helping her mood at all and by the time she was walking into the flat, she was more than ready for a fight.

The first thing she noticed was his key on the mat as she pushed the front door open. She felt her heart rate immediately increase as she quickly started looking around, desperate to confirm her worst fears were misplaced but there was no sign of him anywhere. Clothes gone, toiletries gone, his book on the coffee table gone, the picture of him as a child with his mother, gone.

Anna felt a feeling she didn't recognise overwhelm her as she dropped on to the sofa. The chatter in her mind was deafening while she desperately tried to work out what it was she was feeling and she squeezed her eyes shut in an attempt to make it all stop. When it did, the clarity that followed brought with it no comfort. She felt lost. She felt vulnerable. And all she could think was that she needed to make him come back.

Anna called every friend Warren had. She'd long since copied the contacts from his phone so it was easy enough to call every person he knew but no one had seen or heard from him. At least that's what they told her. She turned up at some of their homes but that was equally fruitless. By Sunday night, Warren's phone had stopped going to voicemail and was now saying the number was unavailable. Anna was subsequently fighting to maintain control as she lay wide awake all night, playing out a million different scenarios of what would happen when they saw each other at work the next day.

By ten o'clock on Monday morning Anna was pacing up and down her small office with no idea what to do. Warren had not only not shown up for work, he had resigned and left, telling no one but his immediate boss who had told Anna that she had of course assumed Anna knew, that she was surely in on whatever had motivated him to ask for complete discretion while he worked out his notice.

When she started to feel there were a growing number of eyes on her, Anna had stopped pacing and sat down at her desk. She looked at her computer screen, her hands resting lightly on the keyboard in front her, doing her best to look like she was functioning as normal while biting down hard on her lip as she did so, desperate to stop the angry, wretched tears that threatened to flood her eyes at any moment as the truth finally threatened to swallow her whole.

Warren hadn't just left, he had vanished. In the space of one weekend he had disappeared so completely that even the most efficient forensics team would be hard pressed to find any trace of him. If she continued to wallow, she would have to accept that he had planned meticulously for who knew how long, with the singular goal of extricating himself from her life. She shut her eyes for a moment and concentrated hard, imagining herself pulling down an internal shutter on her ability to feel, any empathy erased along with Warren.

And then she started to type. She had a report that needed to be shared by the end of the day and there was no way she was going to miss a deadline.

* *

Now

Half an hour after dropping everything and racing from her office, Anna stood completely motionless across the road from the café. Her mouth was still open and frozen in time after the gasp she'd omitted on seeing Warren in such close proximity for the first time in so many years. He looked just as she remembered him but an even better version than the image stored in her memory, if that were possible. He had worn the passage of time well, his hair shorter, his face still soft and kind despite the experiences of life etched around his eyes in the finest of lines. She noticed how well he carried himself, how confident he seemed, how relaxed was his demeanour. She felt her heart inflate in her chest, fearing it may just burst with the anticipation of actually standing in front of him, talking to him, touching him. Her eyes were the only part of her visibly in motion as she followed his every move, chatting and laughing with someone as he bid them farewell, clearing the now empty tables as the afternoon flow of customers dribbled to an end, the early evening rush yet to get underway. The timing was perfect which just reinforced her belief that this was all simply meant to be. Just one final customer to leave and then he would finally be alone.

It felt like an eternity as she waited, impatience building along with the increasing pounding of her heart. She had waited so long for this moment. "Come on, leave!" she urged as she desperately tried to contain a growing anger at this stranger who clearly had no idea she was the only thing stopping the moment when two long-lost lovers would be beautifully reunited.

Anna moved so quickly when she finally saw the annoying woman get up to leave, she was able to nip inside the café before the door had even closed behind her.

"Hello Warren." There was an eerie silence. Two simple words that unleashed well over a decade's worth of the most tortuous pent-up emotion. The sound of herself saying his name and suddenly standing so close to him made Anna gulp as she immediately choked back tears.

With his back to the door as she entered, Warren jumped. "You scared me," he said as his head whipped round and then there was a loud crash as the mug he had been holding slipped through his fingers and smashed on to the floor, taking the colour from his face with it. He stood, ashen, his hand grabbing for his throat as if he were suddenly finding it hard to breathe.

"Anna." It was little more than a whisper.

Anna chose not to register the look of abject horror on his face so consumed was she with her own surge of euphoria. She took a step towards him, arms outstretched and then she stopped as Warren jerked away from her, the table behind him preventing him from getting further away. "Warren?" His displeasure slowly started to sink in. Perhaps he didn't recognise her? "It's me!"

"What are you doing here? How did you find me?"

"Does it matter?"

"Yes it fucking matters!"

"I found you! Isn't that enough?" Another step forward, arms further outstretched.

Warren stumbled backwards. "Keep away from me! You can't just walk in here. You need to go."

Anna looked totally bemused. "I'm not going anywhere! I'm back, Warren. We're back!"

She put her arm out to touch him but Warren pushed it away. "Oh no you don't. Just leave Anna and I'll forget I ever saw you."

"But I don't want you to forget! I just want to hold you."

210

"Anna!" Warren shouted as she reached out to him again. "For fuck's sake!" This time she got hold of his arm firmly and he swiftly made a large sweeping circle with it in an attempt to dislodge her grip on him. She grabbed for the other arm. Stay focused, she willed herself. Any minute now he'll be in my arms! Trapped by the tables surrounding him, Warren could only continue to rebuff, batting her arms away again and again but the harder he tried to defend her advances, the harder she tried to take hold of him.

"I've waited so long Warren. Have you thought about me? I know you have. Not a day's gone by when I haven't wondered, imagined what life would have been like if you'd just given us another chance. I tried so hard to find you. And now I have!" All the while grabbing, being pushed back, grabbing again.

Warren stumbled, a chair falling over behind him, the table acting as an unwanted barrier, scraping along the floor as his weight pushed against it. He was panicking, desperate to get away from her but with nowhere to go.

"You couldn't find me for a reason. I didn't want to be found and I still don't want to be."

"It's overwhelming, I know. It's a shock after all these years but none of that matters now!"

Anna's determination was unshakeable, convinced that the minute Warren recovered from the shock of seeing her, he would fall into her arms, the pain and madness of everything that had happened between them left to melt away with one embrace.

"I don't want you here Anna," Warren shouted. "I don't want you anywhere near me. I just want you to go."

27

Grace

Grace stood just feet away from the door to the café, struggling to understand what she was watching. It appeared to be a full-blown fight between Warren and Anna, however incomprehensible that seemed. She didn't recognise the look in his eyes which she could only describe as the most intense horror. He was clearly afraid too, but of what? She saw him mouth Anna's name again and again as he literally fought her off, desperate to avoid her advances as her arms reached out to him with Warren spitting profanities as she did so. Anna had her back to Grace but it was obvious she was trying to get hold of him. Something Warren was determined to stop. But whatever was going on one thing was beyond doubt and that was that they clearly knew each other.

As Grace had approached and her eyes had confirmed the unthinkable, that it was indeed Warren and Anna engaged in some kind of bizarre combat, there had been a split second when she'd had to decide if she was going to march on in, break them up and then find out what the hell was going on. Her instinct, however, had been to duck into a bus shelter that stood just to the right of the café's door. It had provided the perfect cover and allowed her to continue to watch unseen. She stood now, feet glued to the pavement, unable to move – unable to go in, unable to leave and unable to explain why she felt unable to do either. When her phone suddenly started to ring her dilemma was immediately solved, her paralysis shattered by the loud ringing. Grace quickly turned and walked away as she answered the call.

"Are you in the office?" It was Sam.

"No, but I'll be back in half an hour or so. Is everything okay?"

"You need to come and see me, the minute you get back. I'll explain when you get here."

It was, of course, a tortuous foot-tapping, nail-biting cab ride back to the office with Grace desperately trying to keep a tight hold on her imagination that was straining to break free. She hurried to Sam's office, her heart racing painfully which only worsened when she saw the look on his face. Without saying anything, he handed her print-outs of some pictures that she quickly flicked through, eyes wide, jaw slowly dropping.

"They came in just before I called you. The headline's likely to be 'Does gay Phil Stevens pay women for sex?' I'm sorry Grace but I can't stop it running."

The pictures were of Phil entering and leaving her building. There was a report that had been filed with them, the essence of which was that police had confirmed a brothel had been running in one of the flats with Phil recognised by residents as being a regular visitor to the building. DS Jacobs had only left her a message the previous day to say they had made a number of arrests which meant he wouldn't be back and to thank her for her invaluable help. At least the timing of the coverage wouldn't damage his investigation. Although she doubted that would make Phil feel any better about it. And then her heart started to race again. Phil! She quickly scrolled for his number and hit the call button.

An hour later, Grace was sitting in Phil's flat. They had been due to meet for dinner with Emily but Phil had no desire to be seen out in public. Instead, Grace had picked up a takeaway that now sat untouched on the table between them. He had cried when she arrived and Grace had struggled to support his weight as he'd clung to her, each sob more painful than the last, her eyes squeezed shut in response, her heart breaking. And then they'd sat in silence, Phil lost to his thoughts, Grace simply waiting till he was ready to share.

"I quit. Felt like the right thing to do," he eventually said.

"No!" Grace cried. "Why so quickly?"

"Come on Grace, it was inevitable before this happened. There was no way I was ever going to be able to prove the drug pictures were fake. At some point, I would've had to accept that and then either quit or be fired. This latest bullshit has just meant there's no point drawing it all out."

"But we can prove it's wrong this time! The girls who were working in the flat can confirm you never went in."

"There's no point Grace. There's no coming back from this. The truth won't make any difference now."

Phil's voice was flat and emotionless. Grace would have preferred him to shout and scream. Anything rather than see him look so totally and utterly defeated.

"So what now?"

Phil looked at her. "You know I have to go. I need a fresh start and I can't have that here."

"How far?" She braced herself, hoping for somewhere no further than Manchester.

"America."

Grace attempted a smile and nodded, not trusting herself to speak.

"Do you want something to eat?" Phil gestured at the unopened takeaway bag.

Grace shook her head, pouring herself another glass of wine instead. "Where's Emily?" Grace asked, suddenly finding her voice as she realised Emily was missing.

"She popped over earlier."

Grace was about to question why Emily would do that and why she was so obviously avoiding her but she stopped herself. Now really wasn't the time. Instead, she moved to sit next to Phil and took hold of his hand. He leant into her and that's how they stayed, blended together, until his eyes closed.

It was an hour or more before Phil stirred, during which time Grace had lost count of the number of texts that had pinged their way into her phone. As he stretched himself awake, she took the chance to take a look. "I'm really sorry but I need to go and see Warren. You'll be okay if I go?"

"Of course. I'm shattered anyway so could do with going to bed." Phil watched her as she quickly gathered up her things. "Is everything okay?" Grace put on her coat and then stopped, unsure for a moment if now was a good time to offload. "Grace?"

"I saw him fighting with Anna earlier, the life coach I've been seeing."

"I didn't know they knew each other?"

"Me neither. Warren gives the impression of being so open and there's always lots of conversation but seeing them together, so hostile and angry, it's made me realise there's clearly lots I don't know."

"But everything's okay with you two?"

Grace shrugged. "I guess I'm about to find out."

When Grace arrived back at the café it was almost closing time. Judging by the stale heat and the amount of empty bottles and glasses, it had clearly been a busy night. She did a quick scan to make sure Anna was no longer on the premises and then took the last table. Warren smiled as he saw her but there was a heaviness in his expression. He signalled he would be with her in a minute but there was no light in his eyes. He looked haunted. Grace felt nervous as she waited, realising she hadn't really thought through how she was going to approach this. Should she tell him she saw him with Anna? Would he tell her what it was all about before she even had the chance?

She continued to fret and then suddenly, he was sitting opposite her. He handed her a glass of wine and drank thirstily from a bottle of beer. He was fidgety and distracted so she just waited, desperately trying to look calm, the anxiety swelling inside her until she felt like it was choking her. She coughed. The sound snapped Warren out of his thoughts and he looked at her with something vaguely unpleasant in his eyes. Grace visibly pulled back.

"Why didn't you tell me you knew Anna?" Warren demanded.

"Why are you so angry with me?"

Oblivious to the fact he had been asked a question, Warren continued his attack. "Do you have any idea what that woman put me through? How hard it was to get away from her? And now thanks to you, she's back."

Grace gasped. "Anna was your girlfriend? The one you couldn't escape?"

Warren looked confused, clearly unsure why Grace was even asking. "Yes she was my girlfriend! And after years of looking over my shoulder, you just led her right to me!"

Grace shook her head in disbelief and then she stiffened. His anger was infectious. "What exactly are you accusing me of? I went to see a life coach, selected randomly I might add. And yes, I talked to her about you because you brought something positive into my life in amongst all the shit I was dealing with at work but I had no idea she knew you. I certainly didn't know you'd had a relationship with her or that she'd chased you out of the country. So now that I've made that clear, I'll ask you again. What exactly are you accusing me of?"

For a moment their eyes locked and then, as if suddenly remembering who it was he was talking to, Warren's expression changed. "Grace I'm sorry. It was such a shock seeing her and when she mentioned she knew you and that you'd helped her find me it just felt like....I just thought..."

"You thought what? That somehow I'd colluded with her? I can see how being involved with a crazy, manipulative sociopath could colour your judgement but to assume I was just the same?" She shook her head. "It's unbelievable."

"I didn't think that Grace. I'm really sorry."

"But you did think exactly that!"

And then the stand-off came, both saying nothing, Grace's arms folded defensively across her body, Warren's head down. He didn't look up until he heard her chair scraping along the floor as she pushed it back ready to stand up.

"I know you're not thinking straight but if you really thought I was only in this as Anna's stooge then you really don't know me at all. And for that to be your best explanation for what's happened is just heart-breaking." Her voice cracked slightly and Warren reached for her hand but she snatched her arm away.

"I'm so sorry Grace. Truly sorry. Please don't go. Not like this."

Grace stood up. "Goodbye Warren," she said, and then headed straight for the door.

28

Anna

Anna had moved her car three times, moving ever closer until finally she had a clear view into the café. She'd had no choice but to leave Warren earlier once customers had started to file in, clearly oblivious to the fact they were interrupting something, much to Anna's frustration. Ever the perfect host, Warren had immediately switched his attention, welcoming people as they entered, asking them to take a seat, telling them he would be with them shortly. He had then looked at Anna, eyebrows raised until she had reluctantly admitted defeat. But only a temporary one.

"Perhaps we can pick this up later?" she had suggested but she hadn't waited for a reply. It wasn't really a question that she felt needed answering. She had then raced home, calling ahead to tell Marta that she needed her to stay late, had run into the house to collect her car keys without a word to anyone, run straight back out again, jumped in her car and then raced back into town. And now she sat, watching, waiting.

Her heart was still racing. It had been beating abnormally fast since the minute she'd made the decision to go and see Warren and hadn't calmed since. She had played their encounter over and over in her head. Initially she'd tried to convince herself that it had gone well but, each time she replayed it, she had zoomed in ever closer on Warren's expression when he had first seen her and the sheer horror in his eyes was hard to mistake. Or maybe it was just the shock of seeing her after so many years? They had said some pretty hurtful things to each as their relationship had broken down. He was the only person she had ever opened herself up to and she knew she hadn't handled his rejection well. Perhaps he wasn't able to just put all that to one side? But it was all water under the bridge now surely? She had then convinced herself that it was a blessing their meeting had been brought to a premature end. The enforced pause would give him a chance to get used to the idea that she was back in his life. They would have their chance to talk properly soon. Yes, everything would be different then.

The café continued to pulse with the energetic chat of its occupants until finally, it slowly started to empty. Each time the door opened and a few more people left, the accompanying sound of music, voices and laughter slowly diminished too. Anna was just starting to wonder if it might be time to go back in when she saw Grace arrive. She held her breath, temporarily thrown. This was a scenario she hadn't considered. She had been so singularly focused on just herself and Warren, she had allowed herself to temporarily forget the unwanted third wheel. She quickly shifted position until she could see Grace sitting at a table. Her view was restricted but clear enough to see Warren join her a few minutes later. She squinted slightly, willing her eyes to provide some clarity of their expressions and then she allowed herself the smallest of smiles. She was no body language expert but there was definitely trouble in paradise.

Their conversation seemed animated, and not in a good way. She watched as Warren tried to take Grace's hand, with Grace swiftly moving herself out of his reach. And then finally, she stood up and seemed to be heading for the door. Anna stared at Warren, willing him to let Grace go and then she gasped. Grace was through the door and walking towards her. Anna immediately sunk down in her seat, her hand instinctively up and covering her face, allowing just enough room for her to watch Grace stride past, eyes fixed, expression sombre.

Anna's eyes switched to the rear view mirror as she continued to watch Grace slowly disappear from view. The minute she could no longer see her, she grabbed her bag and hurried into the café, eyes everywhere, searching for Warren.

"Sorry, we're closing."

Anna looked at the waiter in front of her. "I'm looking for someone. I'm looking for Warren," she said, eyes now back in search mode, scanning every face and covering every corner.

"You've missed him," the waiter then said, already heading back to the bar. "He'll be back in tomorrow."

Anna felt every ounce of air leave her body in one large, anguished sigh, leaving her instantly deflated, her head suddenly too heavy to hold up. As she tried to gather her thoughts, cursing Grace for distracting her while Warren had clearly slipped away, she felt a swell of anger surge up through her body and she thumped the table beside her with all her might, causing glasses to shake violently and bottles to topple over.

"Hey!"

Anna was vaguely aware of the waiter shouting after her as she quickly headed back to her car.

29

Grace

Grace woke with a start. She was about to get up when she remembered it was Saturday and instead did her best to relax. Her head felt heavy on her pillow, weighed down by a mass of negativity. Or perhaps self-pity was more accurate. She felt horribly sorry for herself which quickly led to self-loathing before settling on a hollow numbness until she simply felt nothing at all.

Phil was a boarding pass away from leaving the country. Her relationship with Warren was in tatters. And Emily was avoiding her. As Grace let it all sink in, her only conclusion was that if ever she were looking for a moment to completely submerge herself in self-pity, there would never be a better opportunity than now.

She stayed exactly where she was until the stillness became unbearable. She needed to do something. She needed to get up, get dressed and make a plan for the long empty day that stretched out ahead of her. It was a few moments more before she was able to will herself into action but, once she was upright, she found some momentum and within half an hour, she was on her way out and heading for Paddington. She would go to see Gillian.

A train and a cab ride later, Grace was sitting in the bright day room of Oak House, the residential home where Gillian whiled away her time, happily or not, depending on the lucidity of the day. It was a large old house set in its own grounds with any sense of foreboding deflected by the beautifully kept gardens that opened out on either side of the gravelly approach, winding its way from the ornate iron gates up to the imposing front door. The house itself was quite breathtaking and meticulously maintained. It all came at quite a price but it was a place full of compassionate staff, the equipment was state of the art and there was a wonderful sense of calm. It meant a lot to Grace to know Gillian was being so well cared for.

The day room was bright and airy with high ceilings and large dramatic windows providing almost panoramic views of the gardens that were full of colour and texture. Sitting on a small sofa with Gillian beside her, Grace watched a collection of birds swoop onto the elaborate feeding table to enjoy today's treats, providing another layer of activity for tired, lost eyes to focus on. She looked around the room and, as she always did, she tried to imagine what lives had been lived amongst Gillian's fellow residents, sitting immobile, shells of people now, with nothing left to do but wait for the inevitable. Grace shivered and then allowed herself a wry smile. This was possibly not the best place to come when your joie de vivre was currently absent without leave.

Her thoughts were interrupted by a warm hand reaching for her own for the first time since she had arrived that she instinctively took hold of.

"Hello Mum."

Gillian looked at her and Grace searched her eyes for any flicker of recognition. Sometimes it was hard to tell if she was present or not.

"It's a beautiful day. Perhaps we could have a stroll in the gardens later?"

"Is Oliver coming soon?" her mother asked, her eyes full of hope.

"Not today, Mum." Grace put on her most convincing and reassuring smile. She doesn't know me anymore, he had said. She won't miss me. But she did remember. And if not missed, his absence was distressing for her. Not that Oliver cared, judging by the total lack of contact or interest over the years. Grace had received the odd card or email, written, she imagined, when he was drunk when his senses were suitably weakened, leaving him without the strength of mind to ignore the feeling of guilt that, for the most part, was clearly deeply buried. But he had never once asked how Gillian was. Apart from paying for her care, he had successfully wiped her from his life in one selfish sweep.

"We need to talk about when we can visit Grace. He's so busy. But we need to make sure she's on track."

Grace felt her heart contract and she bit hard on her lip. She wanted nothing more than to let out a desperate cry and then let it swell into an angry yell borne out of frustration, resentment and ultimately love. At least she knew now that for today's visit, Gillian wasn't in the here and now but lost somewhere in the past. And despite struggling to shape each word she spoke, at least Gillian was calm. Grace would take that over a mother who was agitated, confused and scared as she had been on many previous visits. For long spells, it would feel like her symptoms had stabilised and then there would be a sudden decline that she now understood was most likely brought on by another stroke. Small in comparison to the first one but debilitating all the same. She knew some of the medical staff thought it was a miracle she was still alive. When faced with a choice of life or death, Grace was no longer sure which would be kinder.

The arrival of a care worker with tea and a selection of pastries and muffins provided a welcome distraction and Grace chatted about nothing in particular as she poured them both a drink. Gillian accepted a cake which she played with, Grace noticed, her appetite clearly on the wane. Occasionally, Gillian asked a random question, her mind flitting from one decade to another and back again, struggling each time to find the words she wanted then, having found them, there was a second struggle while she fought to actually say them. Grace swallowed the growing lumps in her throat and indulged her, responding to whatever Gillian asked, always careful not to challenge or correct her which only made Gillian distressed. And then they settled into a companionable silence until Gillian drifted into a peaceful sleep.

"Shall I take these away?" Grace looked up and smiled at Lucy, one of the care workers she had come to know well.

"Thanks Lucy."

"How is she today?" she asked as she quietly gathered up the cups and plates.

"Stuck in the past. But she's peaceful." Grace shrugged, knowing Lucy would understand her acceptance that it could be worse. "We've chatted so that's something at least."

"Did she give you the necklace?"

"What necklace?"

"She's been carrying it around with her for days. I kept telling her she'd lose it but she wouldn't let any of us take it. It's probably in her pocket."

Both turned to look at Gillian, her head resting lightly to one side, her breathing even. Their eyes moved to the pocket of her cardigan, both knowing the other was immediately wondering if it would be okay to have a gentle rummage. Grace looked at Lucy who gestured with her head for Grace to see if it was there. Taking care not to disturb her, Grace reached into one pocket then the other and then pulled out the necklace. And then she gasped.

"Is it yours?"

Grace nodded, her eyes immediately flooded with tears. "It was a gift. When I passed my A levels. I thought it was lost."

Lucy smiled. "Well that's perfect! Now you have it back."

Grace held it at arm's length, almost frightened to look at it, something Lucy misinterpreted. "It's okay love, you take it. I'll tell her she gave it to you. Better that than risk her losing it." Lucy now had everything loaded on to a tray. "I best take this away. Lovely to see you Grace."

Grace nodded with a tight smile. She watched Lucy go and then, with Gillian still sound asleep, she picked up her things and quickly headed back to reception to call herself a cab.

It was late afternoon by the time Grace arrived back at Paddington. Apart from a small cake, she had eaten nothing all day and was just wondering whether she needed something to eat or just a very large drink when she realised someone was calling her name.

"Grace!" She turned around and for a moment didn't recognise Sam striding towards her, a huge smile on his face. He was casually dressed in jeans, a shirt, trainers and a jacket. "I was beginning to think it wasn't you."

"Sorry. I was miles away."

Aware that Grace seemed to be staring at his clothes, Sam's eyes immediately looked down. "What is it? Am I wearing the wrong brand of trainers?"

"No, sorry. It's just I've never seen you in anything other than a suit before. The casual look suits you."

Sam smiled. "Are you on your way somewhere?"

"No. Just back. You?"

"Been to see my brother and his wife and their new baby. It was carnage."

Grace smiled at the wicked glint in his eye and felt the tight coil that she'd been carrying in the pit of her stomach since the moment she left Oak House, slowly start to uncurl. Just standing next to Sam made her feel better. There was something infectious about his energy, about his physical strength and the kindness in his eyes. "I need a drink. What are you doing now?" he asked.

"Yes, I could do with one too."

"Come on then. Let's go and find somewhere."

They found a pub that within a few hours would probably be the kind of place they would steer well clear of but it was

228

nearby and virtually empty so would do just fine. Once they were settled with drinks and an assortment of nuts and crisps, Sam immediately entertained her with the tales of his amazing sister-in-law who had clearly taken to motherhood like the proverbial duck to water and the apparent ineptitude of his brother who, by comparison, was struggling to adapt to his new role.

"So where've you been today?"

Grace was aware her demeanour immediately changed as the conversational spotlight turned on her. "I went to see my mum."

"Nothing like going home is there?"

"She's in a residential home. She has dementia so I'm never really sure if she even knows who I am."

"Oh God, I'm sorry. I didn't realise."

"It's fine, really." Sam's face was immediately full of concern and Grace smiled. "Honestly, it's fine. She's been ill for years so I'm used to it now."

"Were you close?" Grace lowered her head. "You don't have to answer that," Sam said, his tone suggesting he felt he might have crossed a line. "It's none of my business."

Grace thought for a moment and then before she could decide how best to answer, the words were already spilling out of her mouth, the need to talk clearly far greater than any desire to do her usual thing and politely close the conversation down.

"I want to just say no but it's way more complicated than that. It took a long time for me to realise that she suffocated me as a child. Actually not just as a child but as an adult too."

"She was strict then?"

"Not strict in the normal sense. It was more subtle than that. It felt like I was allowed to do stuff but the truth was I had no real say." Grace stopped for a moment and Sam gave her a reassuring smile. She was struggling to find the right words but he was happy to wait. "She always supported me but everything was done her way and on her terms. She micro-managed me through school, chose what university I went to, dismissed my dreams of becoming a journalist or a writer and then just when I finally reached a stage in my life where I was ready to have it out with her, she had a massive stroke and started to lose her mind." Sam went to say something but Grace hadn't finished. "I got horribly drunk when I was eighteen and lost a Tiffany necklace my parents bought for me for doing so well in my exams. It was a massively rare display of affection and pride. My mum was furious. She kept telling me how disgusted and disappointed she was for months and months afterwards. I did everything I could to find it at the time. Posters, phone calls, emails. There was no Facebook then to help spread the word but I searched relentlessly, day and night but never found it. I didn't remember getting home and she made me so terrified about losing control, telling me in no uncertain terms how lucky I was that I hadn't ended up either raped or murdered that I've never drunk like that to this day. Then today, one of the care workers said my mum had been carrying a necklace around with her." Grace reached into her pocket and pulled out the silver heart and chain and placed it on the table in front of them. "I didn't lose it at all. She took it. Her way of teaching me a lesson I guess." Saying the words out loud released something and Grace felt the first tear fall. "I mean, who does that? I felt so wretched that I'd been so careless and let her down and all the time, she had it."

Sam put his hand on her arm and left it there. "And yet, even in her confused state, she obviously wanted you to have it back, to know it wasn't lost."

Grace's eyes shot up to Sam. "Please don't try to defend her."

"I'm really not. It just makes you wonder if deep down she knew she'd done the wrong thing and maybe this was her way of putting it right?"

"Or maybe she was carrying it around with her and enjoying the memory of how she'd so spectacularly played me?"

Sam said nothing more. Grace knew he was only trying to help but he couldn't possibly know how deep the scars ran. For a moment, they sat in silence until Grace once again felt compelled to share her thoughts. "Friends used to say to me, 'why don't you just tell her what you want, that you want to do things your way?' They just didn't get it. By that point I didn't know what I wanted! She was such a formidable driving force, I never had room to develop the desire to question. And I certainly didn't have the bravery or strength of character to push back. I simply became one of life's passengers." Grace said the word carefully, painfully aware the reference belonged to Anna. "Always just along for the ride, no opinion, nothing useful to contribute, just going wherever I was taken. And she did such a fantastic job that even now, I'm still making the same mistakes. Attracted to boyfriend after boyfriend because of their dominant personalities or because someone else says we'd be a good match, still hoping I've made the career choices that would have made her proud and still looking for someone to lead the way so I can then follow along without question."

"Now hang on a second," Sam said, suddenly sitting up very straight. "I can't begin to imagine what it was like for you growing up but the picture you're painting isn't the Grace I know. The Grace I know is confident and amazing at what she does. She's a strong leader with a team bursting with respect for her. She's the most perceptive person I know, able to negotiate her way through difficult conversations, mediate between conflicting colleagues to a point where everyone thinks they've come out the winner." He paused for a moment. "What she absolutely isn't, is gullible or subservient or hanging on anyone's coat tails. And before you say it, I know it was difficult with Peter but at least you stuck it out. What about all the ones who left? The ones who couldn't take it for more than a few weeks and just quit? You are way stronger than all them put together."

Grace smiled through her tears that she swiftly wiped away. "Have you finished?"

Sam smiled back, his eyes twinkling. "That depends on whether or not I've convinced you that whatever you think your mum did to you, you came out the other side pretty sorted as far as I can see." He stood up. "I'll get us another drink."

Grace was happy to be left with her thoughts for a moment. She looked at the necklace in front of her, wondering how so many huge memories could be held in such a small piece of silver. And painful ones at that. She wondered what other equally despicable means her mother had used to get her way or make a point. She was in no doubt there would be other hideous acts that she was unlikely to ever know about now and, if challenged, she felt sure Gillian would simply say she had just wanted what was best for her, as if that sentiment alone was enough to justify what had felt to Grace like one spiteful act after another.

Sam put a fresh drink in front of her bringing her back to the moment. "I had no idea you wanted to be a journalist." he said as he sat down.

"Fancied myself as a feature writer for a while. Never got past the Uni mag though. Not exactly award-winning stuff but I loved it."

"Well write some stuff for me then."

"What, just like that? No experience, no track record and you'd just accept a feature from me?"

"Don't worry. I'd soon spike it if it was crap." Grace laughed, shaking her head, convinced he was just joking. "I'm serious Grace. Write something for me."

"You're not just trying to make me feel better?"

"I'm insulted at the very idea," Sam said, doing his best to look suitably hurt. "Instinct tells me it will end up being one of my better decisions. But just to be absolutely clear, I'm definitely not doing you any favours. Okay?"

Grace nodded. She wasn't sure she believed him but that wasn't going to stop her putting together some ideas and giving it her best shot. Then checking the time, she finished her drink. "I think I'd better be heading off. Thanks for the drinks. And for listening."

"The pleasure was all mine," Sam said with a smile, his cheeks flushed with a mixture of alcohol and just a little awkwardness. "I'll see you on Monday."

"Actually I'm not in on Monday." Grace hesitated. She was due to meet Matthew and had decided to use it as an excuse to take the day off. She was about to start explaining and then she stopped herself. "It's a long story. I'll save it for the next time."

Grace took a deep breath as she stopped for a moment in front of a large black door. It was just before four o'clock on Monday afternoon. She studied the list of company names alongside a bank of buttons and choosing the appropriate bell, she announced who she was when prompted by a voice through the intercom and then pushed the heavy door as it buzzed. Disappearing inside, she made her way to the second floor and found herself in a smart but fairly basic reception area where she was asked to take a seat by the young receptionist. She sat on one of two large sofas and had a look around. The furniture was minimalist but stylish and all very grey. The place could definitely do with a dash or two of colour. She scanned the pictures on the walls; an abstract selection of fairly nondescript images that gave nothing away about the company or its enterprises. A few people came and went but it was all very quiet and slightly unnerving as a result. However hard she looked, there were no obvious visual clues about what business was going on beyond the reception and, for a moment, Grace wondered if the place had been swept clean in preparation for her visit. A thought she immediately dismissed as ridiculous paranoia.

Although she was sure there should be the odd industry magazine lying around at the very least that would have made her feel less suspicious and on edge. Grace's mind chatter was in full flow, jumping from a question to raising a concern and back again and then she realised someone was talking to her.

"Grace, how lovely to meet you."

Her head shot up and she immediately stood up to take the hand outstretched towards her. As she took it, she looked into the eyes of the man it belonged to who was smiling warmly at her and she gasped. Whoever this man was, he most definitely wasn't the person she'd seen online. Her preparation for the meeting may have been virtually non-existent but she had definitely checked the credits of the photographs she'd seen on Matthew's company website and this was not him. She felt her heart start to race, a thin layer of sweat suddenly coating her hand that she hoped he wouldn't notice as she slipped it away from him. She was aware that he was talking to her but was unable to concentrate on what he was saying. Grace forced herself to focus. "I just have to grab someone quickly and then I'll be with you. Something to drink while you wait?"

"No, I'm fine thank you."

Grace watched him go over to the receptionist and then after a few quiet words, he waited while she called someone for him. What should she do? She was panicking, desperately trying to control her breathing and the loud throbbing in her ears so she could concentrate long enough to come up with a plan. "Come on, think!" she urged herself. And then finally instinct took over and grabbing her phone, she did her best to look like she was reading a message and as discreetly as possible, she took a picture.

When she looked up again, whoever this man was (she suddenly realised he hadn't actually introduced himself when he greeted her) was chatting to someone on the phone. After a minute or two he said goodbye, passed the handset back to the receptionist and then he was heading back to her. "Right Grace. Shall we?"

He gestured towards a meeting room behind the reception desk and Grace dutifully stood up and headed towards it, relieved that it was completely glass-fronted with the receptionist in full view. If he lunged at her or suddenly tried to strangle her, at least there was a chance the receptionist would either see or hear what was going on and call for help. She gave her head a little shake and frowned at her overactive imagination. Bloody drama queen. While her wild thoughts raged, he chatted to her about something and nothing as they sat down, offering water that he then poured, placing a glass in front of each of them. And then they were sitting looking at each other, weighing each other up, both smiling, him seemingly genuinely, Grace masking a growing sense of unease.

Eventually he spoke. "I hope you don't mind but I've done some background research on you. You have a very impressive track record."

"Thank you," she said, not sure in the moment if she minded or not.

"With some insight from you on your ultimate goals and ambitions I can definitely help you, whether just general counselling or helping you into a new role. But I feel I must be honest with you first about the somewhat unorthodox nature of our introduction."

Just as Grace had started to think this was indeed the meeting she was expecting, she was back on high alert. She held her breath as she watched him hesitate, clearly struggling to find the right words to get started. "There's no easy way to say this so I'm just going to get straight to it." And then he stopped again.

"I really wish you would," Grace said, her anxiousness manifesting itself as frustration and making her voice sound clipped as a result.

"Anna says that life coaching is about empowering someone to realise their potential, the emphasis being on a client finding all the solutions to their problems themselves." He paused for a moment. "I think that's a fair summation." Another pause causing Grace to fidget in her seat. "But I had my doubts about Anna, the reasons for which are irrelevant and I'm afraid I felt it necessary to put her to the test. I decided to see if she would enter into an experiment and lead someone on a pre-destined path." Grace was now feeling very uncomfortable, a rising heat creeping through her body until it grabbed at her throat, her neck reddening, her heart racing, her mouth horribly dry but she was too bewildered to take a drink. "All she had to do was build up sufficient trust with you to get you to make contact with me, or at least Matthew," he continued, "in return for a fee." The most dramatic pause of all followed and then he gestured towards her with his hands. "And here you are."

Grace allowed the silence to completely envelop them, her expression fixed, her eyes staring straight at him. His words were spinning in her head, the frustration she had been feeling ceremoniously pushed aside by a growing anger.

"Why would you do that?"

He remained still and calm. "As I said, I had good reason to test her ethics."

"But why me?"

"That, I'm afraid, was less calculated."

Grace was incredulous. "So I was just an unwitting participant in your little game?"

He had the good grace to finally look uncomfortable. "Surely the point is I was right and I can now report her to the association she's accredited to. And a call from you to back up my complaint will see her totally discredited."

"Hang on a second!" Grace knew her voice was rising but so was the cocktail of emotions she was struggling to contain. "Without knowing anything about me, you use me to facilitate some burning desire to rid the world of a rotten life coach and now you want me to push that aside and help you to finish the job?" No response was forthcoming so Grace chose to continue her rant. "And why do you even care? What if Anna has broken a few flimsy rules? It's hardly the crime of the bloody century. Why does it even matter?"

His head lowered temporarily to avoid Grace's penetrating eyes and then, with a renewed sense of purpose, he slowly raised it again, his expression so fierce that Grace visibly stepped back. "It does matter," he said quietly. "It matters very much."

Grace felt her cheeks flush while the rest of her body shivered. She quickly stood up and collected her things together. "Whatever Anna is, you are so much worse. This meeting is over." As Grace reached the door, she stopped suddenly and turned back to face him. "So where does Warren fit in?"

"Warren? I don't know anyone called Warren?"

"No, of course you don't."

As soon as Grace was clear of the reception she pulled her phone from her pocket and stopped the recording that she'd started the minute she had stood up and headed for the meeting room then dropped it back into her bag. When she stepped outside, the rush of fresh air was extremely welcome and she took a few large gulps before heading for the nearest café, cursing as she went that she hadn't thought to ask her supposed future mentor his name.

As she took a quiet table in the first café she found, she wondered if it was too early for alcohol while she rummaged in her bag for her phone. When she finally got her hands on it, she did a quick scroll through her recent contacts and then hit the call button.

"Sam, it's me. That long story I said I'd save till the next time? Any chance the next time could be now?"

It was two beers, a large plate of nachos and a chocolate brownie later before Sam appeared in the café. He smiled as he saw Grace but his apprehension was clear as he sat down, making her kick herself for not at least checking herself in a mirror. She could only hope she didn't look as confused and disorientated as she felt.

"Are you okay?" he said as Grace watched him search her face for even the smallest clue. She'd had nothing to do while she'd waited but eat, drink and wind herself up into a frenzy. It was a relief to finally let it all go. She took a deep breath and then verbally launched herself at him.

"I know you must be thinking what the fuck has happened now but as always, everything is completely out of control and I have no idea what the fuck is going on or how the hell to rein it all in."

"Grace, stop!" Sam took hold of her hands and waited until her manic eyes settled on him. "Let me get a drink and then just start at the beginning."

Sam ordered himself a beer and another one for Grace and then she told him everything. How she had been having coaching sessions with Anna, how Anna had challenged her decision-making process (or lack thereof), how she had questioned her new relationship with Warren, how she had then seen Anna and Warren caught up in some kind of passionate argument only to discover Anna was the dangerous ex-partner who still haunted Warren to this day and then finally, how she had gone to meet Matthew on Anna's say-so only to discover she had become embroiled in a ridiculous plan to discredit Anna.

"Wow." Sam sat back in his chair as Grace watched him try to process it all.

"Would another drink help?" she asked. Sam nodded and Grace stood up, returning a few moments later with two more beers. She handed him a bottle and then watched as he took a large swig. "What are you thinking?"

"Never a dull moment with you, is there?" he said, and Grace raised her own bottle with a rueful smile. There seemed little point in denying it.

"The worst part is I started seeing Anna to repair the damage done by Peter. It was supposed to be about building my confidence, making sure I was on the right path and learning to stand up to all the bullies I seemed to have let into my life." Grace hesitated for a moment. "But while I was taking it all really seriously, it seems Anna was focused only on getting me to a point where I'd call Matthew with no questions asked." Grace felt her cheeks flush as she realised how easily she had complied. It must have been the easiest money Anna had ever earned. "And never mind what she was being paid for this little ruse she agreed to take part in, I was paying for her time too."

"I think you may be due a refund." Sam looked at her for a moment. "Bit strange though that Anna and Warren have history," he said, trying to make sense of the first coincidence.

"That's what I thought. Warren left the country to escape her years ago. He thought I'd helped her find him again. Which I absolutely didn't."

"And what does Anna say about it?"

"I haven't seen her since I saw them together." Grace racked her brain, desperately trying to remember the conversations they'd had about Warren. "Maybe she did use me to get to him? She certainly questioned how we got together. But it was me that found her. Not the other way around. So how could she have known we even knew each other?"

Sam couldn't possibly know the answer to that. He thought again for a moment. "So there's you, Warren and Anna. And then Matthew. Who is he?"

Grace rooted around in her bag for Matthew's business card and handed it to Sam. "Anna was quite insistent that he could help me with my career."

"I didn't know you were looking for another job."

"I'm not. I just didn't think there was any harm talking to him." Grace hesitated, suddenly feeling a little embarrassed. "Anna's very persuasive. It was easier to just do what she suggested." Her voice trailed off, painfully aware of the familiar subservient picture she was painting that Sam had only recently so eloquently denied.

"What do you know about him?"

"Very little." She grabbed her phone and opened up his website. Consultant basically. Involved in a range of sectors. That's him on the left." She held out her phone so that Sam could see a picture of him. "And this is who was waiting for me instead." She switched to her photos and then once again showed Sam the picture.

"So we need to find out who he is and then find out the connection between him and Matthew?"

Grace sat back in her chair, relieved to have made it to a point where a plan was formulating. "Yes, that's exactly what we need to know."

Sam drained his beer. "Right, if you're okay with me doing some digging, I need to get back to the office. Can you send me the picture of our mystery man?"

Grace immediately did as he asked. "I recorded the meeting. I'll send that too."

Sam looked suitably impressed. "And what are you going to do now?"

Grace smiled at him. "I'm going to have another beer."

30

Sam

When Sam walked back onto the editorial floor, there was only a sprinkling of desks occupied by the night shift who were busily updating and rewriting copy for the paper's second edition that would go to press shortly.

He slipped into his office and, sitting down at his desk, he grabbed a pad and pen as he waited for his computer to wake up. He tapped the pen as he concentrated, trying to align his thoughts, writing Anna's name first. A quick online search led him to her website. Nothing unusual there. And then a couple of links to conferences she'd taken part in, followed by some listings in relevant industry directories but nothing of any interest. Sam took out Matthew's business card and tried him instead. He scrolled through the roll call of entries, browsed his website, glanced over a few pompous articles he'd written for some specialist business magazines and then drew the same conclusion. There was nothing of any interest here either.

So that left the mystery man. Sam stared at the picture Grace had taken. His eyes twitched as his mind raced, fired up by a familiar spark of exhilaration that came with the thrill of the chase. He loved a puzzle and this one had certainly ignited his journalistic curiosity. But it was personal too and that put a completely different spin on things. It wasn't simply about uncovering what was going on. There was so much more at stake here. This was about Grace. A woman unlike any other he had ever known.

The first time he'd met her, he'd been immediately struck by her quiet confidence. She clearly knew her stuff but unlike many around her, she had the ability to handle potentially difficult people in a way that meant she almost always got what she needed from them. No mean feat in a place of work like theirs. Not that he would ever call her manipulative. It was simply about getting the job done in the most efficient and painless way possible and keeping everyone on side in the process. She made the print journalists believe they were still king and then with genuine probity and without saying anything negative about their newspaper colleagues, she talked to the online and digital teams as if they were the only departments that really mattered. The result was she had everyone on her side and he had never heard anyone speak of her without genuine warmth and respect.

Now that he knew about her mother, her skills at managing difficult people made perfect sense. With the exception of Peter of course. Sam's blood still ran cold when he thought of the night he had found him leaning over Grace's desk, his face inches from hers, his eyes full of anger, his voice loud and threatening with Grace literally white with fear. He had never allowed himself to dwell for too long on what might have happened if he hadn't walked in when he did, happy not to have had the chance to find out exactly what this abhorrent man was capable of. He knew he should have officially reported Peter but still had no regrets about his

245

undercover exposé which had been far more satisfying and an infinitely quicker way to bring him down than going through official channels. Channels that Peter may well have wormed his way clear of and then what would he have done? It was a risk Sam hadn't been prepared to take.

Watching Grace repeatedly seek refuge from Peter had revealed a completely different side to her. A fragility that sat at complete odds to her normal demeanour. Sam had hated seeing her so vulnerable and it had been an instinctive reaction to try to protect her. Then, just when he felt he had helped her put the whole sorry saga behind her, she had innocently walked into the middle of who knew what. A mess that she only stumbled into because she was trying to take control and find a way to deal with Peter. Sam shook his head. Ironic didn't come close. It was like a perpetual circle of doom. Well, whatever it took, he was determined to help her to understand exactly what she was now a part of.

Uploading the picture to his computer, he set a reverse image search in motion and then rested his head in his hands for a moment, gently massaging his forehead. If this didn't work, he wasn't sure what to try next but he would have to think of something. Having to tell Grace he'd come up with nothing was simply not an option.

When Sam looked up a matter of seconds later, his screen was flooded with pictures. He gasped as his eyes tried to take it all in, his right hand already clicking through to a number of articles that he speed read as the bigger picture slowly started to take shape. And what a story it told. The printer behind him whirred into action. He would have a proper read through everything later.

As he continued to scan through one article after another, he spotted a name he recognised and grabbed for his phone. A quick swipe through his contacts and then he hit call and waited.

"Tom, hi it's Sam……I know it's been way too long. How's the family?……That's great. Yes, I'm all good too. Look I'm sorry to call out of the blue but I think you might be able to help me with something. How much do you remember about Alistair Connor?"

Sam grabbed for his pen. It seemed Tom remembered plenty.

Half an hour later with the call ended and a stack of scribbled notes in front of him, Sam was suddenly aware of raised voices and laughter. He had forgotten for a moment that he wasn't alone. He loved the newsroom banter and missed being an everyday part of it. And the late shift was a completely different dynamic. No grown-ups in the building for starters (the least offensive term they used for the company's management) with the pace of incoming news slowed to a virtual standstill, on a normal night at least, so there was always time to relax and have a bit of a laugh.

"Hey Sam." Sam jumped as the night editor appeared at the door. "Pub in ten if you fancy it?"

"Yes I do!" he replied with a smile. "I'll see you there."

Sam glanced at the clock on the wall and was surprised to see it was already past ten. Picking up his phone, he wondered about calling Grace and then decided not to. They'd arranged to meet early the next morning before work. Better to wait for clear heads before he shared what he'd found and it would be good to have a drink with Ben and the others. It was a while since he'd felt like one of the boys. He had one last scan of his screen to make sure he hadn't missed anything then gathered up the articles he'd printed along with his notes and stuffed them into his bag. He was aware of a weight as he stood up, the kind he used to carry when he was embroiled in a really significant story. The kind of story that really mattered, where no detail could be left unscrutinised, where no alleged fact could be left unchallenged. But the heaviness he felt was welcome because this was an important story. It involved Grace and nothing was more important to Sam than her.

31

Grace

Sam was already waiting when Grace arrived at their chosen café the following morning. She clocked the pile of paper as she approached him, her eyes then quickly searching his face for a hint of how the next hour might play out.

"Good morning," he said with a smile as she sat down. "I ordered your some coffee and there's some croissants here. I wasn't sure what you'd want so I ordered a selection."

"Thank you," she said, as a coffee was placed in front of her. And then she looked at Sam, not wanting to appear rude but desperate to hear what he had found out and unsure what he was waiting for.

"Shall I start?"

Grace nodded. "Yes please."

Sam took a deep breath. "So the person you met was Alistair Connor. We know he wanted to discredit Anna and I'm pretty sure I now know why."

Grace gasped. "This is terrifying. Who the hell is he?"

"It's less about who he is and more about a sequence of events that happened around five years ago. Alistair had a brother, David, who committed suicide. There was an inquest and the Coroner returned a verdict of accidental death. The reporter who wrote one of the pieces at the time is an old contact of mine. We had a chat last night and, in a nutshell, it seems Alistair wouldn't accept the verdict. David was married with three young children but he'd been having an affair. When he wouldn't leave his family, the woman he was having the affair with told his wife. The marriage collapsed and his wife moved away and took the children with her. Not content with that, this woman then started a rumour that David, who worked in a prominent position in the City, was guilty of insider trading. There was no proof but the seed of doubt was planted and his company found a way to get rid of him. Six weeks later he was found hanging in his garage." Sam paused for a moment to let Grace take it all in. Eventually she looked at him and braced herself for what she knew was coming next. "The other woman was Anna."

Grace sat back in her chair, shaking her head in disbelief. "I had no idea what to expect but it definitely wasn't that. And you're sure Anna was involved?" Grace asked.

"My mate had a different surname for her but I've done some basic checking and I'd put money on the fact it's her."

Grace was clearly struggling. "But it still doesn't make any sense?"

"My mate knew the journalist who befriended Alistair when it happened. Apparently Alistair wanted Anna to be prosecuted believing she was directly responsible for David's death but, however badly she'd behaved, she hadn't done anything illegal. The journalist stuck with him for a while but when it became clear the police weren't interested in taking it any further, there was nothing else to write. He wrote up an interview with Alistair but it never ran. Alistair was furious. He felt like no one was listening, that he hadn't had the chance to have his say. The journalist told Alistair to get in touch if anything new came to light but he never heard from him again."

"And what about Anna?"

"She was working in the City too for a financial PR firm but once David was under investigation, she disappeared. I think she was married too with children of her own but working under her maiden name. There was certainly nothing reported at the time that her own marriage had ended. Perhaps she moved away for a fresh start? She covered her tracks well and the journo was never able to find her to get her side of the story and with little interest from his paper, he eventually stopped looking."

Grace still looked confused. "But it still doesn't make any sense. I can see why Alistair would want revenge for his brother which connects him to Anna. But why would she team up with him? Never mind agree to do something so unethical?"

Sam shrugged. "I guess that's where Matthew came in." Sam flicked through his pile of papers and then held up a photograph for Grace to see. It was a picture of five men on some kind of corporate golfing trip and she picked out Alistair straight away. A sharp intake of breath followed as her eyes focused on the man to his left. It was Matthew. "Alistair must have known there was a good chance Anna would recognise him," Sam continued, "so he clearly sent his mate in to get her on board. And I'm assuming he chose Matthew because his line of work meant he could present Anna with a plausible story."

"She just doesn't strike me as someone who would be so easily swayed to do something like this though. Alistair said he paid her. Perhaps I should have asked him how much? I'd like to know how much messing with my head was worth." Grace sat back and closed her eyes. She felt like everything was swimming around just inches above her. One discovery more outrageous than the last, one unanswered question leading straight to another and all swirling in a cyclone of chaos that her brain simply couldn't absorb. Making sense of it all therefore felt, quite literally, out of her reach.

"It's a lot to take in I know." Sam looked at his watch. "We should probably get to work."

Sam paid the bill and they headed outside and on towards the office which was only a short walk away.

"Why don't I come and find you later?" Sam asked. "We can have a drink or maybe something to eat as you rejected my lovely selection of pastries? Give it all a chance to sink in and then we can work out what to do. What do you say?"

Grace smiled at him. "I'd like that." And then without another word, she put her hand out to an approaching taxi which swung in beside them.

"Where are you going?"

Grace opened the cab door. "I need to go and see Anna."

"I'm not sure that's a good idea. She has no idea Alistair is involved."

"Well won't it be fun telling her," Grace said as she climbed into the back of the cab and shut the door behind her.

32

Anna

Anna's day had started in the most heinous of ways. Breakfast with her ex-husband, Julian, or Julie as she liked to call him. Needless to say, it wasn't a moniker he much enjoyed. Anna had watched with disgust as he had devoured 'the treat of a full English' as he called it while she was barely able to swallow the coffee she had ordered. He occasionally suggested these little get-togethers to ensure they remained aligned where the parenting of their sons was concerned. She had initially tried to resist but it had been pointless, eventually deciding it was easier to meet for an hour every now and again than suffer the barrage of calls and messages she was forced to endure when she tried to avoid him. As she sat and watched him, coffee in hand, she wondered as she often did how she had ever ended up dating him, never mind marrying him. He was talking now but she wasn't listening. His main reason for wanting to meet up was the boys' constant swearing that now seemed to have been accepted as the norm (she assumed he meant accepted by her but refused to rise to the bait) and, as always, the amount of time they spent glued to their phones and tablets. At the appropriate moment she would tell him she was on it and he would go away feeling progress had been made.

In the meantime, her mind was on Warren. It had been a week since she had seen him. She had stopped by every day but had been told she had just missed him each time. How was that even possible? She had left her number on at least three occasions and had really hoped he would get in touch. That, after some time to let it all sink in, he would be left with the same hope and desire that she felt. The same sense of a lost love found.

In darker moments, she had been tortured by a nagging thought that she had desperately tried to deflect but, despite her best efforts, it had occasionally wormed its way into her consciousness. What if he didn't want to see her? What if he hadn't been thinking about her, dreaming about her or praying for the moment she would walk back into his life? She felt herself stiffen. Grace. It was the only possible answer. God, how she hated the sound of that name in her head.

"Anna?" Nothing. "Anna!" More insistent this time, jolting Anna back into the moment. As she focused, Julian was staring at her, eyebrows raised. "Have you heard a single word I've said?"

"Yes of course. And you're right. I'll be more vigilant about their phones." The eyebrows were still up. "And the swearing too," she added quickly and finally they lowered.

"Good. I knew it would be helpful to talk it through. We're a team after all aren't we?"

Anna couldn't bring herself to answer. Instead, she picked up her bag. "I have to get to work."

Julian stood up as she did. "I'll get this. Good to see you."

Anna looked at him with an expression she hoped was so bathed in disdain that even idiot Julie would see it and then she walked away. Quickly.

Anna had an hour before her first client of the day and was eager to use every minute of it planning her next move. Feeling she had wasted quite enough time already, she hurried to her office, weaving her way through the busy reception with a quick swipe of her ID card before stepping into a waiting lift. As the doors slowly closed, she felt her demeanour change, a growing sense of nervous anticipation in her stomach as her body prepared to work out how best to move forward with Warren. With adrenaline starting to wake up every nerve end, she was out of the lift before the doors were even fully open. And then she stopped. So abruptly that her bag came off her shoulder and swung forward, its weight causing her body to stiffen to avoid falling forward with it.

"Grace!" Anna did her best not to look flustered although she was horribly aware that her cheeks had immediately flushed the minute she'd seen Grace sitting on one of the sofas opposite the lift. "I wasn't expecting you? What a surprise." And a very unpleasant one, she thought, as she replaced her bag on her shoulder and tried to compose herself.

Grace stood up, her expression deliberately blank and giving nothing away. "Hello Anna. I think we need to talk."

Anna hesitated for a moment, wondering if it were possible to say no, that she was expecting a client and didn't have time to talk but Grace was already moving towards her. "Shall we?" She was suddenly standing uncomfortably close, her eyes daring Anna to do anything but comply. Anna straightened her back. Whatever this was she could handle it and, with that thought firmly in mind, she turned and headed to her office. Opening the door, she quickly took off her jacket and put down her bag as Grace automatically sat on the sofa and then slowly, Anna sat down opposite her. Grace didn't waste a second.

"I know about your little plan with Matthew." Anna's hand shot up to her mouth in an attempt to stifle a gasp. He had told her! Why would he do that? Anna's mind was immediately racing, desperately trying to work out how she could possibly explain herself but Grace wasn't finished. "Why would you do that? Why would you risk everything you've worked for just to mess with me? I know he paid you. How much did it take to make you say yes? And why me? What did I do that made you want to use me as the pawn in your disgusting little game?"

Anna took a couple of slow, deep breaths and then she felt her expression change as the panic she had been feeling was overtaken by raw hatred. "It wasn't a game. It was for a serious piece of research. But despite that, I never intended to say yes, however much money he offered. I'm proud of what I do. Proud of how I help people. There was no way I would jeopardise that."

"So what changed your mind?"

"I saw you with Warren. *My* Warren."

Grace looked totally bemused. "What, that's it? You saw me with a man who literally went to the ends of the earth to be rid of you and what? By manipulating our sessions to fulfil some ridiculous brief, you thought you could get him

256

back?" And then to Anna's complete horror, Grace laughed. She actually laughed! Anna could feel her heart thumping in her chest and she squeezed her fists tightly to suppress the immediate urge to punch her. To hit her again and again until the smirk she now wore was well and truly wiped off her face.

"Yes, get him back!" she shouted. That did the trick. Maybe not as satisfying as delivering a physical blow but at least Grace had stopped laughing or even smiling, the look in her eyes now tinged with fear. That was more like it. She should be afraid! So why was she suddenly leaning forward?

"But that's only half the story isn't it?" Grace whispered, her face low and calm. Anna suddenly felt nervous as she watched Grace reach into her bag and pull out some papers. She held up a picture. "Who's that?"

"Matthew of course! But you know that. You met him didn't you?"

"No, this is who was waiting for me." Grace held up another picture and Anna felt the air sucked from her body with such a force, she feared she might actually pass out. Her head felt light, her eyes fuzzy, her heart pounding ever faster. So, after all these years, he had found her.

"I'm guessing by the look on your face you know him? Seems I wasn't the only pawn in his game, hey Anna?"

Anna didn't know what to do. Fight or flight? Her over-riding instinct was to run but her legs were frozen. She was paralysed. She had no control over mind or body as she tried desperately to hold it together.

"There was no research! Just a plan to discredit you. Alistair's probably making the call right now to your professional body, letting them know how unethically you've behaved, how easily you could be bought to manipulate a client." She paused. "I think that's what they call retribution."

Anna's eyes darted up to meet Grace's. What did she know? "Whatever he told you it's lies." Her throat was suddenly incredibly dry forcing her to speak in what was little more than a whisper.

Grace held her stare. "It all seems spot on so far. But he didn't tell me about David. I found out about him all by myself."

Anna went to say something but then stopped. A million thoughts were clouding her brain. She had been so thrown when she saw Grace with Warren, so consumed with jealousy that she hadn't stopped to scrutinise Matthew's motives or even attempt to get to know him. He had given her the excuse to interfere in Grace's life and she had grabbed it with both hands, focused only on finding a way back to Warren with any semblance of professionalism forgotten. And her actions had become about so much more than just the call to Matthew. But she wouldn't say any more now. However conflicted she found herself, the one thing she was certain about was that she felt no compulsion to explain herself to Grace.

"Seems you have quite a track record in fucking up people's lives don't you?" Grace said. Anna felt the heat coming back into her body until her neck prickled and her cheeks reddened. She was aware that Grace was talking again. Why was she still here? When would she stop? "But driving a man to suicide Anna? No wonder Alistair wanted some justice."

"Shut up! Just shut up!" Anna screamed. She had heard quite enough. "Let's not forget how you sat in that very seat, lapping up whatever I threw at you, just accepting what I said without question. You would have done anything I asked! And now just because you've been exposed as weak and gullible, you come in here trying to laud it over me. Well I won't let you!" Anna let her angry words hang in the air, her eyes never leaving Grace's. Grace was clearly unnerved by the outburst and was trying desperately hard not to look away but was unable to prevent an involuntary glance at the door. Anna followed her gaze and then standing up, she reached out and opened it. "That's enough talking don't you think?"

Grace stood up and then as she reached the door, she stopped, her face so close to Anna's she could feel her short sharp breaths on her own flushed cheeks. And then she smiled and watched Anna draw back. "If you think for one minute that Warren's going to welcome you back into his life you are not just deluded, you're certifiable. He hates you, Anna. Hates you with the kind of passion that sent him half way around the world just to get away from you."

"Get out!"

Anna barely waited until Grace had stepped into the corridor before slamming the door behind her.

33

Grace

Grace was sitting in the dark in her favourite corner of her sofa, a glass of brandy in her hand. She hadn't been aware she even had a bottle and it certainly wasn't her drink of choice but, if ever there was a night when brandy was needed, she felt that this was it. She had been tempted to take up Sam's offer of dinner but in the end, she had just felt so exhausted and unsettled by everything that she just wanted to be in the comfort and safety of her own home. And seemingly with an unfamiliar drink that was burning her from the inside out. She took a few more small sips and although the taste made her grimace slightly, she was starting to get used to the warming effect that slowly spread through her body, deciding it was actually quite welcome and strangely soothing.

What a surreal few days she'd had. It felt much longer. She had gone over the timeline in her head a number of times, unable to accept that her world could be so ceremoniously upended in such a short space of time. She felt completely detached from normal life, trapped in a toxic bubble that felt impossible to burst.

As she sat curled up in the stillness, she allowed herself a moment of complete self-indulgence and felt her eyes blur with tears, suddenly feeling overwhelmed with sadness. Her body ached with it and her heart felt heavy. She struggled to find words to describe what she was feeling and then it struck her and she shivered. Lost. That was how she felt. Totally and utterly lost. Everything felt like such a mess and she desperately tried to work out the exact impact Anna had had on her. She had gone to see her for guidance but now she felt like that had just been an excuse. She had been struggling with work and with Peter and hadn't known how to cope and, instead of digging deep and dealing with it herself, she had chosen to relinquish control. Anna was right about one thing. She would have done anything she suggested – she *had* done everything Anna had suggested. The fact that Anna had abused her trust suddenly felt immaterial. The bigger issue was that she had let her, that she had done as she was told, just like she always had.

Grace felt physically sick. She had wanted her self-esteem boosted but right now she felt nothing but the most all-consuming self-loathing. She had thought of herself as strong and capable but Anna had reminded her that she was fundamentally weak and incapable of managing her own life. She had made her wonder who she was all over again and made her feel vulnerable. Lost.

And of course running alongside all this, she'd had to watch Phil's life unravel in the papers and across the internet. She was now simply waiting for the call to say he needed a lift to the airport, convinced it would come the minute he returned from a visit to see some friends. No doubt saying his goodbyes, she had thought when he told her. And if that wasn't enough, Emily remained conspicuously absent from her life without authorised leave.

Grace took another few sips of brandy and tried to focus on what she should do now. It didn't take her long to realise that there was really only one possible course of action. She would take control, that's what she would do, once and for all and with a strength and determination that she knew was there if she would just give it room to breathe.

Turning on the lamp beside her, she squinted slightly as the room lit up and then took her laptop and her phone to the kitchen table, turning on more lights as she went. Taking her phone first, she scrolled through all the unanswered messages and then she checked her emails, grabbing a pad and pen as she did so. A list was clearly required if order was to be restored and then she systematically worked her way through it. A text to Phil to say how sorry she was that she hadn't been in touch – she would explain when she saw him and suggested they meet the following evening. A text to Sam with more apologies for not getting back to him sooner and the edited highlights of what had happened with Anna. She would catch him for a coffee tomorrow. And finally a text to Emily. Where was she? Was she okay? Then she turned her attention to work. An hour went by as she carefully went through her emails, responding where answers were required and making sure nothing had been missed.

When she hit the send button for the last time, she sat back and stretched, pulling her arms up high above her head to release the tension in her back. She felt infinitely better knowing at least some semblance of order had been restored and then an involuntary twitch below her left eye reminded her that she wasn't quite there. She still had to deal with

Warren. There had been voicemail messages and texts, the sense of panic obvious as he pleaded with her to call him so they could sort things out. She had mentally put him to one side on the pretext she didn't know what to say to him. She was struggling to process how she felt about him, trying to separate genuine feelings from Anna's voice in her head, telling her over and over again that they had only got together because her friends had set them up. It was also hard to ignore the sense of disbelief that Warren had ever been involved with someone like Anna. She imagined Anna had been quite different back then but it was still hard not to see him differently as a result of his connection to her. And then, as if that all wasn't enough, he had immediately assumed the worst of her when he realised she knew Anna. It was a struggle to imagine how they could ever come back from that.

She sat quietly for a moment, her eyes closed as she tried to concentrate on slowing her breathing and clearing her mind. She saw images of them together, relaxed and happy, those moments when he clocked her coming into the café and his whole face would light up, the feeling of his arms around her and how protected he made her feel. And then suddenly she was looking at an image of him with Anna and her expression changed. Knowing they had history made her feel uncomfortable, destabilised almost, anxious certainly.

Slowly opening her eyes, Grace looked at the clock on the wall in front of her. It was past midnight. She closed her laptop and started to clear things away, turning out the lights as she headed for her bedroom. Warren would have to wait.

Grace was at her desk early the next morning. Although she had made sure she had responded to anything urgent, she still had documents to check and meetings to prepare for and she was determined to be completely on top of everything before the team trooped in. As they started to arrive, it wasn't long before she felt totally immersed as people pulled up chairs to her desk for impromptu updates and questions were shouted across the office, the room soon alive with chatter. She could feel the energy, the daily dose of adrenaline in full flow and it felt good. No one had even mentioned that she hadn't been around much and she found herself smiling as she surveyed the room, proud of her team and what they were achieving, almost forgetting for a moment that while it had been business as usual here, the last few days had been anything but for her.

An alarm on her computer caused a Pavlovian response as she immediately stood up and headed off for the weekly management meeting chaired by the big boss, Zac. She still felt like an imposter at the table, the last element of her new role that continued to feel slightly alien. As she walked into the large meeting room, she smiled as she saw Sam. It was widely accepted he was Zac's golden boy, much to the chagrin of his older colleagues but, as the person who was driving the digital success of the business, the intricacies of which were way beyond Zac, the accolade was inevitable and, of course, richly deserved. She slipped into the seat next to him. The meetings were dry and occasionally quite fierce so she was always pleased to be within reach of her kindred spirit.

"You okay?" Sam asked as Grace sat down. She nodded, unable to answer as Zac swept in, always once everyone else was seated and called the meeting to order. Wouldn't do to be caught chatting.

Thankfully it was a fast-paced meeting. The circulation director took a bit of a beating but otherwise there was little to keep them in the room beyond the normal updates and in less than an hour, it was over.

"Fancy a coffee?" Grace asked, knowing Sam would suggest the same but she was keen to get in first. As always, he had been there for her and she didn't want him to have to ask for the full update on Anna. The offer definitely needed to come from her.

They headed to the canteen and Grace told Sam to grab a seat while she got them a drink. As she sat down to join him, she smiled at his anxious face. "You don't have to look so worried! I'm fine. Honestly."

"I'm still struggling with it all," he said as he emptied two sachets of sugar into his coffee and stirred vigorously, "so I can't imagine how you must be feeling."

Grace's smile widened. "I keep telling myself it'll make a great dinner party story, should I ever be invited to one."

Grace could tell Sam wasn't convinced, fearing she was already protesting too much on the 'I'm fine' front. She took a deep breath and did her best to appear as close to normal as possible, without any clear idea of what that actually looked like.

"Thanks for your text last night," he said.

"I'm sorry I didn't make dinner. I was too exhausted I'm afraid. I'd have been awful company."

Sam smiled at her. "I doubt that. But I totally understand. So let me just make sure I'm clear so far before you tell me about your unscheduled visit to see Anna. So we have Alistair Connor, looking to avenge his dead brother, believing Anna to be ultimately responsible for his suicide. Anna discredited David, so Alistair set out to do the same to Anna."

"A perfect summary," Grace said with a smile.

"The bit I still don't get is why Anna agreed to his plan?"

"It was because of Warren."

"I don't understand," Sam said with a shake of his head.

"As soon as she saw me with Warren, I became the only thing stopping the big romantic reunion she'd been desperate for for years. And then Matthew gave her the perfect excuse to mess with my life. Of course, she didn't know it was really Alistair's plan until I told her."

Sam sat back in his chair. "Fuck me. So you're telling me she was so overcome with jealousy that she agreed to manipulate her sessions with you with the aim of achieving what exactly?"

"I'm not sure she really thought it through beyond the idea that I was with Warren and she wasn't. She's clearly deranged so I think we just have to accept it's all as clear as it's ever going to be."

They sat in silence for a moment while Sam mentally placed the final piece in the puzzle. "So what now? What do we do now that we know all this?"

Grace thought for a moment. "Nothing."

"Really?"

"Well what do you suggest? Alistair's never got over what happened and you can't really blame him for that. Anna's behaved unethically yes but no crime's been committed."

"But what about you?"

Grace smiled. "So my confidence has been dented, my feelings have been hurt and I've been left a bit confused about stuff. I'll get over it."

And then he lent in, his eyes full of such respect and kindness that Grace couldn't stop herself blushing. "Well I think you're being fantastically pragmatic about it all. Peter, all the stuff Phil had to deal with and then all this on top, I'm amazed you're still standing."

"Oh stop it," Grace said, mockingly chastising him, her eyes immediately down. She was aware of him looking at her, recognising the sense of feeling safe that came with being so physically close to him. She forced herself to look up. "But thank you. That means a lot." Grace checked her watch. "Come on, we should get back to work. I've distracted you quite enough over the past few days."

They headed back to their respective desks in silence, reaching Grace's department first.

"See you later then." Sam raised his hand with a smile but as he turned to walk away, Grace stopped him.

"You do know I couldn't have got through this without you don't you? And I don't just mean finding out the background to why it all happened." She stopped, unsure suddenly how to articulate what his unquestioning support truly meant to her but before she could decide what else needed to be said, Sam was already backing away.

"I'm glad I was able to help. And I'd have been furious if you hadn't let me."

And with a smile, he turned and walked away.

Half an hour later, Grace was still staring at the same email. She had lost count of how many times she had started reading it but each time, by the time she was half way through it, her mind had wandered again and always back to the same point in her conversation with Sam. The moment when he had asked what they should do now that they had worked it all out. She could hear herself saying, 'nothing', over and over again. Nothing, nothing, nothing. Could she really just do nothing?

Before Grace could think about it any further, she was reaching for her bag, grabbing her coat and muttering that she would be on her mobile if anyone needed her. Without stopping to consider what she was doing, she rushed outside, each stride wider and more purposeful than the one before. She hailed a cab and then sat, tense and rigid in the back, her knuckles white from gripping her bag so tightly, her eyes fixed through the window but seeing nothing.

Grace stood outside the familiar black door and was about to press the same bell that had first led her to Alistair when the door swung open. As a woman came out, Grace quickly stepped inside. When she reached the reception she asked for Alistair with as much confidence as she could muster.

"Is he expecting you?"

"Yes," she lied, giving the receptionist her name and quickly taking a seat.

As she waited, Grace was aware of the receptionist making a call. She was clearly well-practiced at lowering her voice which she was now doing so effectively that Grace was unable to make out how the conversation was going. Neither did she know if the call to him had been internal or not. She still had no idea if he was even in the building.

It suddenly struck Grace that she hadn't really thought this through and she started to feel a little nervous. What the hell was she doing? What was she going to say to him? And more pertinently, what on earth could he say that would make any of this feel better? All he could do was apologise which would achieve what exactly? Leave her feeling even more humiliated than she did already. Humiliation that he wasn't equipped to understand.

"Grace?"

Grace looked up.

"I'm afraid Alistair isn't here. I've made some calls but I haven't been able to track him down I'm sorry. But I can pass on a message?"

Grace stood up. "No. No message."

Grace headed quickly back down the stairs, propelling herself through the large front door and out into the fresh air. She hesitated for a moment, wondering if she should have left a message and then forced herself to just walk away, unaware as she did so of Alistair, standing slightly back from a large second floor window, expressionless as he watched her go.

34

Anna

As soon as Grace had left her, Anna had dropped onto the sofa in her office, normally reserved for those needing help (it had felt appropriate and mildly comforting), wishing that there was someone in her usual seat qualified to guide her through the raging emotions swelling her mind until her head had throbbed painfully. Anna had slammed the door so violently behind Grace that for the first few seconds, the entire room had reverberated. Anna had shaken along with it, completely consumed by a rage that caused her fists to clench and her nerve endings to jingle, so infuriated was she by Grace's parting words that continued to repeat in Anna's ears, over and over again. To consider for even a single moment that Warren might hate her, that he had sought to escape her, was simply too much. In fact it was ridiculous. He may have been overwhelmed by their situation but he didn't hate her! And of course Grace didn't understand! How could she? Their love was so all-consuming, so ethereal, so beyond any love Grace could ever have known. How could she possibly get it?

Anna's heart had raced uncomfortably until she had finally accepted that, as well as rage, there was now something even bigger inching its way into pole position. Fear. A gut-wrenching, hair-raising terror that sent an icy shiver down her spine and made every muscle in her body tighten. Alistair knew where she was.

It had been a very long time since she'd thought about David but now, despite desperate attempts to hold them back, her mind was suddenly flooded with thoughts of him. She sat back and closed her eyes as her mind flicked through image after image, like a slideshow on fast forward, each picture lasting no more than a second or two but it was long enough for her to remember.

* *

Before

Anna had never learnt to enjoy drinks receptions or networking events of any kind, despite working in an industry that thrived on them. Any public relations role lives and dies on contacts and relationships with both clients and the media and the financial sector that Anna inhabited was no different. While most enjoyed the constant revelry, for Anna such events brought together everything she hated, moulded into a couple of hours of pure hell. Small talk, fawning over people who on a good day she felt indifference towards and, on a bad one, anything from mild disdain to utter contempt or, even worse, being fawned over by someone else, being forced to suffer sycophancy and exaggerated emotions of any kind, all just filled her with horror. She had a suite of excuses that she used on a rotating basis to avoid such agony but on the odd occasion, like tonight, she was forced to accept there was no escape.

After twenty minutes, she was already wondering if she had been seen by enough people to negate any doubt as to whether or not she had actually attended. Believing the answer was a resounding yes, she was about to slip away when she was suddenly aware of someone approaching her. Her heart sunk.

"Hi Anna, I'm David Connor. It's lovely to finally meet you."

Anna looked at him and took the hand he had extended towards her. He was tall, smartly dressed in an immaculate suit and highly polished shoes, his hair short and greying. Anna smiled. That was true of virtually every man in the room but there was something in his eyes that grabbed her, her desire to flee suddenly forgotten.

"David Connor," she said slowly. "Well this is an honour."

He laughed. "No one has ever said that to me before."

"I'm sure that's not true," she said, mildly amused that she was slowly turning into the kind of person she hated at these events.

"That was an incredible job you did making the investment scandal go away."

Anna smiled. "I was just doing what you pay me for."

"Well I was grateful and impressed all the same."

The company David worked for was a client of Anna's but he was far too senior to be part of the staff she regularly liaised with. She and her team had successfully negotiated them through one potential crisis after another. On this most recent occasion, Anna had turned around what could have been a public relations disaster when it was revealed that money from one of their funds was being invested in the wrong side of a politically sensitive conflict in some far flung place (she had already forgotten the detail; there had been so many similar situations).

"Can I get you another drink?" he had asked her. "In fact, would it be totally inappropriate to suggest a drink somewhere else? I bloody hate these events."

Anna had laughed, delighted to have found a kindred spirit and a means of escape in one very charming package.

They found a nearby bar and quickly settled into a relaxed and flirtatious conversation. The connection had been almost immediate for Anna. She'd studied him as he spoke, knowing she was being obvious but she didn't care. Just looking at him had awakened something in her, a feeling she hadn't experienced since Warren, a thought that had made her stiffen ever so slightly. She wouldn't think of him now. David had the deepest blue eyes that sparkled when he laughed which he did often. He was confident and self-assured but there was no hint of arrogance. Everything about him was slowly drawing her in. She could feel herself gradually leaning in closer until she could smell the subtle aftershave and the faint smell of alcohol on his breath.

Anna had clocked the wedding ring early on but hadn't allowed it to register as any kind of barrier. Why should it be? She was married to Julian after all with two young children at home under the care of an au pair. She wasn't afraid to admit there was little in this family environment that held any kind of appeal so anything that provided good reason to stay away should be actively encouraged as far as she was concerned.

And so it had begun. Slowly at first but for Anna at least, an affair had been inevitable. With careful manipulation, she had ensured contact between them had continued and then with a lightness of touch, the casual encounters quickly turned into dinners for two and eventually a passionate afternoon in a plush hotel. Within weeks, Anna was already way ahead, imagining a new life for herself, one full of love and passion, a million miles from the suffocating routine she currently endured. A life that she deserved.

Unfortunately for Anna, that wasn't how David saw it. In a flash of conscience, he took a long look at what he was doing and immediately realised he had made a terrible mistake. He loved his wife. He adored his children. So what the fuck was he doing? Having some kind of mid-life crisis, clearly. As quickly as he had fallen into the relationship with Anna, he wanted out. A line drawn. All contact broken.

The shock of hearing the affair was over flipped Anna from passionate romantic to vengeful shrew in the blink of an eye. It was like Warren all over again. She tried talking him round, she tried crying, she tried hysterics and then she'd got angry.

When Anna called David's wife, Jessica, she told her she needed to discuss an award David had been nominated for. She urged her to keep it to herself, telling her that the only way this could work was with the element of surprise. And wasn't that right.

Anna was already waiting when Jessica arrived at their chosen restaurant. It was mid-morning. Anna had anticipated the meeting would be short so a straightforward coffee felt appropriate. Jessica approached Anna with an outstretched hand and a wide smile.

"Hi Anna. Lovely to meet you."

"Please sit down," Anna said, shaking her hand. "Coffee?"

"Yes please."

Anna ordered more coffee and then sat back in her chair, her legs crossed, her back straight. Jessica went to say something but she immediately put her hand up to stop her.

"I'm sorry Jessica but before you tell me how exciting it is that David is up for an award, I must tell you why you're really here. It gives me no pleasure to tell you that your husband has been having an affair."

Anna watched the colour drain from Jessica's face. Her mouth fell open slightly but she seemed unable to form any words. "That must be very hard to hear," Anna continued, "but I know if it were me, I would want to know." Anna stopped. That wasn't true at all. Anna would actually be delighted if Julian had an affair. Anything to show he actually had some spunk left in him. Regardless, it felt like the right thing to say in the moment.

"How?" The word was barely more than a whisper. "I mean when? His routine hasn't changed. He's at home at the weekends. When was their time?"

"There's always time," Anna said. "Afternoon meetings spent in hotel rooms, business dinners to hide behind, endless events to register for but never actually attend."

"And how do you know all this?"

Anna smiled as she waited. And then there it was. A sudden realisation that rippled across Jessica's face causing her eyes to widen and her mouth to fall open, a small gasp escaping the moment the action was complete. She stood up and Anna immediately did the same. As Jessica then stepped towards her, Anna was too quick, catching Jessica's arm in a tight grasp as she swung it towards her, dashing her hope of wiping the smile from Anna's face.

Anna maintained her grip with their eyes locked until Jessica finally stepped back, her body shrinking in defeat. She picked up her bag and jacket and then turned back to Anna. "You're a disgrace. You should be ashamed of yourself."

"And yet I'm not. Lovely to meet you Jessica."

Jessica had left David within days but even with her out of the picture, David had still rebuffed Anna. Worse, he had real hate in his eyes when he had told her repeatedly that he wanted nothing more to do with her and that he would never forgive her for ruining his life. Such dramatics. And all because she had done what he didn't have the courage to do so they could move on with their lives together. He had tried to retaliate by telling Julian and what had Julian done? Forgiven her! Instead of being angry or hurt, he had tried to make her talk about it, wanting only to steer them through a difficult moment to reach better times on the other side. She had found it all repulsive. Grotesque even. It was all further proof if it were needed (which for Anna, it most definitely was not) that Julian was even weaker and more pathetic than she already believed him to be.

As day to day life fell back into its normal pattern, Anna had found herself unable to shake off the sense that she had still been wronged. A few carefully chosen words whispered into just the right ears and the rumour mill leapt into action.

There was no proof that there was anything illegal or even immoral about David's financial dealings but, once in play, doubt smothered him like an oversized coat. And then she had heard David's wife had taken his precious children and moved away which meant David had been left alone, his life suddenly horribly empty. His marriage was over. His children had been taken away. And now his career was finished. Anna had felt an immediate sense of satisfaction. Job well and truly done.

A few days later, Anna had been in a meeting when one of her team came flying into the room, spluttering apologies for the disruption his entrance was causing.

"You're late," Anna said, her displeasure obvious.

"I know, I'm sorry, but my phone hasn't stopped ringing since I came out of the underground. David Connor's dead. They think it was suicide. The press are all over it."

A collective gasp swept around the room in the style of a sombre Mexican wave but it was only Anna who lost all colour from her cheeks, her eyes stinging as if the news had actually slapped her in the face. The room then erupted into a wave of sympathy; wasn't it awful, so terribly sad, his poor family. Anna stayed very still while she tried to work out how she felt. She was suddenly so overwhelmed by an incredible numbness, it was preventing any visible emotional reaction. And then she felt herself slipping towards a place of darkness and immediately sat up very straight and gave her head a little shake. She refused to feel responsible in any way. This wasn't her fault. He had brought it all on himself and shown himself to be weak. And there was no attribute less attractive than weakness. Anna then allowed the thought that he was gone forever to drift into her mind. She immediately batted it away and stood up.

"Okay, that's enough," she shouted above the chatter. The room fell immediately silent. "Organise some flowers from the company," she said to the young woman on her right. "Jake," she addressed the meeting's latecomer, "are we needed or is the in-house team handling the media?"

"They're keeping this one to themselves. No comment at all from us and any queries should be directed to Sophia."

"Let's move on then."

The media interest had been phenomenal, with members of the financial quarter and wider business world falling over themselves to praise this remarkable man who had clearly been wrongly and outrageously accused of misconduct, his professional downfall blamed on nothing more than unsubstantiated gossip. There were pictures of the grieving widow but she refused to make any comment and in the middle of it all there was David's brother, Alistair, shouting to anyone who would listen that they should all look no further than David's mistress, Anna Jackson, to understand why his brother had felt taken his own life was the only option left.

Anna had used every contact she had to spread her outrage and deny all suggestions of an affair as the ramblings of a desperate grieving man. She threatened them with a blackout if they dared to print any of Alistair's claims, making it clear she would deny them access to any press releases, interviews or events pertaining to her very influential clients. The only person who could confirm her relationship was David's wife who thankfully wasn't talking but Anna knew the business and financial journalists she dealt with had no control over the news pages of their papers and websites whose editors would throw her under a bus without blinking. The clock was already ticking on how long she could hold off the inevitable coverage. Whatever she did now, her career as she knew it was over. It was time to remove herself.

Anna was tempted to just pack a bag and disappear under the dark of night to start afresh somewhere on her own but leaving Julian and her children at this point could trigger interest that she didn't want, interest that Julian would be totally incapable of handling. Instead, she quietly resigned. It had then been easy to persuade Julian they needed to move away for a few years, telling him that she'd had enough of the City and that this latest scandal was the last straw. They had done so well, she told him, overcoming her small indiscretion and the last thing they needed was to get caught up in the fallout from David's death. She told him she wanted some space and fresh air to consider a new career path, that a project in the shape of a new home somewhere miles from London would be the perfect distraction while she considered what she might do next. Julian was immediately on board. Anna had then changed everything from her maiden name to her married name, Miller, which had seemed to be the simplest and quickest way to try to disappear. It was something she had never planned to do but Julian had been delighted, mistaking it as some kind of gesture that the affair had indeed just been a glitch and that this, along with a new start somewhere, was her way of showing her renewed commitment to him which had annoyed Anna enormously. If she hadn't needed him to move away with her for this plan to work, this could easily have been the moment when she told him exactly what she really thought of him.

Leaving him would just have to wait.

* *

Now

Anna couldn't remember the last time she'd cancelled clients but there was no way on earth she was heading into work today. She had woken feeling tired and wretched and had initially convinced herself that a day spent at home was just what she needed to catch up on some admin but it hadn't taken long to realise that she simply didn't have the mental capacity to concentrate on anything. She was way too preoccupied and had eventually given up trying to focus on any work-related paperwork. Instead, she just sat in her lounge for hours, once again poring over the past. The affair with David all seemed like such a long time ago now so why had Alistair suddenly resurfaced? So he wanted to discredit her but, in all likelihood, she doubted his actions would cause more than a ripple, if that. So why go to all this trouble?

Far more worrying was whether or not he was now done or if there was more to come. It was a chilling thought that made her sit up very straight but, before she had time to consider what this might actually mean, her eyes were drawn to the clock hanging on the wall opposite. The boys would be home from school soon. She slowly stood up and headed for the kitchen, motivated by a sudden need to drink wine.

If she hurried, she could down at least half a bottle before they came crashing through the front door.

35

Alistair

Alistair was sitting at his desk at home, perfectly positioned so that he could look out of the large window into the beautiful garden, rich with colour and wonderfully calming as a result. Not that he could take any credit for it. The green fingers belonged to his wife, Beth. The garden was her domain, its beauty the result of her daily pottering.

He looked at his computer and slowly scrolled through the waiting emails. Nothing felt very urgent but even if it was, he was too distracted to concentrate on anything. He had dreamt about this moment for so long. The moment when he could ruin Anna's reputation in the same way she had ruined David's, believing it would come with the most overwhelming sense of satisfaction and the chance to finally find some peace. But he felt nothing. Nothing new anyway. The sadness was still all-consuming, the anger bubbling uncomfortably just beneath the surface as it always had and, of course, the regret that he carried everywhere with him – that he hadn't been able to stop David believing that taking his own life was the only option he had left.

Alistair had been really impressed by Grace when he'd done some research into her background and was sure in different circumstances they would have got on well together. He of course felt guilty that she had been caught up in his plans and could still see the look in her eyes as he'd explained how they had ended up sitting opposite each other. He wondered what had made her come to see him again? Of course he might know the answer to that if he had agreed to see her but, in the moment, he hadn't had the stomach for a verbal bashing, convinced she would have been looking for another opportunity to vent her understandable indignation. It would have been pointless so instinct had therefore told him to send her away. He had been so delighted when Matthew had got in touch to let him know his plan was in play that he hadn't stopped to really think about how Grace would be affected which felt churlish now. Maybe at some point he would be able to get back in touch with her to see if she would let him help her? But whether that moment ever came or not, the important thing to hold on to was that Anna had done what he needed her to.

Alistair had made the call to report her and sent a full statement by email as requested but had heard nothing since. He was under no illusion that Grace would help him. That was something else he hadn't thought through carefully enough and it was clear now that she was, of course, far too hurt and angry to do him any favours.

As he mulled it all over, he realised that he didn't actually care one way or the other if he ever got a response to his complaint. Whatever the outcome, it would never be enough. If one association discredited Anna, he had no doubt that another one would give her renewed validation such was the lax way her industry was regulated. And anyway, how could being labelled an unethical life coach ever feel like justice for what she did to David? As he let that thought sink in, he felt thoroughly embarrassed by his rather pathetic and amateur plan.

"Fancy a cuppa?"

Alistair immediately looked up and smiled. He hadn't heard Beth approaching. And then he stood up. "Let me make it. You're the one whose been doing all the work." Alistair kissed her cheek as he passed her in the doorway, her gardening gloves still in one hand, a small bunch of daffodils in the other. "Or maybe a gin and tonic?" he shouted from the kitchen.

"Yes please!" Beth shouted back. "I'll just go and clean myself up."

Alistair busied himself making the drinks hoping the alcohol might do the job and drown the ball of anger that sat heavily in his stomach. He'd had the chance to avenge his brother and he had wasted it. He silently cursed his ineptitude as he tried to get a handle on what, if anything, he had actually achieved. He imagined for a moment that his plan did indeed prove to be successful, resulting in Anna being humiliatingly struck off, shunned by her peers and unable to continue practicing, her career dead in the water. If that turned out to be the case, then he would know, unreservedly, that he had ruined her professional reputation in the same way she had ruined David's.

His eyes came sharply back into focus. The only problem with that was that Anna would still be alive.

36

Grace

Grace was already waiting when Phil came through the door of the bar. She smiled as she saw him. Just seeing him made her feel better about the world, as if everything was suddenly aligned again now that she had her best friend in her midst.

She had chosen a corner table with high banquette seating and Phil dropped himself down next to her, his arms immediately around her. She held on tightly to him as if trying to draw strength from him, attempting to recharge her weary batteries with his energy and all the while breathing in the familiar and reassuring smell of him.

"You can let go now," he said but Grace didn't move a muscle. Eventually he put his hands on her arms and gently tried to release her grip. When finally his efforts were successful, he looked at Grace and was surprised to see tears in her eyes.

"What's the matter?"

Grace did her best to pull herself together. "It's nothing. I'm fine, honestly. I'm just so pleased to see you."

"I've been away for a few days. And aren't you always pleased to see me? It doesn't normally make you cry."

Grace attempted a smile. "It's just been the strangest week but I know you're having a tough time too."

"Never mind that. You first."

Taking a deep breath, Grace did her best to explain. "So you remember last week I said I saw Anna and Warren in some kind of fight?" Phil nodded. "And you remember we talked about Anna and laughed at how she was doing nothing more than making me feel worse about myself? Well it turns out it was deliberate. She took money from someone to see if she could manipulate me. Nothing major but enough to make a mockery of the hours I spent with her. She only agreed because she saw me with Warren, an ex of hers who she's been obsessed with for years. It was enough to make her want to hurt me."

"Fuck."

"Indeed," she said with a wry smile.

"I told you you were wasting your time with her. Can you do anything? She can't get away with that surely?"

"Do what though? Alistair, the bloke who set it all up, wanted to discredit her. He said he was going to report her to whatever body she's associated with but, even if they take action, it won't change anything that's happened."

"But why did he care so much?"

Grace took another deep breath. "He blamed Anna for the death of his brother."

"I'm sorry," Phil said, clearly confused. "He blamed who for what?"

As succinctly as she could, Grace whisked Phil through the highlights, watching his jaw and his eyebrows slowly separate as she did so, a look of complete disbelief shaping up in between. When Grace came to the end of her tale of woe, there was a moment's silence while Phil quickly tried to process it all.

"Wow. What a complete mind-fuck. And you're sure you're okay?"

"I'll be fine. I just can't decide whether to feel hurt, angry or humiliated."

"Angry. Definitely angry." Phil took hold of her hands and gave them a reassuring squeeze. Grace closed her eyes and for a moment, imagined again that she could access Phil's strength through the touch of his fingers and feast on his impenetrable resolve. Just the idea that it might be possible made her feel better.

"Much more importantly, how are you doing?" she asked.

"Actually, I've made a decision. I'm ready to do an interview with Sam."

Grace felt her eyes narrow as she studied Phil's face. In all the time she'd known him, she'd never once known him to volunteer to do any form of publicity, never mind an in-depth interview. "I'm sure he'll jump at the chance," she said, trying to hide her surprise, "but he's going to need to know what you're prepared to talk about."

Phil thought for a moment. "All of it. I know I'll never be able to prove those photos of me taking drugs were fakes but I'd like to try. Proving I was visiting you rather than prostitutes is easier but in lots of ways even more important. I've always been very out and proud and although there was some coverage explaining why I was really in your building, I need to make sure it's still absolutely clear that I'm still very much out and still just as proud." He shrugged. "I'm just trying to clean the slate. I can live with a few smudges but there's no way I can leave with nothing but a stack of lies behind me."

"Leave?" Grace looked him and watched Phil swallow hard.

"I have to go now Grace. You know it's the only way I can start over." Grace gasped, her hand immediately flying to her mouth as if to catch the tortured yelp that was about to escape and shove it back inside. "And it's not as if you didn't know this was coming," he said gently. "The interview will be my way of drawing a line and then I'll be on a plane before it breaks. I just want to be somewhere where nobody knows the history. You get that don't you?"

Of course she did. It didn't mean she liked it though and as the first tears began to fall, Phil immediately took her in his arms. "It's not that bad. I'll still be there when you need me. It'll just take a little longer to get to you, that's all."

"So where are you going?" she asked, swiftly wiping away tears and doing her best to pull herself together.

"San Francisco for starters."

"When?"

"As soon as you let me know when Sam's free. I'll have my bags with me."

Grace arranged for Sam and Phil to meet in a bar that she was confident would be quiet at five o'clock in the afternoon. With introductions out of the way, she organised drinks and then said she would be back in an hour or so. Judging by the surprised looks this prompted, it was immediately obvious both had expected her to hang around but Grace had other ideas. Despite what Phil might have thought, he didn't need her to hold his hand and would be absolutely fine without her there. And, if she stayed, she might be tempted to chip in with the odd opinion or two. She knew Sam would insist he didn't mind but she also knew it would be intrusive and would quickly become annoying. And of course the very last thing she wanted to do was sit and watch the clock inch ever closer to the moment Phil would make his final exit. No, it was better for everyone if she stayed out of the way.

Grace left them to it and headed for the café opposite. She ordered herself a large coffee and took a table outside, feeling the need to be in the fresh air, hoping the gentle breeze would blow away the uncomfortable sensation that was fogging her brain and sitting heavily on her chest.

And then she started to twitch. She looked at her watch and was pained to see that only five slow minutes had passed. It was going to be a long wait. She picked up her phone and started scrolling through her Twitter feed but quickly got bored. She switched to a word game but soon got stuck and immediately lost interest. Next she tried the news. Then a book. Then she stuffed her phone in her pocket.

She watched people pass her by, watched a mother pacify a toddler on the verge of a tantrum, listened to the banter between a shopkeeper and his customer and the chat of two women meeting unexpectedly on the pavement in front of her.

Grace looked at her watch again, an idea slowly developing. She knew if she made the move now, there would be time to do what she had already put off for too long. She hesitated for just a moment and then leapt up, her hand already in the air to hail a taxi.

Grace's eyes were already searching through the large windows of the café for a glimpse of Warren as the taxi pulled up outside. Her heart was pounding and she had absolutely no idea what she was going to say to him or what she wanted the outcome of their conversation to be. She just knew that she had to sort things out one way or another.

As she pushed open the door, she quickly established he wasn't there. She checked the time again. It was possible he would be starting a shift soon but she wasn't sure she had time to wait.

"Hi Mike," she said, catching the eye of one of Warren's fellow waiters. "Is Warren due in?"

Mike looked immediately uncomfortable. "No. He left."

"What time's he in tomorrow?"

As she watched Mike visibly squirm, Grace felt a warm burst of embarrassment crawl up the back of her neck.

"No, he's left. Properly left. The country."

"He's left the country? And gone where?"

"He didn't say." As a customer called out to him, Mike then simply shrugged and quickly went back to work.

Grace stood where she was for a moment, her feet unable to move while all available energy was used to absorb what she had just heard. He's left the country. She said it again to herself. *He's left the country!* Anna had walked back into his life and Warren had run away. Done another disappearing act and run for the hills. What did that say about his feelings for her? Not very much, that's what. And then she jumped as her phone beeped. She grabbed it from her coat pocket to see a text from Phil that simply read: 'Safe to come back'. It was sufficient to get her moving and, leaving the café, she quickly looked for another taxi, texting back that she would be there in ten while she did so.

Grace took the briefest of moments to collect herself before heading inside the bar and then immediately felt herself relax as she headed towards two smiling faces and the sound of laughter as Sam and Phil chatted.

"All done?"

"Yes, all done." Sam smiled at her, sensing her need for reassurance.

"You okay?" Grace looked at Phil. He looked exhausted but exhilarated.

"Yes, it's all down and I feel suitably purged. And I'm starving after all that talking. How about some dinner?"

"I'd love to," Sam said as he started to gather up his things, "but I have to get back to the office."

"Well thanks mate," Phil said, putting out his hand which Sam immediately took hold of. "I really appreciate your time and the opportunity to at least try to straighten a few things out."

Sam held on to Phil's hand, his other hand immediately reaching out to Phil's shoulder which he squeezed warmly. "It'll be a really positive piece thanks to your honesty and openness so the thanks are all mine." He looked at Grace. "I'll see you tomorrow?"

Grace merely smiled and nodded, knowing Sam was only ducking out so she could have Phil to herself.

"So what do you fancy?" Phil asked, already studying the menu.

Grace took off her coat and sat down. "Oh, I'm not sure I'm that hungry to be honest," she said, "but I'll have a glass of wine."

Grace was immediately grateful that Phil simply headed to the bar to order without trying to force her to eat. She didn't want to make this any more difficult than it was going to be but neither did she want to have to pretend it was easy which left them with a precarious line to negotiate.

Phil polished off an enormous plate of fish and chips, intermittently giving Grace a summary of the interview between mouthfuls but, as soon as he pushed his plate away, Grace sensed a growing feeling of unease in him, his shoulders slowly rising until he looked tight and uncomfortable.

"Phil?"

For a few moments, he couldn't look at her. Grace waited until finally, his eyes found hers. "I think it's time to settle up."

Grace watched him go and pay the bill. She couldn't hear the conversation that followed but saw the barman nod towards Phil's waiting suitcases and assumed his raised eyebrows were the result of Phil explaining he was off to start a new adventure. He then shook Phil's hand warmly, no doubt wishing him bon voyage and a happy new life, knowing Phil's enthusiasm for it all was hugely infectious. In contrast, Grace felt numb. But as she clocked the change in Phil's expression as he turned to walk back to her, as she saw the look of excitement and anticipation flick to one of anxious trepidation at how their goodbye might play out, her own demeanour shifted too. In that moment, she was determined not to ruin this for Phil.

"Have you booked a cab?" she asked as he sat down.

"It'll be here in ten."

"I should go then," she said, as casually as she could manage. "The sooner we say goodbye, the sooner I can get over you and find myself a new best friend." She smiled at him and then, standing up, Phil quickly followed, taking her in his arms and squeezing tightly. They had already decided Grace shouldn't go with him to the airport, convinced there was nothing to be gained from a long drawn-out goodbye. As Grace melted into his chest, she realised she had no rulebook for this one, no idea at all how to say goodbye to her most treasured friend who she would miss in a way even she couldn't yet comprehend. What words could possibly express how she felt?

Grace slowly released herself. Two pairs of watery eyes smiled knowingly at each other and it struck Grace that no words were actually needed. She reached up and kissed him gently on the lips and then, picking up her bag and with a smile brimming with love and sadness, she turned around and headed quickly for the door.

37

Anna

Anna was still on high alert. Walking from the tube station to the office, she constantly looked over her shoulder and checked every doorway. At lunchtimes, as she waited in line to buy lunch, she tapped her foot impatiently, eyes flitting from left to right and back again, then she would grab the food she had no appetite for and retreat to the safety of her office. Walking back to the tube station each evening, as the light of the day started to melt away, she merged with the crowds she would normally do anything to avoid, wanting only to be swallowed up by her fellow commuters. She stopped wearing the bright red coat she loved and replaced it with something black. She wore large sunglasses even when dark clouds sat heavily in the sky to hide her frightened eyes and cancelled all social engagements. For the first time in memory, she couldn't get home quick enough at the end of the day, relaxing only once the curtains were drawn and the front door was firmly locked.

When would he strike? Hard as she tried to convince herself otherwise, Anna knew Alistair would be back. She didn't just know it, she could feel it in the pit of her stomach. A heavy uncomfortable sensation that left her feeling permanently nauseous. He had found her and, at some point, he would be back. It was not knowing when that was sending her mildly demented.

As Anna moved around her bedroom one Monday morning, she could hear the usual cacophony beneath her. Heavy feet running up and down the stairs, the banging and crashing of crockery on the granite breakfast bar, shouts from one son to the other, some pleasant, some not so much, interspersed with the gentle calm murmurings of Marta.

And then the house went from loud frenzied chaos to a strangely still silence in the slam of the front door. Anna stopped what she was doing as she felt the calmness ripple through the house, not allowing herself to acknowledge that her sons hadn't even shouted the vaguest of goodbyes. She had heard Marta in the kitchen, tidying away the breakfast things before she'd left with the boys. Anna had no idea where she went or how she spent her days while the boys were at school. In fact she knew very little about Marta's life at all and then reminded herself that was exactly how she liked it. All that mattered was that she knew she would be back before the boys returned from school, no doubt with a cake freshly baked and fruit smoothies perfectly blitzed to wash it all down. She would be ready to help with homework or supervise play dates (Anna had no idea of the boys' after-school activities) and would calmly administer the necessary daily reminder of the rules around the usage of electronic devices. And, perhaps most surprisingly, the boys would listen and, with the odd grumble here and there, would do what they were told not just because they respected Marta but because they genuinely liked her. Anna had seen the warm affection for her in their eyes and for a split second had felt something unpleasant that she had been forced to accept was jealousy. She had dismissed the feeling with a shrug. You reap what you sow.

As Anna wandered along the landing, the walls suddenly felt very bare. She really should make an effort to hang some pictures. She walked down the wide staircase and ahead to the large entrance hall below. She could see into the spacious lounge to the left and the large kitchen to the right, a room that with its breakfast bar, a table that could comfortably seat ten or more (she could only guess; there had been no large family get-togethers or dinner parties with friends to test its actual capacity) and the sumptuous corner sofa, was so much more than just a place where food was prepared. It was the kind of family room that should exude warmth, that should be strewn with paraphernalia telling the story of hectic family life. Not this room. The surfaces were clean and clear of clutter and the air was tinged with a faint hint of disinfectant.

Anna walked into the kitchen and for the first time, the expansive room felt empty. Devoid of personality with no clues at all as to the people who inhabited it. Perhaps she should take a few days off and go shopping for some bits and pieces to liven the place up a bit? She rolled her eyes. She really was losing the plot.

The house had been bought with her parents' money. When she and Julian had divorced he had never challenged ownership. The house had always been in her name and as he was successful in his own right (which had always been a surprise to Anna) he neither wanted nor needed her money. As she looked around the room, Anna suddenly found herself thinking about her father. What would he have made of her life? Would he have been proud of her? Anna wasn't sure why that should matter. Or why she increasingly found herself thinking about him. Her memories of him were sketchy so perhaps this was simply a last ditch attempt to hang on to any memory she still had? But that just made her think about losing him and the fact she'd never felt his presence in her life as powerfully as she felt his absence.

Anna made herself a cup of tea, enjoying the banality of the task but as she sat on a stool at the breakfast bar, she realised she didn't really want the drink at all. She thought about tipping it straight down the sink but she was in no hurry to leave the house and drinking tea was as good a reason as any to stay where she was a while longer.

She let her mind wander, waiting to see what this morning's unease could be attributed to and then she sighed, embarrassed almost as she realised she felt cheated. Where was the love? She knew her sons had wanted to love her. They'd often said the words, telling her as much as she left their rooms at bedtime, but she could never say it back. Eventually they had stopped. She used to hear Julian telling them how much he loved them and how proud he was of them. "It's pathetic," she had reprimanded him. "You sound so weak and needy and all you're doing is making them weak and needy too."

Anna stared into her almost empty cup. She hadn't even noticed herself drinking it. She could hear the large clock on the wall ticking and she focused on the rhythmic tick, tock, tick, tock, terrified of the question that was forcing its way forward until there it was, front of mind and impossible to ignore. Was it possible she had got it all wrong? With everyone but her, the boys were warm and tactile, confident and happy. Being loved hadn't made them weak or needy by any stretch of the imagination. As for herself, she had done nothing but punish the people who had loved her and where had that got her? She was the one who now felt in need of something. She was the one who felt empty, the tea sloshing around in her stomach as if to physically prove the point.

Her thoughts blurred for a moment and then she was thinking about Grace. She was horribly jealous of her but, if she was honest, it was about so much more than Warren. Grace's displays of vulnerability had made Anna silently scoff. Despite her training to get people to open up to her, she had never been able to imagine letting her own guard down to such a point that she might become susceptible to pain and hurt, but what if she had? If she'd let Warren know that she'd been scared by how much she loved and needed him, would things have been different? If she'd given him some space to just be himself, been more confident in his love for her, would he have felt the need to end the relationship at all? If she'd been able to recognise how hurt she was by David rejecting her and had dealt with that rather than focus on a blind determination to just hurt him back, would he still be alive? And if she had looked at Julian differently, seen him as the loving father he clearly was, if she had celebrated the fact that he would do anything to make her happy as something to be cherished and not repulsed by, would this house be full of love and life, with photographs everywhere and piles of stuff on every surface, instead of the hollow shell she currently sat in?

Anna got off her stool and walked slowly to the sink, threw the dregs of her tea into it and then placed the mug in the appropriate place in the dishwasher. Her expression was one of steel. Such self-indulgence! Such over-emotional, sugar-coated bullshit! Her back stiffened. All this thought of lowering guards had the immediate effect of strengthening her own. She would not allow Alistair to intimidate her for a single moment longer. He was nothing more than a stupid old man who was probably only blaming her for his brother's death because, deep down, he knew he was the one who had most likely let David down but was too weak to admit it. Well no more.

Anna put her laptop into her bag and then stopped herself as she reached for her black coat. She smiled as she turned instead for the red one, feeling her confidence grow as she slipped in the first arm and then the second, as if donning a coat of fortified armour.

She left the house with her head high and that's how she stayed for the entire journey. Sweeping into Brockley Court, she exchanged her normal pleasantries with Imogen and then headed for her office. As she unlocked the door, she pushed it open with a smile and headed straight to open the window. Some cool, fresh air was definitely in order.

"Hello Anna. It's been a while."

Anna was not a fan of idiomatic expressions but, in that moment, she felt as if she might quite literally jump out of her skin. She spun around, hoping beyond hope that her ears were mistaken and that wasn't the voice of Alistair rebounding off every wall.

But there he was. He had clearly stepped in immediately after her and was now closing the door behind him.

38

Grace

Grace sat opposite Emily and watched her fidget. Watched her eyes roaming the room, studying the table, her hands, the small vase of flowers, anything rather than actually look at Grace. She watched her play with her drink, swirling the wine around her glass until it swooped dangerously close to the rim. It had never been like this between them. Awkward. Uncomfortable. Tense. And the worst part was Grace had absolutely no idea why.

She tried to remember when she had last seen Emily. It had been weeks. Again, this was unheard of. Their only communication had been voicemail messages from Grace and numerous apologetic texts from Emily saying how sorry she was that she had kept missing Grace's calls. Apologies that had started to lose their conviction as they slowly transitioned into empty excuses.

Grace was desperate to know why Emily looked so distant, why she seemed to be focused only on repressing whatever emotions she was feeling. A growing sense of nervousness eventually made her start to talk.

"I'm sorry I haven't seen you. It's been way too long!" Grace was trying too hard to make light of the situation and then blushed at her own crassness. Regardless she soldiered on. "It's been the most surreal couple of weeks. Maybe if I tell you all about it, you'll understand why I haven't been very communicative?" But she had been communicating. It was Emily who had batted back every approach, who had refused to engage in conversation, rebutting every call with a brief text.

Grace didn't expect an answer and instead, set about telling another rendition of what had happened with Anna and Alistair. She watched as Emily slowly got drawn in, her eyes suddenly up and wide, her mouth falling slowly open as the horror of Grace's story took hold of her with a firm grip.

"I had no idea." It was barely more than a whisper.

Grace held her breath, convinced for a moment that Emily was about to return the favour with her own explanation for why she suddenly looked so uncomfortable in Grace's company. That just maybe, she might now shed some light on why she had clearly been avoiding Grace. But as Emily went to say something, Grace's phone leapt into action, an incoming text making them both jump. Emily sat back in her chair, the newly established communication between them immediately broken. If she had been about to speak, the moment had been well and truly ruined. Grace froze.

"You should see who that is," Emily said, nodding towards Grace's phone but Grace really didn't want to. "Go on. It might be important."

Reluctantly, Grace picked up her phone and was surprised to see a text from Anna. 'Help me', it read. 'At office. Alistair was here and'

And then abruptly, it stopped. Grace felt her body temperature immediately rise as her heart started to pound. She looked at Emily, her eyes full of fear.

"What is it? What's happened?"

"I'm so sorry Em. I've obviously upset you and I have no idea what I've done and I desperately want to sort things out, but I have to go."

Without waiting for a response, Grace quickly gathered up her things and ran for the door, dialling Sam as she went.

A twenty minute cab ride later, she pulled up outside Anna's office building where Sam was already waiting. Without a word, she immediately followed him inside. Imogen was just putting her coat on, her usual seat at the reception desk already filled by a security guard. Sam quickly started to explain that Anna could be ill which seemed less likely to cause alarm than suggesting she might be in any kind of danger but the guard was clearly reluctant to just let them in.

"It's okay," Imogen chipped in, recognising Grace from her appointments, "I'll take them up."

It seemed to take a lifetime for the security barrier to open and then once through, they raced to the lift with Imogen in tow clearly not sharing their sense of urgency. Another irritating wait, a painstakingly slow lift ride and then Grace quickly led the way to Anna's office.

As she opened the door, the first thing she saw was Anna lying on the sofa. Or slumped might be a more accurate description. She was lying on her side but her feet were still on the floor, as if she'd been sitting and then suddenly fallen down. Her head lolled slightly and her left arm flopped towards the floor. Her eyes were neither open nor closed and just out of reach of her hand was an empty bottle of pills. Sam was immediately crouched down beside her. "Anna!

Anna!" He shook her gently and then turned to Grace. "Call an ambulance."

Grace quickly made the call, asked for an ambulance and then blurted out what they had found. "They want to know if she's breathing?"

Sam put his ear to Anna's mouth. "Just."

Grace then answered a few more questions before hanging up. "On their way."

"I'll go and wait for them." Imogen immediately headed back to the reception, grateful for an excuse to be useful and for a legitimate reason to remove herself from the horrifying scene.

Grace could then only watch in awe as Sam pulled Anna on to the floor and put her in the recovery position. He then continued to talk to her, his voice calm and reassuring, telling her over and over again that everything was going to be okay and that help was on its way. Grace could feel herself start to shake, a gentle shiver that was building momentum, spreading through her body with terrifying speed until her teeth started to chatter. She jumped as she heard the ping of the lift in the distance and then Imogen's voice, quickly followed by the sound of feet running towards them.

Sam quickly moved out of the way as two paramedics came into the room which suddenly felt very small. Sam answered questions from one, as the other expertly focused on Anna, pulling equipment from bags, administering who knew what to ensure her life was saved. Grace went cold at the realisation that life was literally hanging in the balance, hypnotised by what was happening in front of her. She paid no attention as Sam moved past her to Anna's desk. He had shared everything he could and she assumed he was simply moving out of the way. And then she was distracted by Imogen who had appeared back at the door, this time with the two police officers in tow.

Grace had lost all sense of time. She shifted uncomfortably on a plastic chair and winced at the sharp pain that shot down her left leg. She stretched it out and then grimaced as she repeated the move with her right leg which was an equally painful experience. And then she sat perfectly still again. She felt emotionally drained, her brain so stupefied that she'd been sitting in an almost comatose state for hours.

As she continued to try to breathe life back into her stiffened body, Grace looked up and down the corridor. It was eerily quiet. The chatter and bustle of visiting hours had long since faded and Grace was left wondering for the millionth time why she was still here and why she had even come here in the first place.

The paramedics had been suitably impressive and in what had felt like minutes, were happy that Anna was stable enough for them to take her away. Grace had thought how much Anna would have hated being carted out on a stretcher amidst a collection of prying eyes. There were only a few people left in reception and in the surrounding meeting rooms but all available eyes were on her as she was hurried away, the many theories as to what could possibly have happened no doubt immediately in play.

With Anna gone, the police had then taken over. They wanted to know how Grace and Sam knew Anna so Grace had explained her relationship with her and then she had hesitated. How much of the stuff with Alistair was relevant? She showed them the text message Anna had sent her and Sam gave a fantastically succinct account of the collective story of Alistair, David and Anna. The younger of the two officers had looked totally bemused while Grace could see the older, more experienced one was busy trying to decide if a crime had been committed.

"What do you think happened here?" he had asked them.

"If it was a suicide attempt, why send a text calling for help? Easy to assume it was a last minute change of heart until you know about the Alistair/David story. Puts a whole different spin on it don't you think?" It was Sam who had answered. In fact he had done all of the talking once Grace had answered their first question. She was way too distracted trying to work out for herself what the hell had gone on.

"So a suicide attempt. Or made to look like suicide," the older officer had mused.

The police had let them go at that point. Grace had felt compelled to follow Anna to the hospital and Sam had said he would see her there as soon as he had dealt with something or other. Grace's hearing had been temporarily impaired along with her ability to speak.

So here she was. Sitting in a harshly lit corridor, the smell of some extra-strength bleach-based product burning the hairs in her nose, waiting to hear news of Anna's fate. She hoped someone would have called Anna's family but there had been no visitors yet. No one tearing down the corridor with a look of panic on their face as they raced to her side.

Grace sighed. Much as she was desperate to be at home, it didn't seem right to leave her. She closed her eyes. She could wait a little longer.

She wasn't aware of Sam until he was sitting next to her, his hand on her arm, gently shaking her awake. It took Grace a moment to acclimatise and remember where she was.

"I must have nodded off. How long have you been there?" she asked him, her eyes struggling to adjust to the lights, her throat painfully dry.

"Only a few minutes. I wasn't sure whether to wake you or not."

Grace stretched and yawned. "What time is it?"

"Almost midnight."

"Bloody hell. Is she okay?"

"Out of immediate danger. That's all they'll tell me."

"Where's her family?"

"Her ex-husband's on his way. He needed to make sure their kids were okay first apparently."

They sat in silence for a moment and then Grace discreetly glanced up at Sam. In a flash, she was wide awake. The look on Sam's face was like an injection of adrenaline and her heart immediately started to race.

"Oh my God, there's more isn't there?"

39

Grace

Grace thought she might actually throw up as she followed Sam to the hospital café. He'd suggested a nearby pub so they could have a proper drink but that felt like it would take too long. Grace just wanted to know as quickly as possible what else he now knew.

She headed for a table while Sam got them some coffees, her chin resting heavily in her left hand, the fingers of the right one drumming on the table, louder and louder as she tried desperately to drown out the manic chatter that filled her head. As Sam sat down opposite her a few minutes later, he leapt straight in, desperate to put her out of her misery.

"So while we were in Anna's office, I took her laptop." Grace's eyes immediately widened and she let out a little gasp. "I know it was risky," he continued, "but I just had this uncomfortable feeling that we didn't have all the facts and that this might be our only chance to find out."

"But you'll get into all sorts of trouble. Won't the police be looking for it?"

"I put it back before anyone missed it so no harm done." Sam rushed the words out, desperate to get back to the point. "Anyway, it seems Anna's desire for revenge ran deeper than we realised." And then he paused for just a moment, teetering on the edge before he threw himself in. "I know Anna told you to keep notes on Peter but she was the one who told him they existed and where he could find them."

"No!" Grace cried, aware of heads spinning towards her and conversations abruptly stopping but her focus stayed firmly on Sam.

"And she was the one who had the pictures of Phil doctored to make it look like he was taking drugs and then sold them on. She also took the pictures of him at your flat when the brothel was being investigated, and sold them too."

"What? So it's my fault he left?"

"No Grace, it's Anna's fault. Not yours."

But Grace wasn't listening. "Everything he went through! He left the bloody country! And it's all down to me?" Grace struggled to take it all in and then started to sink in her seat as the weight of it all threatened to completely overwhelm her. "She was so good at just making me talk." Grace shook her head as she remembered. "I thought we were just chatting. You know, in those moments at the start of a session and then at the end. Just casual chit chat while I put my coat on. I didn't even stop to think about what I was saying."

Sam hated that he was the bearer of such unwelcome news but felt Grace needed to know everything he had found. "There was a draft email waiting for Phil. It was clumsily written so I guess she hadn't worked out when and how she was going to tell him that you were to blame for his downfall, that she could only do what she did because of things you told her. Or maybe she decided your friend moving away was enough?" He fidgeted in his chair. He wanted to reassure her that she wasn't to blame, that she could never have known what Anna was up to but that would have to wait. "I'm afraid there's more." He hesitated for a moment, Grace's eyes wide and staring directly at him. She was still struggling with the idea that she was the reason Phil had gone and then Sam was talking again. She braced herself.

"She also emailed Emily."

Grace knew it was late to be making house calls but this couldn't wait. Impatiently, she shifted her weight from one foot to the other as she waited. After what felt like a lifetime, she blinked at the sudden brightness of the hall light and watched as a dark shape loomed towards her.

"Who is it?"

"Em, it's me."

Grace heard the clunk of a lock being released and then finally, the door opened.

"What's happened? Is something wrong?"

"I need to talk to you." Emily didn't move. "Please Em. Let me in."

Emily opened the door fully and Grace followed her in, closing the door behind her as Emily headed for the kitchen, pulling her dressing gown tightly around her as she went. Emily still had her back to her when Grace started to speak but she was unable to keep the words in for a second longer.

"I should have told you. I know that but how could I? After everything you've been through." Emily swung around, her eyes full of angry tears. Grace's instinct was to put her arms out to her but Emily quickly backed away. "I know I've made it worse now," Grace continued. "It's not just what I did but that I kept something from you for the first time ever." Grace's voice then cracked. "I thought I was protecting you. You must be able to see that?"

"Do you have any idea what it's like when someone finds out you can't have children? I know you do because you've been there when it's come up and mums have suddenly looked horribly embarrassed at the healthy toddler holding on to their leg. Or they've turned their newborn away slightly as if they honestly think I might just snatch it and do a runner. Do you remember those moments? It's not that you had a termination, it's that you thought I couldn't cope with knowing. That like everyone else, you felt sorry for me. Well I don't want your pity!"

Grace flinched. She had never heard Emily shout at anyone before, never mind at her. In fact, shouting didn't feel like the right word. It was more like a scream, full of bitterness and disappointment. "And you weren't protecting me! You were protecting yourself. Scared that I might hate you for such a shameless, selfish act!"

"Yes it was a selfish act. My relationship with John was never going to work and in that moment all I could think was that I couldn't be tied to him for the rest of my life. I wish it had never happened and it's a decision I'll struggle with for the rest of my life. It honestly felt like the only way out. I'm so sorry Em."

"But that's just the point!" Emily's anger had now peaked and was slowly being replaced by a heartbreaking mix of hurt and raw sadness. "You don't have to apologise to me!

What you did changes nothing for me. And I hate the fact you never once stopped to think I might understand. That I might have agreed it was exactly the right thing for you to do. All I would have wanted was what was right for you."

Grace put her arms out again and this time, Emily stood exactly where she was, allowing Grace to wrap her arms tightly around her. She kissed Emily's head and squeezed. "I know you don't want to hear it but I am really sorry that I didn't talk to you. I wanted to. I was so confused I wasn't thinking straight. Finding the courage to finish things with John was such a turning point for me but it had to be a complete break. I hate what I did but I couldn't have his child. It was the worst way for you to find out and if I could rerun it all, then of course I would have found the courage to tell you. Anna's caused such a mess Em. Please don't let her damage us too."

"I could have helped."

Grace finally released Emily enough to look into her eyes. "I know. But like I said, I wasn't thinking straight. I've only just found out the full extent of Anna's carnage. She's done so much damage. Don't let her ruin us too Em, please."

Grace could see Emily was hurting which was truly unbearable. She would do anything for her dearest friend, her sister in all but blood, and the idea that she might have inadvertently ruined their relationship was utterly terrifying. When Grace had found out she was pregnant with John's child, she had felt so traumatised she'd almost lost her mind. She had thought long and hard about how she would cope as a single parent but she was so repulsed by John, so resentful of him, so scared of him, that being connected to him for the rest of her life just seemed bigger than any argument to embark on the parenting journey alone. She had challenged herself and the decision she had made many times since, asking herself again and again a pointless round of 'what if's?' And yes, if she was honest, the decision not to tell Emily had been partly to protect herself. She hadn't wanted to feel any more wretched, any more shameful or guilty than she still did and while of course she knew Emily would have supported her, it wouldn't have been without a degree of disappointment. How could it not be? But having Anna coldly and brutally tell her just added a whole new layer of devastation.

"Em, please."

This time it was Emily who put her arms around Grace's neck and she pulled her close. "It's okay," Emily whispered and then she held on tight as she felt Grace's tears of relief slowly soaked through to her shoulder.

40

Anna

Anna woke with a start. Her body felt heavy, her throat hurt terribly and her mouth was dry. She did her best to pull herself up and as her eyes quickly scanned the space around her, she realised she was in hospital. She let her head sink back on to the hard pillow, giving herself the chance to catch up.

Her first thought was that she was still alive. Something she acknowledged with a huge sense of relief. As the full memory of what had happened then started to take shape, her heart began to race. Alistair had come to see her! And he must have…

"Welcome back, Anna." Anna's eyes jerked towards the door as a nurse approached with a smile. "How are you feeling?" Without waiting for an answer, the nurse picked up a glass of water and carefully placed the straw where Anna could reach it. She drank greedily. "I just need to do a few checks," the nurse said as she replaced the cup and then busied herself taking Anna's temperature and checking her blood pressure. "The police are keen to talk to you when you're up to it."

The police? Anna felt a rising sense of panic as she struggled through the dense fog in her brain to remember the detail. Grace! Of course. Grace must have found her. It was all too much. She coughed. "Your throat will be dry for a while," the nurse said as she straightened her bed and then gently leant Anna forward so she could bash some life into her pillows. "Keep sipping your water and the doctor will be in to see you soon." And then she left, chatting about something and nothing as she went, her words washing over Anna in an unintelligible wave.

It was suddenly very quiet again and Anna didn't think she had ever felt quite so alone. Not just in the moment. The feeling was so much greater than that. Over the years she had ruined everything. Every relationship destroyed, every person who had ever cared for her pushed away and now somebody actually wanted her dead. As she struggled to come to terms with that, the nurse returned to let her know Julian would be in later with her sons and that they were all delighted to hear she was awake and doing well. Anna felt tears sting her eyes. Her sons. She would try harder. She would reduce her working hours. She would show them she loved them every day. And then she was thinking about Julian and the rush of emotion came to an abrupt halt. She shifted position as any feelings of tenderness drained from her body and she shuddered. The cocktail of drugs in her system was clearly taking its toll, making her uncharacteristically sentimental. And then she allowed herself a wry smile. There was nothing like an image of Julian in her mind to return her to her default position of general indifference.

When the police arrived, Anna was more than ready to talk, despite the fact it was still physically painful to do so and exhausting at the same time. There was a detective dressed in a suit and an officer in uniform and having established it was okay for them to take a seat, Anna was encouraged to talk them through what she could remember with plenty of assurances that she should do so in her own time.

"I'd just walked into my office and suddenly Alistair was there. He must have been waiting for me and then slipped in behind me. He said something about how time had been no healer for him and that I needed to pay for killing his brother. Which of course I didn't do." Anna stopped for a moment and took a few sips of water. "It won't take you long to check. I didn't kill his brother, he killed himself."

"We're aware of the circumstances around David Connor's death and the events leading up to it." Anna couldn't remember the name of the detective who'd just spoken but the fact he knew about David had momentarily derailed her. She felt the control of the situation shift slightly. "And then what happened Anna?" he prompted.

"Obviously I was shocked he was even there," she said, trying to keep her voice steady and strong sounding, "never mind accusing me of who knew what, so I reached for the bottle of water on my desk to buy me a little thinking time. I took a few sips and then a few more and he just paced up and down in front of me, rambling about everything that had happened and how he had never recovered from the loss. I didn't know what to say or what to do so I just kept taking sips from the bottle until it was almost empty. And then he stopped pacing and told me to sit on the sofa." She stopped for a moment. "He sat down opposite me, never taking his eyes off me. And then he took a bottle of pills out of his pocket."

For a few moments Anna said nothing. She just stared straight ahead. The detective waited as long as he could and then offered a prompt. "You're doing really well Anna. Can you tell us what happened then?"

"I was terrified," she eventually said. "He told me it just wasn't fair that I was still alive while David was dead and that he was going to put that right. When he shook the pills at me I told him there was no way I would take them." She turned to look directly at the detective and the officer before she continued. "He laughed and told me I already had. He'd put some in the water. I always have a bottle of water on my desk so I never thought for a minute that the bottle he'd watched me drink from hadn't already been there. He'd made sure it was the same brand they sell in the building's café. Smart move don't you think?" When no opinion was forthcoming, Anna finished up. "It wasn't long before I started to feel woozy and I remember feeling so incredibly tired. My head felt very heavy and I must have drifted in and out for a while. I don't know how much time passed but I remember opening my eyes and he'd gone. I was so relieved I think I must have had one last surge of adrenaline. I'd slipped my phone into my pocket when I first realised he was there so I took it out and sent the text to Grace."

By the time Anna had finished talking, the officer was already making a call from his mobile as he hurried out of the room.

41

Alistair

The wait had been the worse part. And of course, the wondering about what had happened once he'd left Anna. How long would it have been before someone found her? In the following few hours, he had tried to imagine how it would all have played out. The discovery of her body and the police arriving. There would be no need for an ambulance. She had swallowed enough drugs to floor a large horse. He wondered if she had been carried out in a body bag for all to see and if it was even vaguely possible that foul play would have been suspected. He had left an empty pill bottle just below where she had slumped, staging it to appear as if it had rolled out of her hand. Who could possibly doubt that such an evil woman had finally given into her conscience and then done the world a favour by taking her own life?

Alistair had been up early after a restless sleep and had continued to scour all the news sites ever since, expecting each time he did so to read about the discovery of a body, the death a result of a tragic suicide. He had the number of the journalist who had been prepared to listen to him all those years ago and was planning to call him the minute the news broke to plant the idea that clearly the guilt of causing David's death had finally become too big a burden to carry.

Once his story was printed, the whole world would then know the truth about what she had done.

By late afternoon there was still nothing and Alistair was starting to twitch. He was no expert but he felt sure it should have been reported by now. Perhaps she was still lying in her office? His blood ran cold at the thought. What should he do? He couldn't afford to call the reception or make a visit. He had to stay away, trapped in his home, waiting, pacing, checking the news, waiting.

As Alistair sat in his study, trying to focus on some work but failing miserably, he was suddenly aware of voices in the hallway. One belonged to his wife, Beth, the other was unfamiliar. And then the door opened and the first thing he saw was the fear in Beth's eyes; the second was a tall suited man, holding a badge up, flanked by two uniformed police officers, one of whom was coming towards him and then firmly encouraging him into a standing position. The suited one was saying something but his words sounded strange to Alistair's ears. Everything had slipped into slow motion. For a moment, he thought he had heard the words 'attempted murder' but felt he must have been mistaken. He felt a pinch and a click and he slowly looked down, forcing his eyes to focus, immediately then surprised to see his wrists had been cuffed together. It was the plaintiff cry of Beth that snapped him back into real time.

"What are they talking about Alistair?"

He couldn't look at her as he was led from the room.

"Alistair! What have you done?"

She was behind him now as he was propelled down the hallway and out the front door but, even out of sight, he could feel her panic, feel the sense of despair. With a hand on his head, he was lowered into the back of a police car and just as the engine started, he couldn't help but raise his eyes. Beth stood, broken and tearful, her eyes full of confusion and fear.

"I'm sorry," he mouthed as the car finally pulled away.

42

Grace

"I wasn't sure you'd come."

Grace had wondered the same herself but here she was, taking the seat she'd been offered beside Anna's hospital bed.

"The nurses said you were here when I was admitted," Anna said. "Thank you for staying around."

"I was in shock. I didn't know what I was doing." The last thing Grace wanted was for this woman to think she cared. "Although I did wonder why it was me you sent the text to?"

"No one else would have understood the threat Alistair posed to me."

That was fair enough, Grace thought and then she waited, happy to sit in an uncomfortable silence. Anna had asked her to visit. If there was something to be said, then let her speak.

"I'm sorry Grace."

Grace wasn't sure how she was expected to respond to Anna's words and was surprised to find herself laughing. A spontaneous belly laugh that made her body shake and her eyes water.

"Did I say something funny?"

It wasn't lost on Grace that Anna looked immediately aggrieved. She pulled herself together and looked at Anna with a wry smile. "Maybe not funny, but pretty ludicrous don't you think? That after systematically setting out to ruin my professional life and the personal relationships that matter the most to me, you think you can just say sorry? How did you expect me to react? Did you really think I'd just accept your apology, shake hands, wish you a happy life and pretend none of it ever happened? I know what you did Anna. I know about all of it. Sending my notes to Peter, the pictures of Phil, the email to Emily, never mind Alistair's little game. I know about all of it!" Aware that her voice was rising, Grace stopped. She didn't want anyone coming in and asking her to leave. Not when she was so close to getting some answers. She took a moment to compose herself. "Just tell me why Anna?"

If Anna was aware of how devastating her actions had been for Grace, or was surprised to discover Grace knew everything she'd done to her, it certainly wasn't obvious. For a moment she just stared at Grace, her eyes cold and steely, but Grace was determined not to concede, prepared to hold her stare for as long as was required. Eventually, Anna spoke. "Let's just say I've always believed my life would have been so different, so much better, if Warren had just given our relationship another chance."

"But you're the one who ruined the relationship! You had him Anna! And then you bound him up so tightly he couldn't breathe. No wonder he ended it! But only because of the way you behaved. And then you went from being simply controlling to a complete psychotic lunatic. No wonder he ran for the hills!"

Grace watched as Anna went to say something and then stopped herself. Grace could almost feel the heat of her anger. She watched Anna take a deep breath and swallow hard, as if literally ingesting the words she had instinctively wanted to say in response.

"But what I want to know," Grace said, moving to the edge of her chair, "is why that turned you so violently against me? Why punish me?"

Grace watched Anna narrow her eyes and instinctively she slid back in her chair. She wondered how it could be that even in a hospital bed with her face pale and her body wired up to all manner of machinery, this woman could still be quite so menacing. "I wasn't punishing you," Anna said, her words laced with surprise that Grace still didn't seem to get it. "I just wanted you out of the way. Sharing your diary with Peter was a bit knee-jerk but I thought if Phil left the country, you might be persuaded to go with him."

Grace waited, searching Anna's face for a clue as to what was coming next but Anna remained tight-lipped. "And then what?" Grace pushed. "Warren would just take you back?" Grace shook her head. "You did all this thinking that could actually happen?"

"When I saw you with him, so relaxed and content, something inside me snapped," Anna spat. "I never gave anyone a chance after Warren. Every relationship was doomed before it had even started. He owed me another chance!"

Grace looked at her in utter disbelief and then she smiled. A smile that spread quickly across her face and up into her eyes until they shone. And when Anna looked back at her with nothing but horror, Grace couldn't help but laugh.

"Don't you dare laugh at me!" Anna shouted.

"You know I thought about going with Phil," Grace said as she slowly stood up. "And then all I could see was me sitting in the passenger seat next to him, something you told me I had to stop doing." She shrugged as she picked up her coat and bag. "All that effort to make me go away and then your words were what stopped me. You have to admit it's a little bit funny?" For the first time since Grace arrived, Anna's cheeks flushed with colour, the heat of her humiliation warming her from the inside out. "Almost as funny as you thinking Warren would ever take you back."

"Just tell me where he is!" Anna shouted.

"Everything alright in here?" A nurse appeared at the door. There had clearly been one raised voice too many. She looked at Anna. "Perhaps it's time your visitor left?"

Grace went to leave but Anna stopped her. "Just a couple more minutes, please."

"I'll pop back in a few minutes then," the nurse said to Grace, as if warning were needed.

As soon as she'd gone, Grace turned back to Anna. "Please Grace," Anna pleaded. "Just tell me where Warren is."

"Well at least I understand now why I'm here. You say sorry, I give you Warren's address and off you go to fuck his life up even more, assuming that was humanly possible. Well I don't know where he is Anna. And if I did, you would clearly be the last person I would ever tell."

Anna went to say something but Grace was quick to stop her. "No more Anna. Like the nurse said, it's time your visitor left."

43

Anna

Anna held her breath for one, two, three seconds and then for one more, just to be on the safe side. As she slowly exhaled, she felt her heart rate gradually return to something close to normal, the pulsing in her chest and forehead easing along with it.

So Grace knew everything. How was that possible? A picture came to mind of Grace rifling through her desk while she lay dying on the floor. Perhaps she had more character than Anna had given her credit for? Which could be why their meeting hadn't gone quite as Anna had hoped. She'd been confident she could convince Grace she was sorry for the Matthew/Alistair indiscretion and had imagined that once that was done, it would then be pretty straightforward to get Grace to tell her where Warren had run off to this time. Instead she'd been forced to explain herself, something she was not happy about at all. And, even worse, Grace had persisted in laughing at her. Anna felt her back stiffen. It had taken every ounce of control – and the odd tube here and there – to stop her leaping out of bed and strangling the stupid woman. How dare she! How dare she laugh at her from her pretty little pedestal that she'd put herself on, lauding over Anna as if she actually deserved an apology! It had almost been too much.

Anna closed her eyes and tried again to relax. She needed to think. She needed a plan. The police had been back to tell her Alistair had been arrested for attempted murder. His fingerprints were all over her office, including the water bottle that had been found to contain traces of whatever unpronounceable drug he had hoped would kill her, so they weren't exactly short of evidence. What a rubbish criminal he'd turned out to be. There'd been some media coverage but no one could get access to her for comments or a picture, Alistair's wife certainly hadn't made herself available and David's wife hadn't resurfaced either, so she assumed any interest in the story would be short-lived. Alistair had admitted to everything so there would be no drawn out trial. Case well and truly closed.

Anna was just thinking it might be good to get out of bed for a while when she heard voices approaching. And not just any voices. Instinctively, she pulled the covers up under her chin and closed her eyes, immediately exhaling loudly and evenly.

"She's asleep," Edward said as he came crashing in.

"Shhhhhhh!" Julian urged, arriving just behind him.

"Now what?" And finally the sullen voice of Charles, Anna's oldest boy, with no attempt at all to keep the volume down.

"Just sit down there Eddie," Julian whispered. "You too, Charlie."

"Her eyes moved!" Edward shouted.

There was nothing Anna could do to prevent the involuntary reaction to Julian's use of 'Charlie' and 'Eddie'. All the times she'd complained to him about Marta

327

persisting in using the annoying shortened names she so hated, and all the time he was bloody doing it too! There was then a flurry of activity with chairs scraping along the floor and the sounds of bags being dropped and then, for a moment, it all went quiet.

"How long do we have to stay?" Charles asked.

"Just a bit longer. It would be lovely to get the chance to speak to your mum, wouldn't it?"

Silence.

Anna was tempted to just tell them to leave if they were such reluctant visitors. She had things to do and people to contact, the beginnings of a plan slowly taking shape that she would need some of her more elusive contacts to help her with. This ridiculous charade was just wasting valuable time.

After what felt like an eternity and several more pleas from her children that it must be time to leave, Anna was aware of Julian standing up. "Come on then boys. Perhaps we'll try again tomorrow?"

More scraping of chairs, more general shuffling and finally the very welcome sound of footsteps slowly receding to nothing. Anna allowed the sense of relief to sweep over her and then she lay quietly with her eyes wide open. It was time to start rebuilding her strength so she could finally draw this hideous mess to a close.

44

Warren

Turning the open sign to closed, Warren stood for a moment, stretched his arms high above his head and indulged in a huge, satisfying yawn. It had been a long shift but he wasn't complaining. The sun was still up, he had sight of the sea, his customers were relaxed and full of smiles and so, therefore, was he.

It had only taken him a few days to land on his feet. He had been into the beachfront café enough times during his first few days in this idyllic French town that he soon struck up a rapport with the owner and couldn't believe his luck when he heard he needed extra help. A quick summary of Warren's experience followed by a trial shift and the job was his.

Initially, France hadn't felt anywhere near far enough. He had told himself it was just a quick pit stop to get himself together and make a longer term plan but within a week he had fallen in love with the place. A small seaside town that felt really authentic. Like a little oasis hidden in the hectic southern coastline. The locals were friendly, loving his determination to speak French, his schoolboy proficiency slowly returning.

Once he had work and a regular income, finding a place to stay had been easy and he was now living in a simple apartment with one good-sized living space that included a small functional kitchen, a bedroom, a bathroom and large French windows that opened on to a small balcony with a view of the sea. He could have got something bigger without the view but for Warren, the balcony was priceless. This was where he spent most of his free evenings, breathing in the smell of the sea and letting the sound of the waves gently wash over him. It was also where he did most of his thinking, picking over how Anna had once again completely upended his life.

He felt suitably wretched about leaving without seeing Grace again but he had no idea how he could ever make her understand what seeing Anna again had done to him. Maybe he would get the chance to try to explain it to her at some point. He really hoped so but, in the moment, leaving Grace high and dry had felt like a small price to pay for his safety because that's how it had felt. That by leaving, he was protecting himself. That as long as Anna knew where he was, he simply wasn't safe. He often wondered what might have happened if he'd stayed but the conclusion was always the same. That staying had never really felt like an option. Where his relationship with Grace was concerned, he had completely fucked it up. Best to accept that responsibility was his and just leave it there.

With so much weighing him down, it was a surprise to Warren that after just a few weeks, he already felt relaxed. The height of summer was still a way off but it was warm enough for him to live in shorts and t-shirts with his skin perfectly sun-kissed and his shoulders tension-free. While he sat on his balcony, as he did most nights, a cold beer in hand, legs stretched out with his feet resting on an as yet unplanted terracotta pot, his mind was wonderfully empty, his thoughts only of the here and now. He lazily scanned the horizon, a lone sail in the distance, the occasional gull floating in the sky and the odd burst of chatter from people passing along the pavement beneath him and he smiled with pure bliss.

Having watched the sun disappear, he was now transfixed by the moon hanging over the sea in spectacular fashion, looking like it could just fall in at any moment, its light caressing the silent water below. A delicate breeze blew in, gently whispering in his ear and making him shiver. It was time to go inside.

After a long, peaceful sleep, Warren was glad to be back in the café by mid-morning the next day and once again surrounded by friendly chatter. When he had first arrived, the voices had all been French but with every day that passed, there was a steady swing towards English. He had been told that in a month or so, he would hear little else, many of the locals heading off on their own holidays to make way for the influx of visitors. They preferred this label to the term 'tourists', clinging to the notion that they could preserve their relative anonymity and keep their precious little town away from holiday brochures. Those that did visit came back year after year, the locals greeting them like old friends which in many cases they now were, bringing with them a sense of hope that a long profitable summer was just around the corner.

By late afternoon, Warren was strolling through the old town where a market was in full flow, the loud banter from stallholders floating on the breeze. The place felt busier again today and he felt the wave of summer energy building, relishing the buzz of the place as the town slowly started to fill. It was like the volume had suddenly been turned up and a sound track had been added, music now playing almost continuously from bars and restaurants, laughter and general merriment spilling from the open doors and windows.

And then he stopped, whipping his head around, an uncomfortable feeling creeping up through his body and prickling the back of his neck. He scanned the faces milling around behind him, then the same to the left and then to the right, narrowing his eyes against the sunlight but no one was paying him any attention. Not that he could see anyway. He shook his head, annoyed with himself for falling foul to paranoia and continued on his way. But the growing sense of unease stayed with him and as the bustle of the town dissolved behind him, he found himself nervously scanning every face, checking every doorway and alley he passed, the prickling sensation now creeping over his whole body causing a series of involuntary shudders in an attempt to shake it off.

"For fuck's sake, get a grip!" he quietly urged himself as his eyes scanned yet another side road and then he stopped, squeezing his eyes shut, feet standing strong and firm. He waited for whatever he thought was behind him to catch up and make themselves known, channelling all his concentration to his ears, straining to hear any sound of approaching footsteps so he could be ready for whatever was coming.

A minute past, maybe two, and then Warren opened his eyes. He sighed, forcing his shoulders to relax as he did so. "Fucking idiot," he muttered. "Stupid bloody fucking idiot," he added, a little louder this time as he strode towards home, shaking his head in disbelief at himself until he arrived at his door.

At work the next day, Warren was still smothered in a cape of unease.

"Everything okay Warren?"

"Yes, all good," he reassured his colleague.

"It's just you've been staring into space for the last five minutes."

"Sorry. Bit preoccupied that's all."

The arrival of new customers provided the perfect distraction. Warren greeted them, immediately chatting about something and nothing as they sat down, talking through the day's specials and making recommendations about local wines. He was aware of his colleague watching him so ensured he put on a great show to reassure him all was indeed fine. He appreciated the concern and for a moment he'd been tempted to share but talking about it all would only breathe life into it again and that was the last thing he wanted.

By the time the lunchtime rush took hold, every table was full both inside and out. Warren couldn't stop himself checking every face that came through the door but once there were no more tables left, leaving him with a café rammed with customers wanting to be served, there was no time for Warren's imagination to embark on even the smallest of adventures, his mind fully occupied for several hours until the afternoon lull finally came.

Handing the reins to a fresh team, Warren finally headed home. Once inside his building, he quickened his pace as he climbed the stairs to his front door, his body fatigued and desperate to rest. It was on his third step into the apartment that he looked up and then stopped, all ability to move lost in a split second, his eyes wide and unblinking, feet glued to the floor, mouth open. The only movement he was aware of was the vibration of his ribcage as his heart thumped violently in his chest and, just a few feet from where he stood, Anna's cheeks spreading to make way for the disturbing smile that was slowly taking over her face.

"Hello Warren. I was beginning to think you were never coming home."

"How did you find me? How did you get in?" And then he put his hand up, suddenly realising he didn't need the answer to either question. She was here, sitting on his sofa, in his home, the place where up until this moment, he had felt relaxed and safe. In fact not just sitting on his sofa but lounging on it, sitting far enough back for her shoulders to nestle into the soft cushions, her legs crossed, arms relaxed and by her side, as if she sat there every evening waiting for him to come home.

"You disappeared. Again. It's starting to become quite annoying."

"You gave me no choice. You wouldn't listen Anna. You never listen." He paused for a moment. "Why are you here?"

Anna looked genuinely bemused. "To be with you of course!"

Anna sat forward and Warren instinctively took a step back.

"Sit down for goodness sake," she chastised. "I won't bite."

Warren hesitated and then sat down in a chair opposite her. "Please Anna. This has got to stop. I'm sorry things didn't turn out the way you wanted but there's nothing left between us and you need to stop imagining there is."

"It's because of her isn't it?"

It took Warren a moment to realise Anna was talking about Grace. "Of course it isn't! It's about you. For a moment in time you were everything to me but that's all it was. A moment in time that was over years ago." Warren watched Anna closely, desperate for a sign that his words were reaching her. "I kept trying to tell you it was too much but you took over my life. You weren't my girlfriend, you were my puppet master."

"Don't be so ridiculous! Puppet master? What are you talking about?"

Warren watched something change in Anna's eyes and suddenly found it hard to swallow. She was never going to understand. It was sad really and for the first time Warren felt pity for her. He felt himself soften. "It's time to let go and enjoy the life you have Anna. And you need to let me do the same. You need to let me get on with my life."

When she said nothing, her head down, her hands clasped tightly together, Warren got up and moved closer, kneeling in front of her but, as her head shot up, her eyes wide and boring into his soul, he felt himself instinctively pull back.

"A life without you?"

"Yes Anna. You've been living a life without me for years....." Warren stopped. The shift in her eyes this time from desperate to icy cold was so terrifying that he was suddenly lost for words. He didn't even flinch as she lunged forward, aware only of a sharp pain. As his hand instinctively clutched at his side, he looked down to see blood seeping through his fingers.

"Anna! What have you done?"

45

Grace

She had never imagined for a single moment that Anna would still continue her pursuit of Warren despite everything that had happened. How had she known where to find him? Grace had never even asked where he was so at least this time, that couldn't be attributed to her.

Grace looked at her watch for the millionth time as she paced the corridor. She almost hadn't answered her phone the night before when the words 'No Caller ID' had flashed up at her but she was mighty glad now that she had. When she heard Warren's dad's voice, slightly shaky and stuttering, she of course knew immediately that something was wrong. There'd been little she could do other than listen, reassure and then book herself on a flight for first thing this morning and a cab to take her straight to the hospital with Warren's dad set to arrive just a few hours behind her. All she knew was that Warren had been stabbed and rushed to hospital with sirens wailing, dispensing dangerous amounts of blood on the way and barely conscious as a result, urgently whispering, "It was Anna", "You need to find Anna", every time he was awake long enough to gasp the words out.

As Grace continued to pace, a door suddenly opened and a nurse appeared.

"Tu peux le voir maintenant," she said with a smile.

Grace looked at her blankly and the nurse's smile widened. She held the door open and gestured for Grace to go in.

"Oh thank you so much," she said as she rushed over. "Merci, merci beaucoup."

Grace slowed down as she entered the room, suddenly nervous about what she might find. What a relief to see Warren propped up and smiling at her. She immediately sat down next to him and carefully took hold of his hand.

"You okay?"

Grace laughed. "You're asking me? You get stabbed by your maniac ex-girlfriend and you're asking me if I'm okay?"

"Well are you? I should never have just disappeared without talking to you."

Grace looked at him for a moment. "Well it's all starting to make sense now we know what the crazy bird was actually capable of. Who found you?"

"I've been working in a café and I told the guys there that I thought I was being followed. I didn't tell them the background so I don't think they took it too seriously until one of them couldn't get hold of me. Luckily for me something made him decide to drop past my flat and check in on me."

"Wow. I think you might owe him a drink. And what about Anna?"

"I spoke to the police but I haven't heard anything since."

"I need to speak to the police too if I can and then they need to speak to the officers investigating the attempt on Anna's life."

"What?"

For a moment Grace had forgotten Warren was now way behind the curve so quickly bought him up to speed with the whole Alistair/David part of Anna's story that he had completely missed.

He rested his head back on his pillow and closed his eyes for a moment.

"Are you okay?" Grace asked. "Do you need something?"

"I need you to know that I really tried to make Anna accept that I could never take her back," he said, lifting his head again, his eyes conveying a deep sense of melancholy, his face pale and drawn. "I told her again and again that I didn't have any feelings for her and that all I wanted was for her to leave and never contact me again but she just wouldn't have it. She kept on and on about how we were meant to be together and how we would never be happy with anyone else." He paused for a moment and Grace squeezed his hand.

"You don't have to do this Warren. I get it, really I do."

"No, I do have to. You need to understand I was genuinely scared. When I first disappeared after Anna and I broke up, I just didn't feel mature enough to cope with the situation. To cope with how controlling she was, how suffocated she made me feel. Running away had simply been the only way I could think of to make it all stop. But this time was different. The look in her eyes when she told me again and again that she still loved me, always had and always would, did more than just send a shiver down my spine, it filled me with such terror that for the first time, I seriously wondered exactly how far she was prepared to go to get what she wanted. To get *me*. I guess we know the answer to that now."

"And what about my safety?" Grace was surprised to feel her back stiffen slightly.

"What do you mean?"

"I understand why you needed to protect yourself but did it ever cross your mind that she might be a danger to me too? She thought the only reason you two weren't back together was because I was in the way so she was already doing a great job of messing up my life – trying to cause trouble for me with Peter, chasing Phil away, trying to turn Emily against me. How do you know physically harming me wasn't next? In fact it still might be as no one seems to know where the bloody hell she is." She stopped, aware that her voice was rising and her anger along with it.

Warren looked at her, temporarily stunned into silence. "I had no idea." he eventually stammered. "And of course, you're right. I was only thinking about myself. I had no idea she was coming after you too."

"Of course she was!" Grace looked away for a moment. When she looked back, her eyes were blurred with tears. "I suppose I should be grateful she only messed with my head but the mental scars will run just as deep, Warren."

Warren squeezed her hand that still lay limply in his own. "I'm so sorry Grace."

"Il est temps pour lui de se reposer maintenant."

Their attention was drawn to the door where a nurse now waited. Grace immediately looked back at Warren.

"She said it's time for me to rest."

340

Grace smiled and nodded as she stood up. She bent down and gently kissed Warren's cheek. "I'm sorry too," she said. "It was me who brought her back into your life, however unintentional that may have been. I'll always regret that."

"No Grace! None of this was your fault! Please tell me you know that?"

Grace didn't know how to answer that so just gave him a small nod.

"And thank you for flying out here. It means a lot."

Suddenly feeling overwhelmed, Grace could only smile and nod again before she turned away. As she walked out into the corridor, she then stopped for a moment. She leant squarely against the wall, letting it take her weight, her legs suddenly weak beneath her. But her mind was racing. Could she have prevented this? She felt like she should have been able to but wasn't sure how. There was no getting away from the fact that it was her decision to see a life coach that had set off this hideous chain of events and the weight of that decision now sat heavily on her shoulders. If she had been stronger, if she had been able to deal with Peter and be more in control of her life, none of this would have happened. And then she was thinking about Gillian, a spontaneous reaction to that word 'control' that continued to taunt her, recognising her default position of blaming Gillian for every bad thing that happened in her life. And then she sighed. This seemed to be as good a time as any to accept that had to stop.

If Warren had died, she knew she would have blamed herself. It would have been impossible not to, despite his protestations that she was in no way to blame for any of it, and the voice in her head reminding her that only one person was to blame here and that was Anna. But then without Grace, Anna would never have found Warren in the first place. Or would she? And then there she was, back at the beginning, wishing she had never felt the need to call Anna, wishing she'd had a different relationship with her mother. Wishing, wishing, wishing.

But Warren was alive and she was desperate to believe that Anna would be brought to justice. And that was what gave her the strength to push herself away from the wall, the power to stand tall on her own two feet and the confidence to turn and walk away.

46

Anna

The last thing Anna had expected was to hear from Grace. She still hadn't decided how she felt about the fact Grace had raced to Warren's bedside. Who did she think she was? Florence bloody Nightingale? And would she ever stop being a threat to Anna's happiness? She was like a bloody human boomerang.

Grace had sent her a text suggesting they meet up if Anna was still around. That meant she knew Anna was in France. Which meant she also knew she'd stuck a knife in Warren. Which, for the record, had never been part of Anna's plan. His constant noise about wanting her to leave him alone had caused a new coldness to embrace her. She shivered as she remembered and then she shrugged it off. He had clearly left her with no alternative.

She still wasn't sure why she'd stayed in France. It hadn't been hard to find out that Warren had survived but, once she knew he was alive, she'd found it surprisingly hard to leave. She was stuck in a bizarre limbo, unsure what her next move should be.

Anna checked her watch. For now, all that mattered was finding out what Grace was planning to do with the information she had. Only then would Anna know exactly what new threat she posed. And then… Anna stopped the thought from going any further. One step at a time.

When Anna arrived at their chosen café, Grace was already waiting.

"Look at us," she said as Anna sat down opposite her. "Meeting for coffee in a lovely little French café like we're old pals on holiday together."

"What are you doing here Grace?"

"You mean apart from making sure Warren's still breathing? Despite your best efforts to ensure otherwise. Will you defend it as a crime of passion? If you couldn't have him then you were going to make sure no one else could either? Was that it?"

Anna looked at her. This was quite a show. "I asked you a question. What are you doing here Grace?" She happily held Grace's stare while she waited for an answer.

"You know I had a really interesting chat with Julian this morning."

Anna slammed her hand down on the table with an almighty bang, sending cups tumbling and coffee spraying across the table and onto the floor, the milk jug, which had been sitting dangerously close to the edge, crashing to the floor along with them. She said nothing, her stare fixed on Grace who was now sitting as far back in her seat as she could while she struggled to maintain her composure.

"Be careful Grace."

"Or you'll do what? Stab me like you did Warren? Or just keep picking away at me until I take my own life like David? And what other evil have you inflicted on the world? I'd put money on there being something else or someone else? Come on Anna, talk to me. Help me understand who you really are."

Anna could feel heat rising from deep within her making her feel clammy and uncomfortable. Grace was still talking, goading her, taunting her. She was too hot to concentrate. She was confused. The relentless sound of Grace's voice was making her feel dizzy and disorientated. Why had she spoken to Julian? What could he have told her?

"Was it something in your past Anna, is that it? Perhaps your parents didn't love you? Didn't show you enough attention?"

"My father did love me!" Anna shouted, her focus suddenly back on Grace.

"But not your mother? That was the impression I got from Julian. That must have been hard to deal with, especially once your father abandoned you. Then she was all you had left. How on earth did you cope with that Anna?"

"I suffocated her that's how!" Anna screamed the words across the table, leaning so far forward that her torso rested on the table which shifted under her weight, trapping Grace in her seat and making it impossible for her to move. "I smothered her until there was no life left in her miserable alcohol-soaked drug-ridden body! That's how I coped! I got her out of my way so I could get on with my life!" Anna bit down hard on her lip. Her breathing was shallow, the air escaping in a series of ragged gasps, her heart banging angrily against her chest. "Are you happy now?" she spat at Grace. "Do you feel like you know me now Grace? I refuse to take any responsibility for David's weakness but yes, I killed my mother, and yes, I stabbed Warren because he became incredibly annoying, just like you have. So what am I to do about you Grace?"

As Anna went to stand up, she was suddenly aware of someone immediately behind her, taking a firm grip of her arms and slapping handcuffs on to her wrists.

"Anna Miller, I'm arresting you for the attempted murder of Warren Fleming with further charges pending following further investigation. You have the right to remain silent. Anything you do say can and will be used against you in a court of law."

Anna stared at Grace in disbelief as the officer continued to speak, his words washing over her and then, to her horror, Grace smiled.

"Sounds rather charming in a French accent, doesn't it Anna?"

47

Sam

Sam and Grace were sitting in silence. It was contemplative rather than awkward, both lost to thought. Sam had been about to tell her life was never boring around her but had stopped himself, convinced he'd been saying that a lot recently. Sitting comfortably as they were in a cosy corner of a pub just a stone's throw from the courthouse, he'd stolen the odd brief look at Grace. Each time he'd done so her eyes had looked slightly glazed, her expression not really giving anything away which he'd taken as a sign that she wasn't yet ready to talk.

Taking a large mouthful of beer he couldn't help another glance in Grace's direction and then he swallowed quickly in an attempt to curtail imminent choking, surprised that she was suddenly looking back at him for the first time all evening. He coughed and then inhaled sharply, his eyes watering.

"Do you need me to pat you on the back?"

"No, I'm fine," he spluttered. "Just went down the wrong way."

Sam took another deep breath and then looked at Grace with a flushed smile. "Sorry. You've been miles away since we sat down. Got a bit of a fright when you were suddenly looking at me." Grace raised her eyebrows in response. "Not a scary fright," he stuttered. "Like there could ever be anything scary about you looking at me. It just made me jump a bit that's all."

Grace smiled with such unexpected warmth that Sam was aware of a slight flutter in his chest. There was a twinkle in her eyes that had been absent for a very long time. He hadn't realised how much he'd missed it.

"Idiot."

Sam raised his glass, happy to accept the label, and hoped it wasn't obvious he was suddenly feeling a little nervous in her company. He wasn't sure why. Or perhaps he was. They had been spending a lot of time together and delighted as he was that Grace's nightmare was now almost over, he couldn't help but feel disappointed that she wasn't going to need him in the same way. He was anxious because he knew he was going to miss her company and he didn't know what to do about it.

"Eight years." Grace shook her head. "I still can't believe it. Alistair Connor is going to spend the next eight years of his life in jail. It doesn't make any sense."

"He pleaded guilty to attempted murder. His actions were premeditated and he fully intended to kill." Sam shrugged. "As far as the judiciary system's concerned, and pretty much everyone in the court room with the exception of you, eight years was a relatively small price to pay."

"Okay, it does make sense," she conceded. "But it's still horribly tragic. And where was his wife? No wonder he looked like he's given up already."

"Anna's turn next. Will we be coming to watch her fate sealed too?"

"No thanks," Grace said without hesitation. "I'm hoping I'll never see that woman's face again. When I close my eyes I can still see her launching herself across the table at me with absolute raging madness in her eyes. Have I told you how terrifying it was?"

Sam smiled at her. "Yes, you have."

Grace drifted back to their last meeting in France and she shuddered. "It's a shame the murder confession proved to be worthless though."

"I know that bothers you but once she denied it and put it down to just wanting to scare you, nothing more could be done. It's not as if there's any evidence to be found after all this time. And it is perfectly possible that she didn't actually do it."

"Possible yes," Grace said, her eyebrows raised at the very idea. "But if you'd seen the look on her face, trust me, you would have no doubt at all that every single word was true." She sighed. "Oh well, at least she accepted there was nothing she could do but plead guilty to attacking Warren, which means no trial. I wouldn't have put it passed her to find a way of convincing a jury she was entirely innocent."

"I spoke to my mate at the CPS again yesterday." Sam hesitated for just a second. "Anna's legal team is arguing strongly that she acted impulsively. That the knife had unfortunately been to hand and she just grabbed for it in a moment of passion-fuelled madness. They're also going to town with character references…"

"From who?" Grace interrupted loudly.

"…..so the expectation is she'll only get three years if they're as convincing as my contact's expecting them to be."

There, he'd said it. He knew he had to pass this new information on, but he also knew Grace wouldn't like it. Sam flinched at the distressed face looking back at him. "I'm sorry Grace. I know that's not what you want to hear."

"You have nothing to apologise for!" She attempted a smile by way of reassurance and then he watched the smile immediately fade. "It just seems wrong that Alistair who, attempted murder to one side, doesn't appear to have an evil bone in his body but gets locked up for eight years. And then the crazy lady who has nothing but evil bones in her body will probably end up doing less than half that time. How is that fair?"

Sam was pretty confident Grace wasn't really asking for a lesson in crime and punishment so decided to just leave the question hanging. The pause was immediately filled by a silence that made him uncomfortable. The last thing he wanted was for Grace to disappear inside her head again, imagining that right now it was a pretty tormented space to hang out in.

"Been quite a few weeks hasn't it?" Sam flinched at how lame his words sounded. "Sorry. But that was the least clichéd sentence I could think of."

Grace smiled at him. "Just don't try and tell me that all's well that ends well."

"I won't. Although I do love a good cliché. When push comes to shove," he mused. "What does that even mean? There's no use crying over spilled milk. I'm just going to nip it in the bud or possibly add insult to injury, when I tell you that things can only get better. Because come hell or high water, leaving no stone unturned and until the cows come home, time really is a great healer."

"Have you quite finished?"

"Sorry. Although you have to admit that was quite impressive. I feel better now that I've got all that off my chest."

"Sam!"

He laughed. "That wasn't even intentional! I can't stop now. Although technically, I think that one's an idiom rather than a cliché."

"I'll forgive you but only because it's all been....."

"Such a rollercoaster?"

Sam ducked as Grace playfully raised her hand. "One more, do you hear me?"

"Oh come on, you have to admit you asked for that one?"

"How about what doesn't kill you makes you stronger?"

The mood immediately changed and a fresh silence threatened to take hold. Sam wasn't sure how to respond but, despite a growing sense of unease, he knew he needed to get Grace to focus.

"You know we really should talk about what happens next." Sam waited but Grace said nothing. "I know you don't want to think about it but this won't wait, Grace, you know that don't you?"

He watched as Grace took in a long deep breath and then slowly lowered her head as she exhaled. "Go on then," she said without looking up. "Tell me what you think I should do."

"Well, if you'll allow me one last cliché, I think when life gives you lemons, you should make lemonade."

Grace's head was immediately up. "Excuse me?"

"The reality is, as far as the media's concerned, we don't know who knows what. Or who's going to write what. Maybe someone has an interview with Anna's husband. Maybe someone's spoken to Alistair's wife? Or maybe no one's interested? So are you happy to just wait and see what trickles out and then react? Or, if nothing comes out straightaway, are you going to scour the news every day, wondering how long you have to wait before you can relax and believe the moment's passed? Or do you want to take control?"

"And how exactly would I do that?"

"By owning the story. You said you always wanted to write, so now's your chance. Anna will be sentenced in two weeks which is the perfect hook. Take control and write it the way you want the story to be told." He shrugged. "Go make lemonade."

48

Grace

Six months later

How could I have missed you again?!!! This time difference is an absolute bastard! Of course you could just move back. It would make life so much simpler. What do you say?!

Anyway, hello my darling friend. How are you? I can't believe I haven't spoken to you for over two weeks which must never ever happen again. In the meantime, I'm resorting to email because I couldn't not be in touch with you on such a momentous day.....I had my last counselling session!

I know I was reluctant to begin with but I'm happy to admit now that you were all right (you especially obvs). Harriet has been truly amazing, soaking up every word and every tear over the last four months or so. It's so easy to see now that proper therapy was what I needed all along. I can't thank you enough for not giving up and continuing to nag me to give it a try, however frustrating that must have been for you with me insisting that I really didn't need it.

I think we all know Mum dying was clearly the catalyst but Harriet helped me see that I always had a choice. Even after she died I could've let our relationship hold me back or choose to just get on with my life on my terms. There are of course conversations I desperately wish I'd had with her, but there's nothing I can do about that now. Learning to accept that was one of many major milestones! Anyway, it's been the hardest thing I've ever done but I feel stronger and more positive than I have for a very long time. Job well and truly done!

Did I tell you Warren's back? (If he can do it why can't you?) He's back in the café and training to be a counsellor. If I was a child struggling to come to terms with the loss of a parent, he's exactly the kind of warm cuddly human being I'd want to spend time with. He's going to be amazing. But he doesn't seem to be able to leave the café behind and I have to admit it is lovely to have him back there. The best part is we're already the best of friends (which is different to being my actual best friend which is clearly a title kept only for you). We have the kind of shared experience that could have completely broken us but it's somehow created a really special bond that I think we both needed more than we realised. There's still an anxiousness in his eyes sometimes and that's horrible to see. If someone bursts into the café it makes him jump and he looks terrified until he's sure it's not Anna. Makes you wonder if that's why she never admitted how she knew he was in France. Her way of leaving him on edge, wondering if some day she'll be back, which is not something I want to think about either. Although she does creep into my thoughts sometimes. I find myself wondering how she passes her days and if she's remorseful in any way. I wonder about her children and how they're coping. I told Harriet that I'd been thinking about visiting her. (I know the idea of that will make you angry but hold that thought and keep reading). We talked about it a lot; what I felt I needed to say and what I hoped to hear back in return. Each time we discussed it I ended up in the same place, believing there was actually nothing I needed to say, and nothing I needed to hear. (See – it all worked out okay in the end).

My other big news is I'm pitching my ideas for my online column to Sam tomorrow. If he likes them (which we both know he will) I imagine we'll have to have that tricky conversation with HR before he can offer me a contract. Writing the odd article after the news feature I did on Anna is one thing but this is something different altogether. I'm not sure what the rules are about work-based relationships. I guess we'll find out soon enough! Imagine if I have to choose – Sam, or the chance of my own weekly column? All jokes aside, I'm feeling very lucky to have the chance to write and continue with my day job which Harriet helped me realise I do actually love. I haven't ruled out making a full transition to writing at some point in the future but for now, if there's a way for me to do both then I'm happy to put in the extra hours to make it happen. Sam's done such a great job helping me rebuild my self-confidence and accept that anything really is possible. He's a fantastic coach. And cheaper than the previous one (I pay him in beer and dry-roasted peanuts) with no craziness lurking in the wings. At least not yet, anyway!

Well that's more than enough about me, how are you? How's the job? Really hope you're still enjoying it. The radio station looks so cool and we all know the Americans love a British accent so I'm sure your popularity is through the roof already. I'm loving the show – thank God for the internet! And how's your fella? Let's do Zoom drinks next week and I can meet him! And I really want you to get to know Sam. And Emily can join in too! (I'm assuming she's keeping you up-to-date on her dating antics? It's enough to make your hair curl! Her new found confidence is both wonderful and terrifying in equal measure.)

It's a beautiful day here. I should be heading for the office but I'm sitting in the reception where Harriet hangs out making myself look very busy on my laptop while I write to you. I've arranged to meet Sam for a celebratory counselling-graduation coffee. In fact I should go. I don't want to keep him waiting.

Sending you so much love my darling friend. I miss you more than you could ever know (if you did, you'd come home!!!!)

Speak very soon,

xxxxxx

Acknowledgements

Being a writer could be a rather solitary existence if not for an incredible and ever-present support network available around the clock. Whether providing encouragement, perspective, a well-needed second opinion or general coffee-drinking companionship, I am so incredibly thankful for every second afforded me from colleagues, friends and family. Special thanks go to Tammy and Emma - you have both been amazing.

This is a constant journey of discovery with so much still to learn. A perfectly executed edit left me refining characters and plot twists until every word could be justified, while another phenomenal polish from proofreader, Alison Parkin, gave me a whole new level of appreciation for the humble comma (all mistakes on this page are entirely my own!). Early assistance from Ailsa Chambers also provided important background research.

I also feel incredibly privileged to have the hugely talented Anita Mangan on board again who has designed another stunning cover. Your ability to capture the essence of a story in a single image is truly mind-blowing.

Of course everyone needs those very special people in their lives whose support and encouragement is as constant as it is unshakeable. For me, that comes from my husband, Steve, and my mum. I will be forever grateful to you both.

About the Author

Elaine spent twenty-five years working in marketing and publicity in the media and entertainment industries. This included seven years marketing national newspapers and a variety of senior executive roles in TV, radio and film. *Bring Me To* Life is Elaine's second novel. Her first, *I Can't Tell You Why* is also available.

Elaine lives in North London with her husband and their two sons.

Printed in Great Britain
by Amazon